Song for a basilisk /
McKillip, Patricia A.
Smyrna Public Library
W9-BYO-268

Song for
the Basilisk

Ace Books by Patricia A. McKillip

THE FORGOTTEN BEASTS OF ELD
THE SORCERESS AND THE CYGNET
THE CYGNET AND THE FIREBIRD
THE BOOK OF ATRIX WOLFE
WINTER ROSE
SONG FOR THE BASILISK

Song for the Basilisk

PATRICIA A. McKILLIP

ACE BOOKS, NEW YORK

SONG FOR THE BASILISK

An Ace Book
Published by The Berkley Publishing Group,
a member of Penguin Putnam Inc.,
200 Madison Avenue, New York, NY 10016.
The Penguin Putnam Inc. World Wide Web site address is
http://www.penguinputnam.com

Book design by Tiffany Kukec.

First Edition: September 1998

Library of Congress Cataloging-in-Publication Data

McKillip, Patricia A.
Song for the basilisk / Patricia A. McKillip. — 1st ed.
p. cm.
ISBN: 0-441-00447-4
I. Title.
PS3563.C38S663 1998
813'.54—dc21 97-46138
CIP

PRINTED IN THE UNITED STATES OF AMERICA

10 9 8 7 6 5 4 3 2 1

for Tom
thanks for all the music

Part One

Caladrius

One

Within the charred, silent husk of Tormalyne Palace, ash opened eyes deep in a vast fireplace, stared back at the moon in the shattered window. The marble walls of the chamber, once white as the moon and bright with tapestries, were smoke-blackened and bare as bone. Beyond the walls, the city was soundless, as if even words had burned. The ash, born out of fire and left behind it, watched the pale light glide inch by inch over the dead on the floor, reveal the glitter in an unblinking eye, a gold ring, a jewel in the collar of what had been the dog. When moonlight reached the small burned body beside the dog, the ash in the hearth kept watch over it with senseless, mindless intensity. But nothing moved except the moon.

Later, as quiet as the dead, the ash watched the living enter the chamber again: three men with grimy, battered faces. Except for the dog's collar, there was nothing left for them to take. They carried fire, though there was nothing left to burn. They moved soundlessly, as if the dead might hear. When their fire found the man with no eyes on the floor, words came out of them: sharp, tight, jagged. The tall man with white hair and a seamed, scarred face began to weep.

The ash crawled out of the hearth.

They all wept when they saw him. Words flurried out of them, meaningless as bird cries. They touched him, raising clouds of ash, sculpting a face, hair, hands. They made insistent, repeated noises at him that meant nothing. They argued with one another; he gazed at the small body holding the dog on the floor and understood that he was dead. Drifting cinders of words caught fire now and then, blazed to a brief illumination in his mind. *Provinces,* he understood. *North. Hinterlands. Basilisk.*

He saw the Basilisk's eyes then, searching for him, and he turned back into ash.

"Take him to Luly," he heard the white-haired man say clearly. "No one will expect to find him there. If they ever suspect he is still alive."

"To Luly? That's nowhere. The end of the world."

"Then it might just be far enough from the Basilisk."

"But the bards—they're scarcely human, are they? They live on a rock in the sea, they go in and out of the hinterlands, they can turn into seals—"

"Tales," the white-haired man said brusquely. "Go before they find us here. I'll finish this."

"You'll be killed."

"Does it matter? Tell them to call him Caladrius. After the bird whose song means death. Go."

He looked back as they led him from the room, and saw

a ring of fire billow around the dead. The eyeless man turned in the flames to look at him. A dark word flew out of his mouth, spiraled upward through the smoke on ravens' wings into the night.

He closed his own eyes, made himself as blind, as silent, so that he could enter the kingdom of the dead.

It was a long journey. The wind's voice changed, became harsher, colder. It began to smell of sea instead of light-soaked stone or earth. The moon grew full, then slowly pared itself down until it shriveled into a ghostly boat riding above the roiling dark. Then it fell out of the sky. They climbed into it, left land behind, and floated out to sea.

Over the shoulder of the stranger who rowed them through the waves, he watched a dark mass separate itself from the night. A constellation of vague, flickering lights formed among the stars. The small boat veered erratically into hollows between the waves. Wood smacked water; brine flicked across his face. He opened his mouth, tasted the odd, dank mingling of bitterness and fish. He swallowed it, and felt a word form in his throat, the first since he had died.

"Where," he heard himself say. No one else did, it seemed for a moment. Then the man behind him, whose hands braced him against the fits and starts of tide, loosed a long breath.

"That is Luly," he said softly, his voice very close. "The school on the rock. You'll be safe there among the bards. Just learn what they teach you, and stay out of the hinterlands, and don't swim with the seals. If you remember your name, keep it secret, lock it away somewhere until you are old enough to know what to do with it."

He saw fire on the rock then, and words died again.

Ghosts began to form in the flames. He closed his eyes, hid himself and his memories in the ashes of a ruined palace. He burned; he watched himself burn until he knew that he was dead, and that the boy in the boat who saw fire on the rock had no memories, no past. The boat bumped against something. He opened his eyes, stared unflinchingly at the windblown flames on the dock while the boy buried himself in the ashes, until he turned into ash, until the ashes themselves disappeared.

He rose then, stepped out of the boat to meet the fire.

It turned itself into torches. Men and women circled him, questioning in lilting, sinewy voices. Their long hair and windblown robes flowed in and out of the night; the uneasy tide spilled against the rock behind them, tossed a glittering spindrift over them, so that they seemed to reshape themselves constantly out of fire and wind and sea. Their faces resembled the faces of animals in old tapestries: lean-jawed wolves and foxes, golden-eyed owls, falcons, even a unicorn, with white skin and hair, and eyes like ovals of night. But they spoke and smiled like humans. Their words, holding no shadow of grief, weariness, despair, seemed of another language, that he once knew, and still recognized.

"Caladrius," said one of the men who had brought him, in answer to a question. "Call him Caladrius."

He felt a hand under his chin, met eyes that seemed, in the torchlight, as gold as coins. She was a sea creature, he saw: half fish, half woman, who rose up out of waves on the backs of his father's chairs, with a shell in her hand and a mysterious smile on her face. The woman drew damp strands of hair out of his eyes. Her own hair, the color of wheat, fell in a fat braid over her shoulder. It seemed to him like some rare, astonishing treasure; his fingers lifted of their own accord, touched it. Her mouth smiled, but her eyes, not quite smiling, searched for the past he had abandoned.

She said slowly, "It's a complex name for one so young."

"That's all we were told." The man's hands lay gently on his shoulders, still holding him; his voice was dark and taut with past. "After we found him in the ashes. The farm in the provinces burned with everything in it. His family. Everyone. Tell him that when he asks. He doesn't remember anything."

"Then who told you his name?"

"His great-uncle. I doubt that even he lived much longer, after he told us to bring the child here. Will you keep him?"

He heard tide gather and break, far away. Gather and break. His breath gathered; he waited, watching the woman's face. She spoke finally, her slender fingers, white as spindrift, sliding over his head.

"We'll call him Rook, for his black, black eyes." She glanced around the circle, her gold brows raised, questioning silently; there was no dissent in the strange, wild faces gazing at him. "Rook Caladrius. And if he begins to remember?"

"Then he will name himself."

The man's fingers tightened on his shoulders, then loosed him abruptly. He turned, saw all that was left of his past get back into the boat. For a moment ash sparked, flamed in his chest; he swallowed fire, watching until the boat was only a tiny, glowing lamp swaying above the waves. He turned then, feeling nothing, empty as the air between sea and stars. He followed the strangers up the endless stone stairway along the face of the rock, his eyes on the next step, the next. Near the top he stopped abruptly, staring up at the tiers of fire-washed windows carved out of the stones. The woman behind him, keeping a hand at his back, asked, "What is it, Rook?"

He said, astonished, "The rock sang."

The ancient school on Luly, he learned, was older than the name of the rock, older than the language of humans. It rose out of rock like something sculpted by wind, shaped by storm. It was never silent. Sea frothed and boomed constantly around it. Gulls with their piercing voices cried tales passed down from bards who spoke the forgotten language of birds. Seals, lifting their faces out of the waves, told other tales to the wind. Wind answered, sometimes lightly, sometimes roaring out of the northern hinterlands like the sound of all the magic there, if it had one word to speak, and a voice to speak it with. Then the rock would sing in answer, its own voice too deep to be heard, a song that could be felt, running from stone into bone, and from there into the heart, to be transformed into the language of dreams, of poetry. Rook heard the rock sing again the first night he slept there. Later, out of stone, he made his first song.

He played it one day on a single-stringed instrument whose unpredictable sounds, sometimes tender, sometimes ragged and eerie, said best what he saw. Bard Galea, the woman who had named him, was pleased. Bard Trefon, whose deep eyes and dark skin reminded Rook of the seals that peered out of the waves around the rock, was not.

"I hear seagulls squabbling in it," she said. "And the wind. And ravens calling your name."

"I hear the picochet," Bard Trefon protested. "I am trying to teach him the harp."

"Well, he was born in the provinces, of course he would

be drawn to the picochet. It's the farmers' instrument; he must have heard it in the womb."

"He has an ear for the harp." They argued amicably, their voices spirited and strong, tide tangling with wind on a bright day. "It's the harp that the land barons will want to hear in their courts, not the peasant's instrument."

"I think," Bard Galea said, looking deeply into Rook's eyes, "he has an ear for whatever he touches. Can you put words to your song, Rook?"

"They burned," he said briefly.

Her eyes changed, became strange with thought, like birds' eyes, or the unseeing eyes of students lost in their music. "Then you know something that's hardest to learn. Words change, here. You must make them new as if you had never spoken them before."

He looked at her, his eyes gritty, charred with sudden anguish; an ember flared out of the ashes. He plucked the single string; past and terror receded, blocked by sound as tuneless as a wave. "I never have spoken them before," he answered, remembering the taste of the sea on his lips, the first word forming in him as they rowed toward Luly.

Bard Trefon broke off the piece of a word in the back of his throat. He took the picochet from Rook gently and set it aside. He wore a harp at his back like a butterfly's wing, as if it had unfolded there and never left him. His eyes consulted Bard Galea's in the way that they had, saying things silently. She said softly, "They were right to bring him here, I think. This may be where he belongs. Rook, do you know the story of how the first bard came to this rock?"

"No."

"The first bard in the world learned all his words new; he had no father and no mother, and no one to teach him. So he went exploring the world, to put names to all the wonders in it. He was following the path of the sun across the sea to find the land where it set, when an enormous whale rose out of the water and swallowed him, coracle and all. The bard began to sing in the whale's belly, a song of such heartrending beauty that the whale could not bear to stop it. It swam toward the setting sun until finally it came to a barren rock. The whale opened its mouth and the bard stepped out, still singing, this time to the rock. At the song, the rock loosed its fierce clench on itself and grew hollow, letting the song carve chambers and doors and long hallways that caught wind in them like breath and molded it into music. The whale, unable to leave the bard, fed itself to the birds and the fish, and left its backbone for a bridge between rock and land, and its ribs for boats. One day, the bard, ever curious, walked across the whale's backbone and disappeared into the hinterlands.

"A thousand years later he returned, pursued by all the magic in the hinterlands for the magical instrument he had stolen. That's the one you played for me. The picochet."

"It depends," Bard Trefon said to a passing gull outside the window, "who tells the tale. I think he stole the harp."

Rook looked curiously at the picochet's square painted belly and the long, single string that wound around a peg above his head. "What is magic?"

She paused. "A word. It changes things, when you know what it means. The magic in the picochet makes things grow. So the tale goes, and so the farmers of the provinces south of the hinterlands believe."

"The picochet," Bard Trefon said, "would hardly be worth picking a quarrel with all the magic in the hinterlands."

She smiled her sea smile at him, her eyes catching light. "That's how the tale goes."

"But what is the truth of the tale?" He took the picochet gently from Rook and set it aside. "Magic comes from the heart, and it's the heart that plays the harp. Come with me, Rook. I'll show you."

Her smile left her, like light fading on the sea. "Be careful," she told them both.

Bard Trefon took him out in a boat, rowing away from the rock until they were safe from the exuberant swell and thunder of breaking waves. Then he dropped an anchor stone over the side, baited a line, and let it drift. He took the harp out of its case and handed it to Rook. "See what comes," he said, his dark face sparkling with brine, his eyes intent, like the seals when they rose out of the water to watch. The boat, veering and darting around its anchor stone, nearly tossed the harp out of Rook's hands before he struck a note. He positioned it awkwardly, plucked one tentative string after another, the haunting scale Bard Trefon had taught him. The land beyond them dipped and rose, the flatlands to the south luminous with morning, the northern forests still receding into shadow. In the distance, a misty blur of hills rose out of the forests, rounded like bubbles. They seemed to float above the still, dark trees. He narrowed his eyes against the light, tried to see beyond. Bard Trefon, tugging at his line, said, "You're looking at the hinterlands. They go north to the end of the world."

"Who lives there?"

"You never know until you go there. Everyone who goes returns with a different tale."

"Have you gone?"

"No." He pulled up his hook. The bait was gone, so was the fish that had taken it. "Not yet. It's where you go to ask a question. About your life, perhaps. Your future. Or your past. People there tell you. If you listen. If not, you come back at least knowing some odd tales, very ancient songs. Some never come back."

"What happens to them?"

"They go elsewhere. They may return to Luly, many years later, and tell what happened to them. Sometimes the bards only hear of them in a song." He let his line drop again. "Play the song you made for the picochet. See if you can find it on the harp."

He tried, but the sea kept getting in the way of the song, and so did the hinterlands. He gazed at the floating hills, wondering what he would see if he walked across them, alone through unfamiliar trees, crossing the sun's path to the top of the world. Who would he meet? In what language would they speak to him? The language the sea spoke intruded then, restless, insistent, trying to tell him something: what song he heard in the seashell, what word the rock sang, late at night under the heavy pull of the full moon. His fingers moved, trying to say what he heard, as the sea flowed like blood in and out of the hollows and caves of the rock, trying to reach its innermost heart, as if it were a string that had never been played. He came close, he felt, reaching for the lowest notes on the harp. But it was his own heart he split, and out of it came fire, engulfing the rock in the sea.

He cried out. A string snapped, curled with a wail like wood in fire. Bard Trefon, staring at him, reached out, catching the harp before Rook flung it into the water. "No," he said quickly. "Rook."

Rook stared at him, his heart still burning. "It was on fire."

"I know," the bard breathed. "I heard. Rook. Try again. But this time—"

His fingers curled into fists. "I will never play it again."

"But you have a gift for it. And there are other songs."

"No." He added, as the bard watched him, brows crooked and questioning, "There is a fish on your line."

"Rook."

He turned away, tugged at the dancing, thumping line until Bard Trefon finally put the harp away and helped him.

The more the bards taught him, the farther back he drove the fire and what lay within it. He built walls of words against it; he charmed it away with music. There was nothing, it seemed, he could not learn in order to escape. He changed the meanings of words without realizing it. Becoming a bard meant becoming someone who knew no past but poetry, he thought. A bard changed the past to song, set it to music, and made it safe. So he learned the tales of the hinterlands, the provinces; he played their instruments even in his dreams, until he woke with strange cadences and ancient languages he almost understood fading in his head. He was taught, in cursory fashion, of the city south of the provinces, which had a sheathed, dangerous paw on the world around him. But its music made him uneasy. Like the harp, it led him back, toward the past; it smelled of fire. Its bright, sweet, complex language was not rooted in wind and stone; it was too new. It held no word for bard. So he reached back, finding past and eluding it, as far as he could, to the first words, the first tales, the first sounds fashioned out of the language of birds and insects, the whine of wind and wolf, the sough of the sea, the silence of death, all the sounds the first bard had woven into his song. After eight years on Luly, he could spin poetry from his dreams, and play anything his hands touched. After three more years the bards of Luly said that he was ready to choose his future.

He had grown tall and muscular, his long, fair hair usually a rook's nest of wind and brine, his rook's eyes, beneath level brows, so dark they seemed without pupils. His rare smile softened their grimness. When he played, his face lost its usual calm. Someone else, the boy in the boat perhaps, staring unflinchingly at fire, looked out of his eyes; they reflected what he did not remember seeing.

"You should call yourself Caladrius," he was told sometimes. "It's a name more suitable for a bard."

He would shrug. "Rook suits me." And when he played, they saw the raven in his eyes.

He sat on a grassy slope outside the school one sunny day, imitating birds on the clay pipes, when the bards summoned him to make his choice. The summons came in the form of Sirina, a land baron's daughter from the northern provinces. She had been at the school for three years; she had a restless nature and a spellbinding way with a harp. "You're wanted," she said, and sat down on the grass beside him. He looked at her, still playing, and realized in that moment how she had changed, from the slight, freckled girl he had first met. Her harper's hands were pale as sea spume; her long hair gleamed like pearl. She knew things, he thought suddenly. She held secrets, now, in the long, slender lines of her body; she held some music he had never heard before. "Rook," she prodded while his pipes spoke back to a passing gull. He lowered them finally, still gazing at her.

"Who wants me?"

"Bard Trefon, Bard Galea, Bard Horum. They want you to make a decision. About your future." She had a northerner's way of chopping sentences into neat portions, as if they were carrots.

"There's no decision to make," he answered simply. "I'm staying here."

"It's more complicated. They said. What you must choose."

"Staying or going is one or the other. It's not complicated." He added as she sighed, "I'll stay here and teach. It's what I want."

"How can you not want to be a bard? How can you want this rock?" she asked incredulously. "You could have the world. If you would only learn to harp. It's what the world wants."

"I don't want the world." The spare, taut lines of his face softened at her bewilderment. "Sirina." The color of her eyes distracted him suddenly; he forgot what he was going to say.

"You can play anything else. You can tell any tale. Sing any song. Why do you balk over a harp? Anyone can play it. You don't have to play it with your heart. Not to please the land barons. Just with your fingers."

"I prefer the picochet."

"Peasant."

He smiled. "Very likely." Her eyes had changed at his smile, become shadowy, mysterious. Their color kept eluding him. "Mussels," he decided, and her gaze became skewed.

"What about them?"

"It's a riddle," he said, following an ancient formula. "Answer: I am the color of mussel shells."

Her eyes narrowed faintly, holding his. "Is that so," she said softly. "Answer: I am the color of a starless night."

"Is that so." His hand dropped to the ground, very close to hers. Neither of them blinked. "Answer: I am a son without a father, a bird without a song. Who am I?"

He watched her lips gather around the first letter of his name. He bent his head, gently took the rest of it from her. She opened her eyes as he drew back; they had grown very dark. He heard her swallow.

"Rook." Her fingers shifted in the grass, touched his. "They're waiting."

"Will you?" he asked as he stood. He had an impression, as her hair roiled away from her into the wind, of someone rising out of foam. "Will you wait?"

Her eyes answered.

He felt something leap in him like a salmon, flicking drops of water into light on its run toward home. I'm never leaving, he thought, striding toward the ancient, drafty pile of stone in which he could still hear, late at night, between the wind and the wild burst of the tide, the final cry of the bard imprisoning all the magic in the hinterlands. Never.

"You have three choices," Bard Galea told him. Her hair was more silver now than gold, but she still had the mermaid's enchanting smile. "You may choose to stay here and teach. Which is what I think you want."

"Or you may choose to master the harp and be called bard," Bard Trefon said. "Which is what I think you should do. Then you will leave Luly and find your future with some house or court or school in need of a bard. If you choose that, remember that the farther you go from Luly, the more the word 'bard' changes, until, if you go far enough south, you will hardly recognize yourself." He waited, dark brows lifted, still questioning, after so many years, still hoping. Rook turned to Bard Horum, a tall, very old man who looked, with his pure white coloring and ancient, oval eyes, as if he might once have been a unicorn.

"Or," the third bard said, "you may take the path across the sea to the hinterlands, and let what comes to you there decide your fate. If you choose that, remember that you may not find your way back to Luly."

Rook started to answer. The unicorn's eyes held him, powerful and still. Did you? Rook wanted to ask. What did you find there? "I choose," he said to Bard Horum, and caught himself, startled and breathless, as if he had nearly walked over a cliff. He blinked away from the ancient gaze, and it dropped, hid itself. He turned back to Bard Galea's smile. "I choose to stay."

That night he dreamed of fire.

He woke not knowing his own name, consumed, as with a sudden fever, by the knowledge that he had a past hidden by fire, another name. Somewhere on the mainland, the blackened, crumbling walls of a farmhouse held his name. He could not find his future without his past. He could not play a true note, even on the picochet, or sing a word that meant itself, without his past. He lay awake in the dark, staring at it, listening to the rill of the tide filling hollows beneath the school. When night finally relinquished its grip of him, he still felt blind, memoryless, as if he had only dreamed his life, and had wakened to find himself among ashes, without words and understanding nothing.

"I can't make a choice yet," he told the bards in the morning, trembling with weariness, rubbing at the rasp behind his reddened eyes. "I'm going to the provinces." This time the seal's eyes watched him, curious, approving. The unicorn's eyes were still hidden.

He left three days later at dawn. Sirina rowed him to shore. They did not speak until the boat scraped bottom and he jumped into the waves to run it out again on the outgoing tide. She said, softly, her face quiet and pale in the new light, "I'll give you a thread. To find your way back."

"Or for you to find me," he breathed, and she nodded. She leaned forward abruptly, kissed him before tide pulled the boat out of his hands. He watched her row halfway to Luly while he stood knee-deep in surf, pack and picochet dangling from his shoulders, still tasting her sea-salt kiss.

Finally he turned, found a beach littered with driftwood and mussel shells, without a footprint, human or otherwise, anywhere in the sand. Beyond it lay the wild land north of the provinces, the forests and hills flowing to the end of the world. He felt its pull, its mystery, as strong as the tide carrying his heart back to Luly, as strong as the name waiting to be found in the provinces. He waded out of the water, shook the sea out of his boots, and began to walk south toward the villages and farmlands, the great houses of the provincial barons. Ravens cried at him from the ancient forest, raucous, persistent. He did not know their language, he explained silently to them; he did not understand. Later, when they dropped a black trail of feathers to guide him into the unknown, he refused to see.

He played the picochet in farmhouses, in inns, the flute and the lute in barons' courts all over the provinces. Sometimes he stayed a night, sometimes a month or two, playing whatever he was handed, singing whatever he was asked. He was given lodgings, coins, new boots, new songs, a strange instrument that had found its way out of the hinterlands, a haircut, an embroidered case for his picochet, many local tales, and offers of positions ranging from tavern musician to court bard. But he could stay nowhere. His rook's eyes searched for fire everywhere. He was shown charred, ruined farmhouses, or the place where they had been before they were rebuilt, or the cornfield where the farm had stood before it burned and its ashes were plowed under. Solk, their name was, or Peerson, or Gamon. They had lost a baby, or a cat, or all their horses, or everything but each other. A terrible fire with only one child, a son, left alive? That sounded like the Leafers, but no, only the grandmother had been left alive in that one. She had wandered out of the house in her nightgown in the middle of the night, thinking she heard her baby son crying. She woke to hear him crying to wake his own children inside the burning house. The Sarters in the next valley had lost their cows when the barn burned, but . . . The Tares' girl had lost her parents, but there were those who said she had started the fire herself.

He couldn't say who had taken him to Luly?

He couldn't say why Luly?

He couldn't say why the name Caladrius and no other?

He couldn't say.

"But you must belong here," he was told many times. "The way you play the picochet. You must have heard it in the womb."

He was certain he could not stay? Not even if—

He was certain.

He returned at night, nearly two years later, alone, on foot. He lit a fire on the beach and sat there, listening to the dead silence in the forest behind him, waiting while a star moved across the water in answer to his fire. Before the boat entered the tide, something spoke in the dead silence of his heart. He got to his feet without realizing it. When the tide caught the boat, and the lamp careened wildly on the prow, he left pack and picochet on the sand and ran into the water.

Sirina caught him as he caught the boat. Tide poured between them; the boat tilted, spilled her into his arms. An oar went its own way; the star was doused.

"You're here," he kept saying, stunned. "You're still here."

"You came back." A wave broke over them; she laughed, wiping her face with her wet sleeve, then his face. "You took long enough."

"You waited for me."

"We waited. Yes."

"You." He stopped, heard the boat thump hollowly as a wave flung it upside down on the sand. Beneath that, he heard silence again, as if the trees were listening. He said, "We."

"I called him Hollis. After my grandfather."

His knees turned to nothing; he sank suddenly under a wave. She tugged him out, laughing again. "Don't be afraid. You'll like him. He has my eyes."

He tried to speak; words turned to salt. She pounded on his back as he coughed. Brine ran down his face like tears. "Hollis," he said finally. Then he heard the strange, deep song of the whale weltering up all around him from sea to sky, and he shouted, loud enough to crumble rock, to overwhelm the magic of the hinterlands, send it fleeing from his heart.

He picked her up, carried her out of the sea.

And so the years passed.

The child in the ashes waited.

Two

In the Hall of Mirrors at Pellior Palace, within the walled city of Berylon, Giulia Dulcet lifted the instrument in her hands many times in many different mirrors and began to play. The hall was soundless but for the music; the hundred richly dressed people in it might have been their own reflections. Arioso Pellior, Duke of Pellior House and Prince of Berylon, stood with his three children across the room from the musicians. Giulia caught brief glimpses of them now and then as she lowered the sweet, melancholy lavandre to pass the prince's melody to Hexel on the harpsichord. The prince's compositions seemed predictable but never were: he scattered accidentals in music, Hexel commented acidly, as in life. Above Arioso's head, the basilisk of Pellior House, in red marble and gold, reared on its sinuous coils and stared back at itself in the massive frame of the mirror behind the musicians. All around the room the basilisks roused and glared, frozen in one another's gazes, while mortals, beneath the range of their stony regard, stood transfixed within the prince's vision.

The composition ended without mishap. Playing the prince's music kept Giulia concentrated and on edge: a note misplaced in his ear would be enough, she felt, to get them tossed, by the irate composer, out of the Tormalyne School of Music into the gutters of Berylon. But the muted tap of fans against gloved fingers reassured them. Arioso Pellior acknowledged compliments with a gracious inclination of his head. The hall quieted for his next composition. Giulia exchanged the lavandre for a flute. She and Hexel played a duet. Then Hexel sang a love song, a stylized piece with vocal frills that he tossed out as lightly as largesse. Giulia sat listening, a slender figure in her black magister's robe, her straight, sooty hair neatly bound in a net of gold thread, her tawny, wide-set eyes discreetly lowered as she listened. Only the lavandre moved to her breathing, its spirals of rosewood and silver throwing sparks of light at its reflection.

The song ended. The prince's younger daughter, the Lady Damiet, lifted a folded fan to her lips and swallowed a yawn. Her broad, creamy face revealed nothing of her thoughts; she was reputed to have few. On the other side of the prince stood his son Taur, twenty years older than Damiet, offspring of Arioso's first marriage. Taur, looking slightly disheveled in his finery, brooded visibly while the music played, applauded a trifle late when he noticed it had stopped. Taur's wife, a thin-lipped woman with restless eyes the color of prunes, seemed to search perpetually for the cause of her annoyance in the mirrored faces. Taur's younger sister Luna Pellior stood behind Arioso's shoulder, nearly as tall as he, with her hair the rich gold of a dragon's hoard, and her eyes, like her father's, lizard green. She had his face, Damiet her mother's. The prince's wives had both died, having done their duty to the Basilisk, and being, so it was widely believed, no longer required.

The hall quieted again. Giulia turned a page and raised the lavandre. Its liquid voice imitated hunting cadences, announcing the beginning of the pursuit. Hexel, she noted, had forgotten his loathing for the composer and was galloping over the keys. A strand of her hair slid free and drifted above the lavandre's mouth, fluttering with every note she played. She ignored it, though the prince's daughter Damiet, her eyes opening slightly at Giulia, seemed to have found something at last to interest her.

The hunt reached its climax; something was slain by an unexpected chord. The harpsichord paced itself to a peaceful walk, while the lavandre sang a pretty lament for the dead. Midway through it, Giulia saw the prince's eyes, beneath slow, heavy lids, fix on her face, as if she played jewels instead of notes, and every one belonged to him.

He came up to her afterward, while the musicians were putting their instruments away, and the guests picked daintily at what looked like butterfly wings and hummingbird hearts. Giulia, who saw the Prince of Berylon rarely and at a distance, swept her magister's robe into a deep curtsy, wondering if she had mortally offended him with a turn of phrase.

Rising, she looked into his eyes. The skin around them was lightly crumpled with age, but they were still powerful, at once searching and opaque, like a light too bright to be looked at, but which illumined everything. This year would mark his sixty-fifth birthday, the thirty-seventh year of his ascent to power over Berylon. His fine face, gilded by sun and symmetrical as a mask, seemed not so much aging as drying. It was as if, Giulia thought, his skin were a husk within which blood and bone were busily transforming themselves into something else entirely.

She lowered her eyes, wondering suddenly if he had read her thoughts. He said only, "You play my music very well."

"Thank you, my lord."

"As I would play it, if I were that proficient. As if you like it."

"Then I must," she answered in her low, clear voice. Years in Berylon had smoothed the provincial quirks out of her speech. "I don't play well what I don't like."

"Did you think the lament a trifle long?"

Surprised, she lifted her eyes again, to glimpse the tentative composer behind the ruler. "No, my lord. You made me see a stately animal, maybe with mythical qualities, that had been slain. Something to touch the heart. Not just something to be viewed as supper. A stag?"

"Or a griffin," he suggested, with his tight, still-charming smile. "I have heard you play here before. You teach at the school."

"Yes, my lord."

"How long have you been there?"

"Five years as a student, my lord, and five as a teacher."

"You are a northerner." She hesitated, surprised again; his smile deepened. "I hear it in your voice. You came to the school young, then. And were given assistance? You are not a land baron's daughter."

"Yes—no, my lord. My grandfather still farms on the northern slopes. He sent me here at fourteen, thinking that I would astound the magisters of the Tormalyne School with my music."

"And did you?"

"Yes, my lord. They had never heard such noise in their lives."

For a moment his smile reached his eyes. "What were you playing for them?"

"My picochet. They locked it in a closet, and forbade me to touch it for five years. They taught me to play more civilized instruments."

"I am not familiar with the picochet."

"It is a peasant's instrument, my lord."

"And one you still play?"

For a breath he caught her wordless. She felt the blood gather in her face, under his bright, unblinking gaze. She said finally, "Yes, my lord."

"I know many uncivilized instruments. . . . But not that. You live at the school?"

"Yes, my lord."

"Good. Then I will know where to find you."

"My lord?"

"When I need you."

She blinked. He turned away; she curtsied hastily, lost sight of him when she straightened. She put the lavandre into its case, her straight dark brows puckered slightly.

Hexel came to her side; she said with relief, "I can't believe we got through that with no bigger disaster than my hair falling down. He was pleased."

"What exactly was he pleased with?" Hexel asked suspiciously. "What did he say to you?"

"Pleasantries . . ." Still frowning, she snapped a case latch with more force than necessary, and saw blood bead along the quick of her thumbnail. "He has such strange eyes. They seem to see everything, even what I'm thinking. Or don't know I'm thinking. He said that he would know where to find me when he needed me."

"And what did he mean by that?" Hexel's blue eyes were narrowed, his long, black hair looked suddenly windblown, though the candles behind him burned still. As a dramatist and composer, he had an exhausting passion for dramatics. He was lean, moody, intense; students at the music school constantly pushed notes under his door, or set his discarded scribbles to music, or dropped roses or themselves across his work. "What kinds of pleasantries did he have in mind?"

"Oh, Hexel." She wiped blood on her robe and began to put her music in order. "He meant music. That's all we talked about."

"Then why are you frowning?"

She tapped the manuscripts straight slowly. "Because," she said finally, "of who he is. Whatever it is he needs of anyone, how do you say no to the Basilisk? I never had to think of it before. He never looked at me before, with those eyes." Something dragged at her attention from across the room; she added nervously, "The way he's looking now. As if he hears us."

"He is an aging tyrant who gets his music played free," Hexel said without compunction, "since he had the foresight not to destroy the Tormalyne School. You are my muse, not his. He can find someone else. I need your inspiration. Tonight."

"For what?"

"For the prince's opera, what else?"

"Oh. Hexel, I can't. I'm playing the picochet in the tavern tonight."

He gazed at her, exasperated. "Not again."

"It's this day every week."

"But I need you!"

"Tomorrow."

"You are merciless."

"So you are always telling me. Why can't you find someone else to be your muse instead? All I do is inspire you with horror, headaches, frustration, and despair."

"That's why I need you," Hexel said briskly. "Without proper proportions of despair, how can I tell if I'm doing anything right?"

"Come with me. We'll talk on the way. You might like what I play."

"I would rather have hobnails driven into my ears. You are only doing this to prove some obscure point, because no one could possibly want to listen to you."

"Northerners do," she answered simply. "They miss it."

Hexel snorted so audibly that faces across the room turned, exhibiting exquisitely raised brows. "It's a foolish and dangerous thing you are doing, Giulia Dulcet, and if anything happens to you it will devastate my work—" He sensed a distraction hovering at his elbow, and found a page there, bowing to the music stand. "What?"

"Master Veris Legere will make a formal presentation of the prince's music to the school, if you will please. . . ."

They followed him across the room. The prince, formally presented with Hexel, looked at Giulia over Hexel's bowed head, the faint, sharp splinter of a smile in his eyes. She thought in horror: He heard. . . . Veris Legere, the silver-haired Master of Music for Pellior House, who knew Giulia, greeted her more pleasantly. He presented the musicians with scrolls tied with gold ribbon, about which they all, even Hexel, made proper noises. Hexel ate a hummingbird heart; Giulia drank, in two swallows, most of a glass of wine while she responded to Veris Legere's polite interest in her work at the school. The mirrors around them began to lose movement, color. The musicians in their scholarly black detached themselves from satins and pastels to gather their instruments and music. Small clusters of courtiers, like elegant bouquets, drifted in the wake of the prince's departure. Finally the mirrors emptied even of servants, who left them to reflect themselves, while the onyx-eyed basilisks turned one another into stone.

Later that evening, Giulia made her way alone through the streets of Berylon. She still wore her magister's black, beneath a flowing hooded cloak. The stone streets, broad and lamplit in front of the music school, grew narrow and twisted as she neared the north wall of the city. Tiers of closed doors and bright windows rose above shops and taverns, smithies, tanneries, market stalls covered for the night. Each street had its own particular odor: she could have smelled her way by now to the tavern at the gate of the Tormalyne Bridge.

Four bridges led across water into Berylon, each named after one of the ancient ruling Houses. To the west, the Iridia Bridge crossed slow moat water in which the frogs would be singing. The plain beyond that was treeless, grassy, the long, dust-white road curving through it flowed visible from the horizon. To the south, the Marcasia Bridge spanned broad deep water to the docks, where fishers moored their boats and cleaned their catch, and the trade ships, sails colored according to House or province, took their wares downriver. East, the Pellior Bridge rose over slower, shallower water, where goods and passengers were carried by flat-bottomed barges. The Tormalyne Bridge crossed the river at the beginning of its long curl around the city, where the rushing, silvery water had sliced a path through shelves of rock, torn earth away and swallowed it, scoured the sides of the ravine into cliffs as sheer as a knife blade. There were no docks on this side of the city, no river traffic. Travelers crossing the bridge passed into a forest that stretched between Berylon and the northern provinces. The smells that roamed into the tavern beside the bridge were redolent of raw pelts and tanneries.

She was stopped once by the night watch. The long instrument she carried had made a suspicious silhouette in their torchlight. Bloodred basilisks on black tunics cast baleful stares at her; neither they nor the watch saw farther than her magister's robe, and they let her pass.

On Tanner's Street, she opened a weather-beaten door beneath a faded sign: a griffin poised between broken halves of shell. The Griffin's Egg, the tavern called itself. At that hour it had a scattered crowd of trappers, tanners, a few dusty travelers out of the provinces, shopkeepers, tired women with barefoot children at their knees. Giulia eased through the crowd to the back corner of the tavern, where Justin was fitting pieces of his bass pipe together, and Yacinthe unwrapped half a dozen small drums of various sizes from their cases. Ionia, who played the flute, set a brass bowl on a table with a few small coins in it to inspire their audience. She smiled at Giulia, showing a sapphire fang over one eyetooth. Jewels glinted through her hair, down her shoulder, from the studded rein that she had trimmed from some horse's fine harness. Yacinthe, beating a drum, danced around Justin, the gold rings on her toes tapping on the floorboards, blue feathers trying to fly in her dark hair. He tossed her a grin, his eyes on Giulia as he went to meet her.

"I'm sorry I'm so late," Giulia said. "I had to—"

He stopped her with a kiss. Then he said softly, "I know what you had to." She looked closely at him. His eyes were lowered, his smile troubled. He was tall and fair-haired, with a sweet ruffian's face that was a misleading combination of innocence and danger. His hatred of Pellior House was genuine and unremitting. She had met him in the Griffin's Egg one night when she searched for a place outside the school to play. Like the instrument she brought there, he was an indulgence and a passion; she knew little of his life outside of the tavern where they played, the tiny room above a shop where he lived. She laid a hand on his chest; he clasped it, but still did not meet her eyes, busy swallowing his protests, she suspected.

"I play where I'm told," she reminded him simply. "You know that. It's my work. And I can't help loving the music. You know that, too."

"I know." His fingers tightened on her hand. He raised her palm to his mouth, before he loosed her. He looked at her finally, his brows crooked. "I worry about you in the Basilisk's house. He is unpredictable and ruthless. And you were alone on the streets. There's a full moon tonight. They're coming in here to drink hard. The watch challenges anything that moves."

"They stopped me," she said. She slid off the magister's black beneath her cloak, and then shrugged off her cloak. "They thought I was armed."

"They killed a man near Pellior Bridge. They thought he was armed."

Giulia, on one knee, froze for half a breath, then continued unbuckling a shoe. "They don't kill magisters."

"Not yet."

She kicked off her shoes, then pulled the gold net out of her hair so that it fanned darkly over her bare shoulders, nearly reaching the waist of the short, full skirts that skimmed her knees. Justin watched her, his smile surfacing again. Someone rattled a cup against a table like a drumroll. Yacinthe imitated it. Justin pulled the gilded, beaded leather tie from the mouth of her instrument case. He looped it around her neck carefully, tied it, while she watched the mottled light slide over his brown, muscular hands, and catch in the tangled cloud of white-gold hair. He pulled the instrument out of its case and handed it to her.

"Magister," he said gravely. "Don't break the windows with it."

He picked up his pipe again and blew a deep note. She plucked the string, listening until she heard its solitary voice clearly beneath laughter and argument, the roll of dice and clank of pewter on wood. She tuned it to a note out of the north.

They began to play.

Three

Sirina waited until Hollis was fourteen before she left them. Rook had sensed her going long before. Like tide turning, drawn by the moon, by the mysteries of the deep, she had ebbed, little by little, away from him, so that he stood once again on a lonely shore, watching the distance widen between them. She asked him, in many ways, to come with her, before she got tired of asking.

"Luly is growing tiny," she had said to him. "There's not enough room. For all of us."

He thought of the stone chambers, tiered like a beehive, the walls so thick not even the sound of the picochet traveled between them. They might have been living there with only the wind and the sea shouting poetry at them in forgotten languages. "There's room," he had answered absently.

"I thought I would take Hollis home," she said another

time. He had stared at her, oddly perplexed by the word, as if what he had thought it meant was wildly inaccurate.

"He is home. Luly is his home."

"I mean to see my father. For a while."

"How long is a while?"

"Just a while. Just a few months. So he can see what it is to be a court bard. In a house planted on earth instead of stone. With people coming and going. So that, when he's older, he can make choices."

"I made choices without knowing."

"I know," she said softly, her brows crooked at something he could not see. She had grown, he thought, more beautiful through the years: tall and supple, with a line beside her mouth left there by laughter, by pain, by thoughts she did not reveal.

"Come with us," she begged.

"I can't leave my students."

"It's this rock you can't leave," she said, turning abruptly, gazing out at spindrift as pale as her hair. He thought only that she was probably right.

When she finally made it clear to him that she was leaving, he felt, stunned, that the rock was the only safe and changeless thing he knew.

"I can't stay," she said. "I love you. But I never meant to stay here. I want the world back."

"I'll come," he said, without moving. She separated her skirts from his tunics, folded them neatly on the bed. "I'll come," he said again. "When you find a place. Send word to me—"

She made an exasperated noise. "You'll come when the

quarter moon falls out of the sky. You'll come when you can row it to land like a boat."

"Hollis—"

"I'll let him choose."

He stared at her, breathless at the thought. "How can he? He's a child! How can you ask him—"

Her face twisted; tears appeared seemingly at random, beneath her eyes, on her cheekbone, beside her mouth. "It's all I can do!" she cried. "It's the best I can do. I only stayed for you and Hollis. I am a bard of Luly. I must find my place. As you never did. Ever. Ever. I tried to tell you." She turned to him blindly; he held her fiercely for a moment, a silky roil of froth, the undertow. Then she slid away from him and was gone.

Hollis went with her. He came back five months later, looking taller, older, and prickly with moods. "I want to be a bard," he told Rook tensely. "Like her." He looked like her, Rook thought; he had her eyes, her tall grace, though his hair was the color of his father's name. He did not say much more for years, it seemed to Rook.

And then, like his mother, he became a bard, finding music in a shinbone, poetry within the oyster's shell. Like her, he was torn between love and land; he became articulate, and began, Rook thought with amazement, to sound exactly like her.

It was in that spring, he saw clearly later, when the young man with the surprising name came north from Berylon, that the Basilisk's eye turned toward Luly.

He was in the middle of a desultory argument with Hollis when he saw the fire on the shore across the singing dark. He started to comment; Hollis paced a step, stood in front of the window, the distant flame a tantalizing question beside his hand. The world was still on the edge of spring. The winds came that day out of the provinces, mingling newly turned earth with the smell of brine around the rock. Rook, who by now had spent thirty-seven years on Luly, rarely felt the cold. His passage through the school, except on the roughest days, trailed a wake of open windows. Hollis, stars and fire at his back, shivered without realizing it.

His young face was taut and stubborn. He looked, Rook thought with some sympathy, exactly like Sirina commenting on Rook's life. Hollis had grown broad-shouldered and lean, like his father; he wore his black hair long and wind-knotted. Unlike his father, he was methodical rather than impulsive; he had known exactly what he wanted for years. Rook, still compact and muscular from climbing up and down the cliff to the dock and hauling in fish when he had to, kept his silver-gold hair cropped short now. His raven's eyes had not changed; their blackness hid expression, while Hollis's face changed expression as often as the sea.

The sight of the harp in Rook's hands had provoked Hollis, already restless at the smells coming out of the mainland. What they were arguing about seemed nebulous to Hollis and very clear to Rook. He was trying, as Sirina had done, to bring himself to leave Luly and Rook. "I don't understand why you never learned to play that," Hollis said tautly. "You could have left this place long ago. Can you explain?"

Rook loosened a cracked peg on the harp, remembering the day, thirty-seven years before, when he had played Bard Trefon's harp in the fishing boat, and had set his world on fire.

"There is something I want to forget," he said slowly. "Once, when I was harping, I came too close to remembering."

Hollis gazed at him, openmouthed, nonplussed. "What is it you want to forget?"

"I don't remember."

"But don't you think—"

"No," Rook said evenly. "I don't think."

"But if you—"

"If I remember, and learn to harp to please the land barons, then I can leave this rock. Yes. But I don't want to leave. I'm content here, teaching. You want to leave. Your mother had ambitions and so do you. I don't."

"So you always say."

"So I always say." He unwound string from the peg, looking perplexedly at his son. "Since that's what I always say, why can't you believe me?"

"I don't know," Hollis said tersely. "Maybe because you play everything else like the first bard must have played, and even he got himself off this rock for a thousand years. You belong in the world."

"It's you who should leave," Rook said patiently. "You belong in the world. Maybe you should row yourself ashore and join your mother for a few months. Leave the boat for whoever is out there in the dark."

"I don't want to go to a land baron's court."

"Why not? The change might—"

Hollis made an impatient gesture, ending his sentence. "It's too warm, too soft. I'll forget what I've learned here. I'll forget to come back. I'm not ready to leave yet."

"Well," Rook said softly, meeting Hollis's eyes with his

raven's stare. "Neither am I." He loosened another peg, added more temperately, "You'll have roots in both worlds: me on this rock, your mother at court. When you need to leave, you'll always know where to find us both."

"It's not that," Hollis said tightly. "I'm not afraid of leaving."

"Then what is it?"

"I don't know. You let my mother leave you—you'll let me leave you. For this rock. I just feel—sometimes—that I don't know you at all."

Rook was silent a moment, his eyes straying back to the window. "Your mother used to say that to me," he murmured. "I never understood what she meant, either."

Wind flew like a bird around the workroom, skimming over broken or half-finished instruments, sounding overtones, leaving scents of fish, salt, night. Hollis turned to latch the frame of thick ovals of glass and lead against it. He paused, peered out. "There's a fire on the shore. Are we expecting anyone?"

"A young man from Berylon."

"I'll go."

"No," Rook said, rising, wanting the peace and quiet of elements that might complain of him, but not in any language he felt obliged to understand. "I'll go. You finish this; your heart is in it."

He heard Hollis draw a preliminary breath as he took the harp. Rook shut the door before he had to listen, and went to get his cloak.

Outside, he descended the hundred stone steps from the school to the dock. He lit a lantern from the dock light, hung it from the prow of a boat, and stepped into it. Rowing in the easy tide, facing the little coracle of the moon, he remembered that on the night he himself had come to Luly, so many years before, the moon had been dark. As he neared the shore he smelled meat, heard voices, the fierce cry of a seabird begging. A wave seized the boat, shook it; the sighing became a slow, sullen roar. Rook leaped into the foam. Someone splashed out to help him heave the boat out of the tide. Laughter around the fire encouraged them. Dripping, Rook stepped into the light.

Three strangers faced him, all young, all wearing their patched mantles and boots, their wild, untidy hair, like some proud livery. Small harps, in and out of their cases, leaned against driftwood, along with skins of water or wine. A hare crackled on a driftwood spit above the fire. In the farthest wash of light, Rook saw large, gentle eyes, the wink of harness.

He studied two faces, one dark, one fair, then turned to the slighter man beside him, wringing the brine out of his mantle. "Griffin Tormalyne?"

"Yes," the young man said instantly. And then, under Rook's dark gaze, his eyes flickered and he said, "No."

The other two were silent now, no longer laughing, watching Rook as if they had handed him a riddle to solve. Rook said slowly, remembering scraps of news, gossip, that had been washed up along the northern coast or carried back to Luly from someone's travels, "It's not a name common this far from Berylon. And I would guess not spoken often even within the walls of the city."

"It will be," the young man with the troublesome name said fiercely. "It will be heard." He hesitated again. "Tormalyne is not my name. But I am of the House, and it's the name I have chosen and it can be spoken here. Not even the Basilisk can hear this far. In the name of Tormalyne House I have come to learn magic."

Rook blinked. He opened his mouth, found himself wordless. Odd memories glanced through his mind: the music from his hands setting the world on fire, the fierce, sweet strings no longer strung to wood but to his heart; the powerful inhuman gaze of the ancient bard who had nearly turned his path toward the hinterlands, where the first bard had trapped all the forces of magic.

"Here," he heard himself say.

"Here." Then the lean face, browned with southern light, again lost its certainty. "Are you a bard?"

"No."

The young man's face cleared. "Then you wouldn't know."

"No."

"What are you, then?" the dark-haired young man asked curiously. "The ferryman?"

Rook looked at him. In memory the bard's dark, challenging gaze hid itself again, freeing him for the moment. He smiled. "Sometimes. I saw your fire first, so I came to get you. We all read the letter from Griffin's father—"

"We?" Griffin asked.

"The teachers."

"So you—"

"I teach, yes."

"But you're not—"

"No."

"Why not? Did you come here too late?"

"No," Rook said, refusing to justify himself, even to the engaging stranger, for the second time that evening. Sea was stirring the boat, washing almost to the fire; he picked up the rope looped to the boat's prow. "We should cross; the tide is turning. I can bring you all over, to rest for a few days. You've had a long journey. But there are no stables on Luly."

The other two eyed the school on the rock with a certain wariness, as if they expected even the beds there to be made of stone. "We're returning to Berylon," the dark-haired man said. "We just rode with Griffin to keep him out of trouble. We'll take his horse back with us. His family will want to know that he got here safely." He paused, rubbing one brow puzzledly. "It's a barbaric wilderness up here," he added. "What can you learn on the edge of nowhere that you can't in the middle of the civilized world?"

"That's a good question," Rook said. "I have no idea."

Griffin picked up his saddlebags and harp out of the litter of shells and tossed them into the boat. He hugged his companions farewell, promising to send letters with the southerly migration of birds, for lack of more practical means. Then he ran the boat into the sea and said promptly, lighting in it, "I'll row."

Midway across, he finished zigzagging north and south, and found a rhythm for his rowing. By the lamplight swaying behind him, illumining indiscriminately a hand, a cheekbone, some pale gold stubble, Rook pieced him together: neat-boned, strong, his expressions honed by a dedication to something that had brought him this far out of his known world. His family had hated his leaving. His father's letter had been nearly incoherent with exasperation.

Reading his mind, Griffin spoke finally. "What did my father's letter say?"

"Roughly: he could not imagine why you wanted to waste your youth on this barren rock among raddled, flea-bitten bards who probably never washed, and who, on the pretext of teaching you anything remotely useful, would force you to grow onions and milk goats."

The light slid behind Griffin's head; Rook heard a grunt of laughter from the darkened face. "He has never understood anything. I'm sorry he was offensive."

"How do you know that he was? For all you know, we may be just that. Luly is a wild, lonely place, and your father has a point: you are very far from everything you know."

"I came to learn," Griffin said simply. "From you, from anyone. I came to take something from you and bring it back with me to Berylon."

"Magic?"

"Power."

Rook was silent, listening to the tide flowing and breaking against the rock, flooding into hidden channels, rifts, underwater caves. He said, slowly, "It's an elusive force. It's not taught here. It can be glimpsed, in songs, in tales. If you take it, you must find it yourself."

"But it exists."

"I don't know."

"You wouldn't know." He pulled too vigorously, skimming the surface; brine splashed over Rook's face. "Not being a bard."

Salt stung his eyes. He closed them, hearing Sirina again in the stranger's words, hearing Hollis; for a moment he glimpsed what they had been trying to tell him. With the sudden vision came fire, rilling through him as it had through the harp, turning itself into music, music turning itself into fire. Into power.

He stirred, trying to see. "Why do you want power in Berylon?"

The young man's brooding face lifted abruptly."You don't know?" Rook waited, watching the rock slowly mass itself out of the matrix of the night. He heard Griffin's breath, a patient sigh. "You wouldn't know, this far from Berylon."

"I know that Tormalyne House was destroyed decades ago. No one bearing that name was left alive. Yet it's a name you want to bring back to life. And that, after all this time, you must still travel this far to say it safely."

"Arioso Pellior missed a few minor relatives when he destroyed Tormalyne House. My father is one of them. He is afraid—" The young man's jaw clamped hastily.

"Of what?" Rook asked, then: "Afraid for you?" He received no answer; Griffin's face, bent to his rowing, remained in deep shadow. Rook felt a deep twist of sympathy for Griffin's father. A forgotten name, a passionate longing for nebulous powers would likely be far more dangerous to the child of the fallen House than to the Prince of Berylon. But Luly might keep the dreamer safe for a time, until he realized that all he learned among the bards was music.

"Do you know," he asked, "the tale of how the first bard came to Luly?"

Griffin's head lifted. "No. Tell me."

"It has something to do with what you are searching for." He told Griffin the tale, adding, after the first bard disappeared into the hinterlands, "The light to your left is the dock lantern."

An oar splashed again, carelessly; Griffin twisted in the wrong direction, then saw the light. "An odd tale," he murmured. He slewed the boat toward the dock erratically; Rook watched the light swing out from behind one shoulder, then the other. "Is it the truth? That he carved stone with his singing?"

"It's the truth in the tale."

"Then there is power in what you teach. . . . Was that the end of him? He vanished in the hinterlands and was never heard of again?"

"No, that was not the end of him yet. A thousand years later the bard returned, pursued by all the magic in the hinterlands for the magical instrument he had stolen."

"The harp?"

Again he found himself wordless. Then words came to him: the truth of the tale. "No. I think he was pursued for the magic he had stolen; it gave power to anything he played. He crossed the bridge to Luly and cried out a word. The sea rose up on both sides of the whale's petrified backbone and pounded it into sand. The magic remained trapped in the hinterlands and Luly became a rock isolated once again by water. The bard, having sacrificed his voice in his great cry, spent a day playing the stolen instrument, the sound of which crumbled stone all around the school into earth. Out of the earth grew, on that day, grasses and wildflowers, and the vegetable garden behind the kitchen. At twilight, the bard put the instrument down and stepped into a whale rib. The ghost of the whale, freed at last, carried the bard down deep beneath the waves, singing, as it reached the bottom of the sea, the song that had hollowed stone on Luly.

"Which is where the whale got its song, and why farmers love the picochet."

The boat bumped against the dock, slid into another boat. Rook caught the rope at his feet with one hand, an iron dock ring with the other. He stepped out, knelt to tie the boat. "Don't drop the oars in the water," he advised. "You row not badly for a city dweller."

Griffin pulled the oars into the boat and clambered out. "What in the world is a picochet?"

"It has a square, hollow body, a very long neck, and a single string. You play it like a viol, between your knees, with a bow. If you stayed on any of the farms in the northern provinces, you probably heard it."

"We stayed in taverns along the coast." He hesitated. "I remember a caterwauling one night, like cats fighting—"

"That would be the picochet." He dropped a hand on Griffin's shoulder, turning him. "The steps are over there."

"You play this picochet?"

"I am fond of it."

"Were you a farmer, then?"

Rook took a torch from its sconce at the end of the dock, illuminated the steps. "I was born in the provinces. I came here very young. My home and family were destroyed by fire. I don't remember anything of them. When I try to look back, I see only fire."

He heard Griffin's breath gather and stop, then gather again. "Those of Tormalyne House who were not slaughtered by Arioso Pellior died by fire."

"So I've heard."

"He should have killed us all."

Rook frowned suddenly, disturbed by the flatness in Griffin's voice. He angled the torch to see Griffin's face. "Us?"

The young man turned away from him toward the steps. "It's secret," Rook heard through the fire. "It's deadly."

Rook, still frowning, watched his uncertain ascent. "Then don't tell the wind," he said softly. "And don't tell the waves. And above all do not tell the birds."

The winds were gentle that night to Griffin, who might have been blown off the steps in a different season. Even so, he was provoked, by the steep angle of cliff and the nagging, edgy persistence of wind, to ask, "Why this lonely place? What possessed the first bard to build his school here, instead of some civilized place where you don't have to climb down off the edge of the world to buy an apple?"

"I suppose because that long ago no one had invented the word 'civilized' yet."

"It's been around now for some time." He was panting, Rook heard; they were very near the top. "The Tormalyne School of Music was built on one of the busiest streets in Berylon. Aurelia Tormalyne didn't believe you had to wrest music with your hands out of wind and sea and stone."

"Then why did you not go there instead?"

"There is no magic in that music." He left Rook in blank contemplation of that, and took the last few steps alone. He stood silently then, gazing at the sheer wall of stone rising in front of him, with its firelit slits of windows and its massive weather-beaten door, the oak slats bound together with bands of iron.

"There are two doors," Rook said, joining him. "One west, one south. Winds are fiercest from the north. The south door opens to the garden. The first bard's picochet inspired even an apple tree to grow in it."

Griffin turned. Wind shook him, pulled the torch fire into strands, hiding his face, then swirled it together to reveal the vague, stunned expression on it. He said, "I can believe this place is older than words."

"It is said to be the place where words begin. You can go or stay," he added gently. "I'll row you back to your friends now, if you choose. You may find what you want here, you may not. I don't know. Not being a bard." He stopped, the word suddenly strange to him, having transformed itself somehow, during their brief journey across the sea.

The young man who had taken the name of the dead opened his mouth, closed it on a silent word. He bowed his head beneath Rook's fire and crossed the threshold into stone.

Four

In Pellior Palace, the Prince of Berylon's dragon-eyed daughter stood beside him in a chamber without a door. The chamber was the heart of the palace, a secret known only to the two of them, for the prince, having discovered it, had eliminated those who helped him furnish it. Luna had penetrated it, to Arioso's surprise, at a very young age.

"I wanted to be with you," she explained when he found her unexpectedly at his elbow. She was unable to explain the powerful conjunction of logic and desire that had transformed the impossible into the only possibility, and led her there. He questioned her as to her methods; she said vaguely, "I watched you." Pressed, she added, "I was there, where you could see me. But it was me, so you didn't see." Then she gave him back his own captivating smile, and he let her stay.

He did many things in that chamber, she discovered. He

read and wrote and drew, made potions and poisons, invented weapons, traps, instruments of torture. He studied the human body, and charts of tides and stars. He played peculiar musical instruments that seemed to be the cause of strange effects. He kept wild animals in cages, killed them in subtle ways. He made lovely gifts: carved wooden boxes, glass roses, pens, jeweled rings, magnifying lenses. They all contained some deadly trick to them: the blade that flew out of the box, the scented ink that ate into the skin, the lens that, held to the eye, wept acid. These gifts left the room soon after they were made, and often preceded an elaborate funeral. They accounted for other funerals, she suspected, that were swift, bitter and held in odd corners of Berylon unknown to her. She never questioned his actions; she only watched him and became adept at whatever he would teach her. Thus she learned many odd things that, her father said, she might find useful one day. She did not doubt that.

Along with his peculiar gifts and labyrinthine mind, she had inherited his charming manner, his green, almond-shaped eyes, his deceptively pleasing smile. So like him was she that there were those who believed that she had not been born but conjured by him, a changeling made to his specifications, to replace a hapless child born for no other reason than to account for Luna's existence. A pity, others murmured, he had not replaced his heir instead. With her heavy, copper-gold hair, her sun-gilded skin, her movements as graceful as wind, she seemed, even to her father at times, something formed out of light and air and precious metals melted and molded into a wish.

He was watching her mix certain powders and solutions

which, in correct proportions, would clear to a pale amber that looked and smelled like wine.

"It produces no immediate effect," he explained as she stirred. "A day or two later the one who drank it will find a sudden and bewildering difficulty controlling the spoken word. Anything might come, with no resemblance whatsoever to coherent thought. Only one drop of that. So."

She measured carefully, and asked, when the drop had elongated, turned pale, and dissolved, "And then what happens?"

"After a week, the exasperated family and friends find a dark, quiet place, far from civilized society, for the unfortunate sufferer. It's crude, but effective."

The glass rod Luna stirred with slowed briefly. She remembered, suddenly, a great-aunt so afflicted, years earlier: her face purple gray with rage and fear; the nonsense that came out of her; her abrupt disappearance. Luna wondered what her great-aunt had done to offend her father. The swirling mixture turned, like dawn, as innocent as light. She said only, "It seems quite subtle to me."

"The results are uncontrollable and far too memorable. It should be used rarely, once or twice in a lifetime."

She raised her eyes, his own faint, opaque smile reflected in them. "I will give it to Taur," she said. "And then I will rule instead."

"You will do no such thing. Taur will have his uses. Besides, he has three children. What do you propose to do with them?"

She considered. "They could be drowned. They aren't very interesting, anyway. But then, neither is Taur."

"Taur," his father said, mildly annoyed, "has a lover outside of the palace. His wife complains to me."

Her gold brows flickered. "He should be more careful."

"He has no sense. Brio found her."

"What will you do with her?" He shrugged slightly, not answering, not caring, she guessed. "Then what will you do with Taur," she asked, "if he finds out what you have done to her?"

He smiled briefly. "You will see." He glanced at a timepiece he had made, an intricate arrangement of cogs, wheels, bands, to mark the position of the sun in a place without light. "Very shortly. Join me for breakfast."

She began to fit stoppers on an assortment of jars and bottles. Dawn, they had found, was the easiest time to disappear within the palace. Arioso did not trust night; he wanted it within eyesight. Once he interrupted her, warned her what that lid might do, misplaced on that jar. She left his marble worktable immaculate; a crumb, he had taught her, from the wrong powder fallen into a careless splash, could have a disastrous effect on the occupants of the rooms that surrounded and hid them. "The air itself is dangerous," he told her. "It carries words, it carries invisible poisons. Trust nothing. No one. Except me."

The chamber, built of massive blocks of white marble behind the walls of other rooms, had been the last refuge of rulers of Pellior House who had exhausted every other method of dealing with troublesome neighbors or relatives. According to family history, it had been last used two centuries before. Then it had passed into family lore until Arioso had discovered a need for it, and, in his methodical fashion, discovered it. Luna, bereft early of her mother for varying reasons to which she paid little attention until later, followed her father's brightness like a small golden cloud drifting after the sun. There were times when he seemed to disappear even under her careful, eager watch. He invariably reappeared, she found. That resolved, she set her mind to the problem of where he actually went, and how. He always went into the same council chamber before he vanished, she learned. Though he let no one else see him step into that room at such times, he never seemed to conceive of a pattern in her presence. That he had gone through a wall in the room seemed obvious. How became less obvious after she bumped her head. So she used her wits and her eyes, and had seen an unfamiliar expression on his face when she joined him in his secret place. He looked, she realized later, as if he had seen her for the first time in their lives; he had finally recognized her as part of him.

Passing back into the council chamber involved a block of marble turning noiselessly on a disk, and a tapestry with a peephole where an animal's eye should have been. The room was empty, the door closed. The prince's bedchamber adjoined the council chamber; it was known that he liked to work there at odd hours. He opened the hall door, spoke a syllable to the page standing there. Breakfast followed soon: figs, smoked fish, hot sweet cakes, butter, honey, spiced wine. Luna had chosen a fig, he had just poured wine, when the door opened again.

A man seemingly made of twigs, with cracked front teeth and a face entirely seamed with wrinkles, closed the door carefully behind him. He crossed the room soundlessly. His leanness, his slight stoop, drew the eye away from his height, the strength hidden in his bony frame. Lizardlike, he made no unnecessary movements. Even blinking seemed a rare and deliberate action. He was plainly dressed, seemingly unarmed, though Luna knew he could bristle like a porcupine with weapons, if needed. He was a distant cousin, Brio Hood, devoid of charm, and fanatically loyal to the Prince of Berylon.

He bowed sparingly, said nothing, nor would he speak unless required. Arioso picked a fig from the bowl, split it with his thumbnail. He asked without preamble, "Who is she?"

"Her name is Jena Aubade." Brio's voice was at once sinewy and unexpectedly soft; he was habitually silent. "Her father is a wharfman with a clear connection, on his mother's side, to Tormalyne House. Her grandmother was careless; someone of the House was indiscreet. Money changed hands. The bastard was reared among the docks at Pellior Bridge and never told his father's name."

Arioso gazed at the glistening seeds in their dusky purple skin. "Tormalyne House." His hand closed abruptly; he flung the crushed mess onto the silver tray, reached for linen. "For the second time in a month an ember has flared out of that charred name."

"Yes, my lord."

"That patched boy calling himself Griffin Tormalyne—"

"He's far away, my lord, among the bards in the north. They'll keep him quiet for a few years."

"Will they." He fell silent; Luna saw the expression he showed only to her and Brio: the mask of skin and muscle slackened, the skull showing through like thought. "They still cling to that rock like barnacles?"

"Yes, my lord."

"They should have stayed as unobtrusive. Why does he call himself Tormalyne? To whom?"

"I will find out."

"And this woman—I will not have my son embracing even a ghost of Tormalyne House. Where did he meet her? Serving ale in some tavern?"

"Yes, my lord."

"He vanishes from dusk to dawn; he can't keep a thought in his head. He is too old to be drowning himself in a head of hair. I suppose she is beautiful. Is she?"

"I don't know, my lord," Brio said. Arioso glanced at him sharply; he added simply, "I have never understood beauty. I don't recognize it. She doesn't resemble her family. She seems to have inherited her face and bearing from Tormalyne House."

"Does she know who Taur is?"

"Yes, my lord."

Luna watched her father's eyes grow fixed and lightless; color seemed to recede in them. "Then you must take her a gift," he said softly. "From Taur. A glass rose, perhaps. Luna will prepare one. Come to her here at noon. Be very careful of the thorns."

Brio Hood bowed his balding, wrinkled tortoise's head and left noiselessly.

Arioso summoned his heir.

Taur Pellior appeared a quarter of an hour later, red-eyed and dazed, wincing at the sun breaking over the wall into the windows. He had not brushed his hair; he was still buckling the belt around his tunic when he entered. Luna smiled brightly at him; Taur only blinked at her, as if he could not quite see her in all the light. He had inherited their mother's soft oval face and slightly protruding blue eyes that failed to see beyond the moment. His dark hair, Luna noted, had begun to thin. He had their father's height, his strong bones, but his strength was sagging. The worn notch on his belt had yielded to the next.

He eyed his father a little warily, but Arioso spoke mildly. "Sit down." He pushed smoked fish, pink and glistening, toward his son. Taur glanced at it and swallowed dryly. "Eat with us."

"Thank you." He splayed a hand over his face. "I'm scarcely awake. It's very bright in here."

"It's called daylight."

Taur's hand shifted to free his eyes; he looked at his father silently across the massive table. Then he sighed and poured himself some wine.

"You didn't wake me up to share your breakfast with me." He reached for an oatcake, scattering crumbs as he broke it, and dipped a piece in the wine. His voice found a querulous note. "You haven't wanted to see my face in the morning for years. You don't trust me."

The charge was true, so Arioso ignored it. "I want your help."

"Really."

"There is a rumor slipping through the provinces that Raven Tormalyne's heir was not killed in the fire," Arioso improvised glibly. Luna, listening, restrained a blink. "That the child was spirited away somewhere north."

"To the provinces?" Taur's brow wrinkled. "What's he been doing for thirty-seven years? Raising sheep?"

"I am sending a delegation, as a courtesy, to the provincial barons, to extend gestures of goodwill, and my hope that their dealings with us in matters of trade and shipping will continue to be peaceful and so forth. I want you to go with them."

Taur coughed painfully on a crumb. "To the provinces?"

"Today."

"Me?"

"The delegation will leave at noon. It only occurred to me this morning that you should go."

Taur was still coughing. "Why?" He stared at his father, his eyes watering. "Why me?"

"A gesture. They are very important to us, the provincial barons; they could strangle Berylon if they stopped trading."

"But—"

"They have never met my heir. I am no longer young and you must deal with them when I die. Even if this rumor is absurd, that Griffin Tormalyne has lived among them since—"

"It's preposterous!"

"I want no attention drawn to that name instead of to Pellior House and you. It's time you took your duties seriously."

"You never wanted me to before," Taur complained. "You thought you would live forever." He paused briefly, blinking. "At noon."

"I've given you very little time to prepare. But you must see that this is vital to Berylon, to me, to you, that Pellior House maintains strong ties to the provinces. While you are there you could ask a question or two, find out how the rumor began. Subtly, of course. It's time you learned some subtlety."

Taur was silent, all his attention focused, it seemed, on the crumbs floating in his wine. As if, Luna thought, he saw a face among them. She read her brother's expressions as he tried to think of an objection, failed, wondered if he had time, in the scant hours left to him, for a visit to the taverns in the shadow of the Pellior Bridge. Or a message—he could send word to her. . . . He met his father's eyes abruptly.

"How long will I be gone?"

"Perhaps a month. Perhaps longer." He indulged in a thin smile. "Don't worry; you'll be home for my birthday."

Taur rose heavily, nearly overturning his wine. He held Arioso's eyes a moment longer. Luna wondered curiously, in that moment, if Taur would fight him, refuse to leave, reveal the truth, or find a lie that would ease him out of the web of Arioso's lies. But there was only a question in Taur's eyes, half-formed and stillborn, as if he had caught a fleeting glimpse of the true object of the Basilisk's deadly stare.

He only said, "I must tell my family."

"Go, then," Arioso said, choosing another fig. "My apologies to your wife."

At noon, from a high window, Luna watched the delegation, laden with gifts and provisions, leave the yard of Pellior Palace. Taur Pellior, speechless and glum, was flanked by the House guards, as if he had been caught in some mischief. The gates closed. Her thoughts strayed down to the docks at the Pellior Bridge, where a woman expecting Taur Pellior would find a gaunt, silent man made of twigs instead.

She turned, slipped as noiselessly as Brio into the council room, and disappeared once again into stone.

Five

Rook dreamed of fire and woke screaming.

He glimpsed something black flying out of the flames just before he opened his eyes. The night itself ignited as he looked at it. Bewildered, he cried out again. Then he pieced himself back out of the winds and sough of the sea, the trembling dark; he fell back into time. He found Hollis's stunned face, his hand controlling the flame at the doorway. Faces beyond him crowded into shadow, mute, startled. He was in bed, Rook realized; he had dreamed; he had tried to waken stone with his voice.

He said to the motionless crowd, "It was a dream."

Hollis stepped into the room. He dropped the torch in a sconce beside the hearth and Rook sat up, drew his hands down his face. Someone closed the door. Hollis closed the window, through which rain was weeping onto the floor. Rook felt rain on his face. He drew breath, leaned back against the stones. Hollis sat down on the bed beside him. His face patchy, uncertain, his hair awry, he looked suddenly very young.

"What was it?" he asked. His expression changed. "It wasn't—it isn't—"

"No. It was nothing to do with your mother." He stirred, trying to remember; as always, he saw only fire, except for the black that flew. Bird, he thought. Raven. Rook.

"Is it what you came too close to when you played the harp that time?"

Rook gazed at him. He felt the harp strings again beneath his fingers, taut, sweet, warning; he felt the fire threaded into the strings. He sighed. "Maybe."

"But why now?"

"I don't know." His hand found Hollis's wrist, closed around it. "Go back to bed. I'm all right."

But Hollis frowned at him, not moving, wanting more than that to be reassured. "What did you dream?"

"Nothing. Fire. That's all I remember. A childhood memory."

"You sounded as if you were burning in it."

Rook was silent. Black flew out of fire, escaped, left what burned behind. He shuddered suddenly, his fingers tightening on Hollis. "I tried to find out before you were born. That's why I wasn't here to see you born. I was out searching for my past."

"Where?"

"The provinces."

"You didn't find it."

"No."

Hollis opened his mouth, hesitated. "Maybe—"

"Say it."

"I don't want to say it. You might not come back. But—" He waved at the thought, perplexed, confused. "Anyway, it's only tales. Isn't it?"

"The hinterlands?" Rook guessed.

"Yes."

"No. I don't believe it's only tales. But I can't imagine finding past there. Future, perhaps. But past is past." He stared back to where it should have been, his eyes gritty, weary, and felt the warning again, the fire threaded into his bones. He forced his fingers open, his voice calm. "Go to bed," he said again, evading Hollis's eyes. "You're shivering."

"You're afraid."

Rook looked at him, astonished in some deep part of himself, as if Hollis had spoken a word he had been looking for all his life. "Is that it?" he breathed. "But of what? It's done." He paused, wondering. "Maybe I burned them," he suggested. "It was my fault."

Hollis pushed his hands against his eyes, sat blinking at his father.

"Maybe," he said doubtfully. "You should—"

"I know."

"No, you don't know. Not yet. Not with your heart. You can still live without knowing. Or you think you can live that way." He stood up, stifling a yawn; Rook watched him cross the room, take the torch. Sirina, he thought suddenly, bleakly, seeing her grace in Hollis, her long fingers lighting the candle beside his bed. "You sounded," Hollis commented before he left, "like the first bard crying his last word to escape all the power of the hinterlands. He played the picochet, too."

"And I taught you that tale," Rook said dryly, to the closing door. The candle had burned nearly to a frozen pool before he slept again.

"What lies behind the word?" he asked a handful of young faces, the next day. Griffin Tormalyne's was among them. "Say a word."

"Fire," Griffin said.

"Is the word fire?"

"Yes. No. Fire itself is fire."

"The word is fire," a lanky farmer's daughter said reasonably.

"The word is the memory of fire," Griffin argued. "The image. The word is what you see and say when you mean fire."

"Think of fire," Rook said. "Without the word. Is it fire?"

"It doesn't burn."

"It is fire in your mind."

It burns, Rook thought.

"It burns in your mind," Griffin said. "Why? What are you trying to tell us?"

"What you say, when you say a word. What you think when you say it. What I see and hear when you speak. Words are ancient; visions and echoes cling to them like barnacles on the whale's back. You speak words used in poetry and song since the beginning of the world we know. Here, you will learn to hear and to speak as if you had never listened, never spoken before. Then you will learn the thousand meanings within the word. What you say when you say fire." He heard himself then, as for the first time, and stopped abruptly. The students gazed at him, waiting, expectant; he wondered suddenly what clutter of images their minds held, and if words they used ever came close to speaking the burning image.

"What do you say when you say fire?" Griffin asked, breaking Rook's odd silence.

"Here," he answered, "you say all the poetry that makes you see fire. Hear it. Smell it. Feel it. Become it."

"Poetry," Griffin said. "Not power."

Rook smiled, and the flames receded. "One thing at a time."

Three nights later he woke them all again with his dreaming, and again, a few nights after that. In the morning, weary and desperate, he found Hollis again and said tersely, "Let me borrow your harp."

He saw the relief in Hollis's eyes. He went wordlessly to get it, said, when he put it into Rook's hands, "I'll come with you. Maybe you shouldn't be alone. You don't know what—"

"I do know what." Rook sighed. "I have always known. Take my students today; that will help me most." He put his hand on Hollis's shoulder. "Thank you."

He sat alone on the eastern face of the rock, emptying his mind of every word until it became the blank, illimitable face of ocean. And then he played, waiting for memory to burn through the sea into his mind. But though he felt his fingers moving, pleading with the strings, his heart, guarded for so many years, refused to yield its secrets. Only the powerful, unfathomable eyes of the dead Bard Horum surfaced in memory, open again, holding his gaze, showing him what path he must choose.

At dawn, he filled a small pack with clothes and food, slung cloak and picochet over his shoulders, and woke Hollis for the second time that night. Hollis looked at him groggily over the long, bright hair hiding the face on his chest.

"I'm going," Rook said softly. Hollis shifted; Rook put a finger to his lips. "Don't wake her."

Amazed, he saw tears gather in Hollis's eyes. "Don't forget your way back," Hollis pleaded. "Those tales—"

"I won't forget. Tell my students. If you leave Luly—"

"I'll wait for you."

"If you leave—"

"I'll wait," Hollis said obdurately. "Just come back."

He rowed alone across the water, pulled the boat ashore, and left it upside down behind a driftwood log. He walked into the forest, leaving his footprints in a line as straight as the line of raven's feathers he had once ignored. Not even they broke the silence as he left the world behind.

He did not know how long he wandered before he met the old woman beside the shallow stream. He had not seen a road or another human being since he had left Luly, only the hawk and the owl and wolves who howled back at his picochet. All dreams had stopped, in that place, as if he had entered a waking dream. It was mid-afternoon. He had passed through the ancient forests and began to climb. He followed the stream up a rocky slope toward green hills scalloped like waves breaking toward a mystery of blue beyond them. He recognized them: the floating hills he had seen from Bard Trefon's boat. He looked back at all the years that had passed since he been that child wondering if he would ever walk alone through those mysterious hills, and what he might find there. And now I am here, he thought grimly, feeling the sun beating down at him, the ground hard and dry beneath his steps. The old woman's face turning toward him out of the shadow of a scrubby tree startled him. His foot slipped off wet moss, splashed down in three inches of water. She smiled at that, showing few teeth and no fear whatsoever. He regained his balance, wondering if he still had a voice after such silent days and nights, or if he had left that behind him along with the rest of the known world.

"Good day," he said. She did not answer, just gazed at him out of eyes as bright and shallow as the stream, until he felt of no more substance in her mind than his reflection in the water. There was something birdlike about her, he thought. Her nest of hair drifted; a downy feather floated out of it. Her hands, tipping a copper bowl to catch the water, might have been claws. She opened her mouth to speak finally. He expected a greeting in the language of birds, but she surprised him again.

"Cool your feet," she said. "I'll tell your fate." She patted the ground and pointed. "Sit down. There. In the shadow. Where I can see your face."

Her voice, so thin and wavery the mild air might have blown it away, seemed remarkably clear. He let pack and picochet slide from his shoulders as he stepped into shadow, bending into the low curve of branches. Trees on that hill dug deep into earth and clung to stone, hunched over themselves against the bitter northern winds. Sun-warmed now, the tree loosed a scent as sweet as honey at his touch, and dropped a tiny seed cone, like a gift, into his hair.

He sat, and pulled his boots off, propped his feet among

the stones in the shallow water that glided out of shadow into burning light, slid like molten glass down the hill. He looked at the old woman and found her watching him, wind in her hair, water in her hands, her garments mossy and gray, as if she had picked up a patch of the landscape and swirled it around her.

"I'll tell your fate," she said again, and tilted her copper bowl back into the water.

"It's not my fate that's troubling me," he said, suddenly curious about her, in this desolate wilderness. "It's my past. Can you see back that far?"

She only shook her head a little, mute, while the water trickled into her bowl. He wondered where she lived. Nothing under that vast sky seemed human but the two of them, and he was not sure about her.

She righted the bowl carefully when it had filled, and balanced it among the rocks where it reflected the sky. Then she drew a little copper hammer from a sleeve or a pocket. She caught his eyes in an animal's wide, expressionless gaze, and he felt as if she had reached suddenly into him and plucked a deep, taut string.

"Bard."

The hammer hit the bowl at the word; copper rang like a sweet bell. The water trembled. She loosed him abruptly to watch its patterns. He drew breath noiselessly. It seemed both a likely fate, and a shrewd guess: she must have seen bards and students from Luly wandering around the hinterlands for most of a century.

"Can you see dreams in there?" he asked her.

She ignored him. Copper rang against copper again; she

hunkered over her visions, her skirt dragging in the water, her reflection piecemeal among the rocks. Wind blew a complex scent over him, of something flowering, something dead.

"Your past is your future." She added, after a few more moments, "Your future is your past."

He was silent, waiting patiently while she moved in vague circles around his life, seeing nothing, it seemed, any more clearly than he did. She murmured a few words he didn't catch: her language, maybe, words as old as the stones on the hill. He wished she would produce his fate, glittering and improbable, out of the bowl, so that he could talk to her.

She spoke again, still peering into the water. "I see the eagle and the snake, on your road. The cock and the goat. I see the raven in the fire."

He stirred slightly. And then sweat broke out over his entire body, as if the fire had come too close, had burned its way out of memory into light. Wind brushed over him; he trembled in a sudden chill. He brought his feet out of the water and sat straight. She was murmuring again, in her strange language. Or maybe, he thought, his body prickling again, the words were strange only to her.

"City," he understood. "Bridge. Moon. Mirror." And finally, very clearly: "Griffin." She struck the bowl again; the single note seemed to reverberate out of the water and send its slow waves flowing outward around them, as if they sat at the bottom of the bowl. Motionless, he felt each wave melt through him, his bones echoing the ring of copper.

And then she was looking at him without seeing him. Again he had the eerie feeling that some creature whose name he did not know looked out of her eyes.

"You will face the basilisk."

Her eyes cleared. He said, stunned, "What does that mean?"

She tipped the bowl, spilled his future back into the stream. "What?"

"Why did you say—"

"I said nothing." She put the hammer into the bowl, set it beside her. "I never speak."

She rose, pulling her shreds and tatters back out of the wind. He still could not move.

"Then who speaks?"

She smiled, her face wrinkling like a dried pool, a piece of the hard brown earth around them. "You do." He stared at her wordlessly; she studied him as silently, her eyes her own now, and filling, he saw, with sadness. "Do something for me."

"I will," he promised breathlessly.

She turned a little unsteadily, pointed up the slope. "Over and down the other side. Among the trees. That's where they are."

"Who?"

"The dead." She picked up the bowl, and moved away from him, tugged by hem and sleeve and tattered shawl into the wind. "I saw them in my bowl. They need you. You must play for them."

She trudged on bare feet across the stream. He rose quickly, calling after her, "Are they yours? Are they your dead?"

Or, he thought incredulously, are they mine?

She did not speak to him again; the path she chose led down the hill. He watched her for a long time, until she was as small on the hill as the stones at his feet. Then he put his boots back on, slung pack and picochet over his shoulder, and turned.

He took the slope with long, easy strides, following the water to the top of the hill, where the stream burrowed suddenly underground, leaving him high and dry. All around him, green, brown, stone gray spilled into one another, blurred across distances into secret, shadowy hills. To the north he saw water again, vast as an inland sea, a glint of deep blue beneath heavy, lowering cloud, like a partially opened eye. No one had ever returned with the name of it.

He saw the trees on the other side of the hill, halfway down, a flow of delicate green unbroken, it seemed, by village or field. Above the trees, threads of smoke frayed into wind. He smelled it; his throat tightened. A sudden drift of smoke stung his eyes. He closed them and saw the raven flying.

He followed smoke down the hillside into the wood. The bitter pall thickened within the trees; beneath the trembling, chattering leaves, he heard the silence of the dead.

He entered it.

Six

Justin Tabor, red-eyed from a night at the Griffin's Egg, stood in a grimy alley between two battered marble mansions, looking across the street at Tormalyne Palace. The mansions had seen better days. Clothes fluttered, drying, on balconies where once banners had hung. Children wailed above his head, cats fought, men and women shouted at one another. The alley stank. The palace, behind an iron railing spiked with black lilies, held no life at all.

Two griffins guarded the gates; one had lost a wing, the other its head. The gates sagged under the weight of massive chains wound between them, locking them shut. Skull-like, the palace regarded the world out of empty sockets, charred black where fire had billowed out from every window. Only a brilliant shard of glass still clung, here and there, to a rotting edge of frame, flashing unexpected color within the ruined face. A bottle with a few dead marigolds in it sailed out of a window overhead, smashed at Justin's feet. Slivers of crockery and water sprayed his boots; a battle above him escalated furiously, voices locked together and clawing. Picochet and viol, he thought sardonically. The picochet had the last word. A door slammed; a burly man passed him a moment or two later, muttering, blind with anger. He ground the marigolds into stone without noticing them, or the young man watching him within the shadows of the alley.

Justin's eyes went back to the palace. Once every few weeks, very early in the morning, a ribbon or a scrap of cloth blew against the gate and clung there. Invariably the cloth was black. It wrapped itself unobtrusively around a lower hinge, hung there until noon, when a musician carrying a lute in its case over his shoulder stopped beside the gate to shake a pebble out of his shoe. The musician was Justin's firebrand cousin Nicol, who had drummed the history of their House into Justin's head since they were small. Nicol was named after the second son of Duke Raven Tormalyne. Nicol Beres knew everything there was to know about Nicol Tormalyne, who, together with his two small sisters, had suffocated in a marble bathroom during the fire in the palace. There had been no question of their identity. Another child had been found huddled against the blackened remains of the favorite dog of the duke's heir, Griffin Tormalyne. The dog had been identified by the stones in its collar. The child was burned beyond any kind of recognition, though Raven Tormalyne, dragged out of the dungeons below Pellior Palace, was commanded to try. After seven days of imprisonment, the duke himself had been battered nearly beyond recognition. He had lost an eye and his right hand; he could barely walk. He could still cry and curse, which he did; his tears were considered identification enough. He was permitted one last glimpse of his wife, haggard and maddened with pain and grief, as she was slain in front of him. The executioners of Pellior House removed the duke's remaining eye, and then his life.

Duke Arioso Pellior had emerged from the bloody brawl between four Houses with the crown of Berylon in his fist. He named himself Prince of Berylon, promised death to any members of the other Houses found bearing arms within the city walls, and pardoned the scattered remains of the Tormalyne family for their relations. Two years later, in a magnanimous gesture, he invited the survivors to his birthday feast.

Over three decades later Tormalyne Palace was still empty and the birthday feasts had turned into an autumn festival which the entire city celebrated, or pretended to. Justin, a scion of Tormalyne House whose own father barely escaped the Basilisk's War, had his imagination inflamed from an early age by his cousin Nicol. Nicol inflamed well, even better, Justin thought, than he played the lute. He had become a magister at the music school, which Prince Arioso had appropriated, down to its last demisemiquaver, for the good of the city, though he at least allowed it to keep its three-hundred-year-old name. Nicol taught the lute and the harp, gentle instruments that disguised his true soul. His bitterest moment in life had come early, when he realized he had been named after the wrong son. He was a griffin, born to fight the basilisk, and toward that end he left black ribbons on the gates of Tormalyne Palace, summoning his followers.

Justin watched his cousin make his customary stop at the

gate, bend to loosen his shoe, let fall an imaginary pebble, then free whatever he had left on the gate and drop it into his shoe before he pulled it back on. He was never careless; he would no more fill the weedy palace yard with windblown scraps of black than he would have let a light show from within the charred maze of cellars and dungeons on the nights they gathered there. Griffin's Claw, they called themselves, the scions of Tormalyne House whose parents had managed to elude the Basilisk's eye. Their parents, stunned by the devastation of the House, were content simply to be alive and left unnoticed. In secret, their children dreamed the downfall of Pellior House. For years they did nothing but dream. Gradually, growing older and more astute, they began to buy arms.

Nicol straightened, and Justin slipped out of the alley. They walked a block or two apart, before Justin crossed the street and gave his cousin a genial greeting. Nicol, an ascetic, red-haired hawk, seemed even leaner in scholar's black. He answered Justin somberly. He rarely smiled, and had little patience with common social noises.

"There was trouble on the Tormalyne Bridge last night while you were playing at that place—that Griffin's Beak—"

"Egg."

"A man died."

Justin's brows rose. "How?"

"His horse threw him off the bridge."

"That's unfortunate for him, but hardly trouble."

But Nicol still frowned, walking rapidly even in his magister's robe. He saw trouble everywhere, Justin knew; he was seeing it now, trying to make trouble out of a horse unnerved by the drumming echoes of water welling up beneath the bridge.

"They were armed."

"Who were?" Justin asked, used to Nicol's elliptical habits.

"Three men, riding across the bridge. All of them trying to carry weapons openly into Berylon."

"Perhaps they were strangers to the city. They didn't know."

"Or they didn't care."

Justin was silent, puzzled. Nicol, striding vigorously on the scent of motives, mysteries, possibilities, blind to the world, did not enlighten him. It was a wonder, Justin thought, the cobblestones he never saw under his nose didn't send him flying.

"Why should we?" he asked finally.

"Care?" Nicol stopped abruptly, gazing at his cousin; someone behind him nearly fell into his lute. "Maybe you're right. Maybe we shouldn't. I only wondered how far from Berylon you would have to come to try to ride armed through the Tormalyne Gate." He paused, lowered his voice. "Gaudi has been trying to find them." As abruptly, he began to walk again. Arms, Justin thought coldly, and caught up. Nicol scented them like some aberrant animal.

"I don't think it could have been personal."

"What?" Justin asked patiently.

"I mean an angry husband, an act of passion, revenge, something like that. That would have begun within the city, or close enough to it that they would have hidden their weapons."

"Were they allowed in?"

"They had to have the body brought up, identified.... Of course their weapons were taken at the gate. They were questioned, but accused of nothing. Armed men trying to go unnoticed would have crossed another bridge."

"So either they were ignorant, or they were trying to be noticed."

"Or they didn't care," Nicol said, with his bloodhound persistence.

Justin drew breath, held it. "Well," he said finally, "that's one bridge they'll never cross again. Why wouldn't they care about having the Tormalyne Gate slammed in their faces?"

"If they were deliberately creating a diversion, sending a message that they are willing to bring arms for a price into Berylon."

Justin was silent again, refusing to rise to that bait. Nicol could find portents everywhere, even in someone careless enough to be tossed into a ravine. Nicol took his attention off the faceless stranger in his imagination and looked at his cousin suddenly, as if he had just noticed Justin. "You could find out about them," he said. "You have nothing else to do."

"I play nearly every night," Justin protested. "I dragged myself out of bed early for you—"

"I don't have time to stop to eat."

"I didn't ask you."

"You'd be far more use to us if your life was less erratic. You're throwing your talents away on drones up to their ears in ale and so sotted they probably think you're twins."

"Or that I'm playing a double bass."

"You should work. Or study, and teach."

"I do work!"

"I mean a real—"

"Nicol, if this is leading toward an argument about what is real music, I'll be forced to remind you who comes in her magister's black to play with us every week. She thinks it's real music."

"She plays the picochet," Nicol objected absently; the frown inched down between his eyes again. "That mocks her other talents."

"You play together. Do you think her talents are questionable?"

"They're formidable," Nicol conceded. "It's her taste that's in dubious—taste."

Justin snorted. "She risks her formidable reputation to play with us, for no other reason than that nobody at the school can stand the picochet."

"It only has one string. It refuses to mingle in harmonious fashion with anything. Besides, there is no proper music for it."

"So she is forced to take down her hair and bare her shoulders and knees to drunken tanners."

Nicol blinked. "Really?"

"Just to play an instrument that caught her heart."

"Her heart. Nobody plays the picochet by choice. Except in the barbaric provinces. Maybe she spies for Pellior House. Beware of her. Give her nothing. What do you talk about with her?"

Justin evaded the question. "Nicol, do you think I would babble in a tavern about—"

"Lower your voice. You get drunk there. How do you know what you say?"

"She comes to play the picochet," Justin said tightly. "We talk about ballads. Nicol—"

"Don't trust her," Nicol said peremptorily. "Never trust anyone not of the House. That reminds me, though, of something you might do with your life. We could use someone coming and going in Pellior Palace. For legitimate reasons." He ignored Justin's sidelong stare. "You could work there." His hand, closing on Justin's shoulder, checked an exclamation. "They want—"

"No."

"Listen to me."

"No." He unclenched his jaw after a moment. "Be satisfied with my life, Nicol. I'll change it for myself, but not for you."

"Listen," Nicol said.

"I'm not working for—"

"It's the music library from Tormalyne Palace." He paused; his grip suddenly became uncomfortable. "They stole it."

"I thought it had burned," Justin said blankly.

"So did the school. Three hundred years' worth of manuscripts and scrolls so valuable that they were not even kept in the music school. Veris Legere sent word to the school that he needed a librarian to sort and catalog them. Just that. No excuses, no explanation—they burned children, but not before they rescued the music library—"

"Yes," Justin breathed, his eyes flicking down the walk. "Nicol. Why did they wait thirty-seven years—"

"Did he bother to explain? Does he think there is anyone left to care? Someone opened a closet and there it was, a treasure in manuscripts, smelling of smoke, a trifle bloodied, and now he wants a librarian." He shook his head a little; his hand opened, dropped. "I'd do it, but I don't trust my temper," he admitted with rare candor. "But you—"

"Me," Justin said thinly. "I'm just the one to stand around in Pellior Palace trying to read three-hundred-year-old signatures on music stolen from Tormalyne House. Thank you. I would rather gut fish."

"It would be temporary," Nicol said, with his infuriating obtuseness, and for a moment Justin felt the family temper shimmer behind his eyes. Then he laughed, which was easier than fighting Nicol, and which Nicol found equally baffling.

"No. You'll have to use what talents I have. I can keep an ear open in the taverns for gossip about the riders on the Tormalyne Bridge. But sorting musty manuscripts in some marble room in Pellior Palace—I might as well be dead and buried. I'd get drunk from boredom, pass out among the scrolls, and Veris Legere would drop me out the nearest window like a bawdy song."

"Well," Nicol said, unconvinced. "Think about it. We can speak later." They were, Justin found to his surprise, nearly at the steps of the music school. "Everything has its dangerous edge. Even you."

Justin watched him. Among the students he moved gently, gracefully, giving out spare, melancholy smiles to those who greeted him, People trailed after him up the steps; even here he had his following, mostly pale, limpid-eyed, mouths daintily pursed as if they carried quails' eggs on their tongues. Justin turned finally, wrestling with the familiar knot of exasperation and affection that Nicol invariably left in him, and crossed the street to the tavern there to find breakfast.

Seven

Rook stood in fire.

He burned in it; he watched it burn; it had already burned the charred, blackened heart of the wood around him. The dead, twisted and melted by flame, were unrecognizable.

Trapped in memory, he could not move. He was what the fire had left behind it: the ashes in the hearth. He felt sound growing in him, but he could not make a sound, not in the wood, not in the hearth, not with the Basilisk with his golden face and his deadly eyes saying again and again: Is this your son? His father had only one eye to weep sorrow for the faceless child on the floor with its arm around the dog. The other eye wept blood. The child hidden in the vast marble hearth, covered in ash, breathing ash, stared at the mangled ember of the child on the floor, clutching the jeweled collar of the dog in its brittle fingers. Yes, said his father's tears. Yes, said the dog. Yes, said the dead. I am your son.

The dead child watched.

The palace, the wood, had finished screaming; there was only this to finish, that. His sisters had stopped, and his brother. His mother had screamed at the Basilisk; she screamed at the dead child, gave him his name. Then she stopped, and there was only that to finish, because the child was already dead. His father had no more words; he had nothing left to see. The Basilisk finished finally, left the dead in their silence.

He still could not move. He felt a breeze like silk, like the hands of the dead, on his face, on his wrists. He felt his fists clenched, his body shaking in the sunlit wood, as if he stood in all the fury of winter. He could not move, he could not make a sound. The child still hid in the hearth, breathing ash, swallowing it, the bitter taste of being dead. He stared at the child on the floor, himself, and knew he was the child's dream; he was only a dream of being alive. The dead had taken his name.

They had understood, those who had found the dead on the floor. When he came out, covered in ash, unable to speak, they knew that he was the child on the floor. He was ash; he was no one; he had no name. They had given him another. He stared at the eyeless raven on the floor and could not weep, because he was dead. The white-haired man made a circle out of lamp oil around all the dead, himself and his dog, his mother and father. The other men, guards wearing dark cloaks over the torn and filthy griffins on their tunics, led him out of the room. He turned at the threshold and looked back. The white-haired man, his father's uncle, set a torch to the circle.

Fire swarmed over the dead. His father moved, turned blindly to look at him. Something rose from him—a dark flame, a word, his name—flew upward out of the fire. Then flames hid him, hid them all, hid everything, the house, the city, the world. He turned away from the fire, walked a step or two before he stumbled.

Someone picked him up. He could not see, he could not hear. He was dead. They took him out of the world to the kingdom of the dead.

The raven in the fire.

Raven Tormalyne.

He heard himself make a sound, a rook's harsh cry. Blinking, he saw the dead among the trees, faceless and silent, as if they had appeared out of his dream. But they were not his dead: a beaded leather shoe told him that, a cooking pot, a piece of striped cloth, an odd painted drum. He wept then, still shaking, unable to move. Tears broke out of him like rain; he wept blood, he wept ash. Ravens circled him among the trees, cried his cries, dropped feathers like black tears. The dead waited, but he had nothing to play for them: the picochet meant life.

The drum, as silent as the dead, played itself in his head.

It stood oddly in the midst of the dead, for no reason, dropped like an egg on the floor of the wood. It was made of glazed pottery and painted with eyes. The eyes spoke, as he stared at it. The dead were wordless; their eyes spoke. The ravens spoke.

He moved then. There was nothing to play it with, so he played it with bone, bringing a charred thighbone high up over his head and then down, and down again, and again down until the drum broke like an egg and the dead flew out of it like wind, poured among the shivering trees, and passed away, followed by a black wind of ravens. He watched them, his eyes as black, his breath still full of ravens' cries, with ash from the fire, from the hearth.

He dropped the bone after a while, and sat with the husks of the dead.

Hours later, in the night, he remembered the picochet and played it in memory of their lives.

Near dawn, he tasted his name like ash in his throat and swallowed it. I am alive, he realized, amazed. All this time I have been dead.

He fell asleep finally among the dead.

In his dreams, he went north.

He knew the tale his dreams told then: he was both the teller and the bard in the tale. His heart eaten by fires that would not die, he had left Luly and walked through the hinterlands until he found the place at the top of the world where winter was born. There, he thought, would be the cold fires to spawn the instrument to play the ceaseless raging in his heart. In the tale, the bard carried a twisted knot of love and betrayal in his throat; he could not swallow it; he could not sing. In the dream, there was no love, only hatred, and the torn, empty eyes of death. He could make that cold sing for him; he could freeze his own bones and play fire out of ice. He moved into the barren, deadly land without feeling the killing wind: his own fires kept him alive.

Out of mist and burning cold came the monstrous beast that the powers of his rage had summoned. It was white as winter, red as blood, black as night. Its eyes and breath were fire. It had wings and talons like the raven, and spurs as sharp as knives along the bone from neck to tail. Even dead, it could kill: its skin was venomous; its teeth and scales were sharp as swords. The fire in the marrow of its bones never died.

The bard said: *Give me a bone to play.*

It said: *I will give you one. Your life is mine.*

He said: *Take my life.*

It turned its flat head and sinewy neck, bared its teeth, and snapped off a small bone in one wing. The bone dripped; snow hissed at its blood.

It said: *Your heart will take my shape when you play. You will summon me out of your bones. I will do whatever your heart asks. And then you are mine. And then you will live where I live. Your bones will be ice; your blood will be fire. Every song you play will become the song you play out of me.*

The bard said: *There is no other song.*

He woke. Night lay thick and dark as feathers over his eyes; the wood around him was soundless. He felt something in his hand: a twig, or a small bone. He closed his eyes, slept again. In his dreams, the lion rose from the ashes, the eagle flew out of the fire. The blind raven spoke his name.

He could not find his way out of the hinterlands. East turned into south or north; the moon and sun had changed direction; he had misplaced an ocean. The hills were no longer empty. He kept meeting people living in small villages, who pointed him in one direction or another, and then distracted him. They offered him food, asked him to sing a story, and gave him odd things to play. He told them the tale of the bard in his dream; they knew the tale, and the fire-bone pipe. There was one in the next village, they heard, and told him how to find it. In the next village, he found the same vague rumors of the pipe: in the next valley, there was one, or perhaps beside the lake. "I must get home," he told them urgently; they pointed him east and he got lost. They all seemed gentle, kindly people; he could find no reason for the dead. He asked them, but they listened as if he told some long-forgotten story, or a dream. He had traveled into the land of the dead and played for them: that, they somehow knew. Now he could play anything. The trees listened to his picochet and opened new leaves. Birds answered bone pipes he made, and he understood their language. He played a whistle made of a raven's feather and asked the ravens to find his way back to the sea. They led him here and there, to listen to a flute that only women could play, to gourds that hissed and rattled the language of snakes. Home, he told the ravens. But they could not follow his heart's path, he knew. Luly was no longer home.

Home was south, under a burning sky, in a city of stone ringed by water. Home was a place where his name could not be spoken. Home was a reflection in the Basilisk's eye, into which he must move without being seen. Beneath the summer sun of the hinterlands, he felt his heart take the griffin's shape, cry the eagle's challenge. But he must return to Luly for Hollis; he could not vanish out of his own son's life. And Griffin, with his dangerous secrets and deadly name, filled him with sharp apprehension. Luly was not far enough from the Basilisk to speak that name. Death itself was not far enough. . . . His fierce desire to find Luly grew more compelling by the day. He walked the sun's path from morning to night, and still daylight left him in an endless wood, or beside a nameless river, among people who gave him shelter, and taught him tales so old he scarcely recognized the language. In the morning, they pointed toward the sea and told him he would smell it by day's end. At day's end, he would smell the smoke of another village, and hear, not the boom of the waves and the echo of the whale's song, but another instrument he did not recognize, another song.

Finally, when it seemed he had played every instrument made since the beginning of the world, and had begun to learn tales from the birds, he walked out of a wood one afternoon, up a hill, and found himself at the top of the rocky slope where he had found his future.

He stared at it bewilderedly, then turned to look back at the trees, wondering if all the woods had been hidden within that wood, if all his days had been the same day. He found the shallow stream spilling out from beneath the stones, and followed it down the hill. Midway, he saw, beneath a stunted tree, the glint of copper, and a streak of white, windblown hair.

He came to her without surprise, looked at her silently, his face hollowed and gaunt now, with the memories and the sorrow that burned within, eating at him.

She smiled, showing her three teeth. The way the world smiles, he thought wearily. Showing teeth.

He said, "Can you tell me the way back to the sea?"

"You'll find it," she answered, slanting her bowl to catch the water.

"I've been lost for weeks. I can't find my way out."

"You found the dead."

"Yes."

"You played for them. I heard."

"Yes," he said again, his face tightening. She heard everything, he guessed. Every spoken word, every word left unspoken.

"I have a message for you," she said. "Bard." She lifted the bowl out of the water, and he felt his breath catch.

"Is it my son?" he asked, moving closer to her. "Did he come here?"

She only answered, "You'll find your way now."

She struck the bowl with her copper hammer. The note melted into him, sweet and pure, not dying but growing in force until he felt it in the stones underfoot, until the twisted tree shook with it.

The water in the bowl burst into flame.

He stared at it. And then terror raked a claw across his heart, before he could find a word for what he feared. He shouted, "Hollis!"

Turning blindly, he smelled the wind from the sea.

He walked out of the forest accompanied by the croaking of ravens, telling him of fire, of death. In the long summer dusk, the school on the rock seemed to have turned itself back into rock. He could see no light in the windows, no smoke from the kitchens, no movement anywhere. On the shore, boats lay scattered like shells; footprints in the sand fled north, south, into the shadows of the forest. He heaved a boat over, found oars, pulled it grimly into the waves. Tide flowed with him to Luly. As he neared it he saw the thick windows shattered, the stone beneath them streaked black with fire.

There were no boats at the dock. They had escaped. Or they had been trapped. He refused to let himself think. He tied his boat, his hands trembling, and cursed the hundred stone steps that he could not outrun. He smelled the dead before he saw them.

They had been asleep, he found; the fire had caught them at night. He moved through the charred rooms noiselessly, as if he, too, were dead. Fire had left the school hollow as an old bone, had transformed blood and song into ash. He did not let himself feel, or name, or weep for any of them, until he found Griffin Tormalyne's blackened, broken harp beneath the open window of his room. Looking out, he saw the bright-haired, tide-washed body on the rocks.

He slid to the floor, sat with his back to the wall, his eyes as black as the acrid stones behind him, and as tearless. He shaped a pipe in his heart made of bone and fire, and played it for the dead. For the boy who had taken his name, he played the stringless harp on the floor beside him. For Hollis, he played nothing: the thought of him dead might make it true.

As the moon rose in the empty window above his head, he heard a step in the hall. Frail wings of firelight brushed through the dark. He lifted his head, feeling the movement of his bones heavy, unwieldy, as if he were slowly turning into stone. He heard more steps, quiet, tentative. The fire burned more brightly along the stones, limned the charred doorway. He pushed himself up, shaken back to life.

He heard Hollis's voice: "Where are you?"

He tried to speak; a raven spoke. He heard Hollis again, an inarticulate sound, and then the fire found him.

He held his son while Hollis wept, saying brokenly

against his shoulder, "I saw the boat from the shore—I didn't know—I hoped it was you. I saw your picochet when I moored—"

"How many—"

"Over half got out. Some died on the rocks—jumping from the windows, or thrown back onto them by the waves." He lifted his head, watching them again; Rook saw the horror frozen in his eyes. "Some never woke."

"I saw. When did it happen?"

"Four nights ago. The bards that were left took the students to the provinces. I waited for you. I couldn't let you come back alone. Not to this."

"Who did it?"

Hollis blinked. He pulled back a little to see Rook's face. His hands closed on Rook's arms. "It was an accident. What makes you think—" He stopped, his eyes locked on the raven's eyes. His fingers dug into Rook, feeling for bone. "No one would—" He stopped again; Rook saw him shudder. "Someone," he whispered, "said he dreamed fire moving across the water early in the morning. Before the moon set."

"He dreamed it?"

"He—we said he must have dreamed it."

"No."

"How do you—who—" His voice rose. "What do you know? What did you find in the hinterlands?"

"I know my name."

Hollis stared at him. Blood flushed into his face; he shouted incredulously, shaking Rook, "Who are you?"

"My name is Caladrius." He pulled Hollis to him again, quickly, tightly. "You are still alive," he breathed, amazed.

"And so am I." He turned then, to pick up the blackened harp beneath the window. He gazed a moment at the dark, moon-laced swirl of tide below, trying to free the stranded dead. "We'll bury them," he said, "before we leave."

"Why?" Hollis whispered. "Why this? Why the bards? It's like—setting fire to birds."

"They took in Griffin Tormalyne. And now he is dead again."

Hollis, quieter now, gazed at Rook silently. He opened his mouth, drew a breath, but did not ask the question that was dawning in his eyes. He said instead, "He never told us his true name."

"It was in his father's letter. I remember it. I want you to go to the provinces. Your mother will hear of this; let her know we both survived. Stay there. You'll be safer, there."

"I know." His face, still struggling with grief and shock, was easing into more familiar lines as he began to think. "So will you."

"I'm going south."

"Yes. I know what Caladrius means. I want to hear you sing in Berylon."

He began to hear the song then, wordless yet, formless and powerful as the wind and waves that, grain by grain, had sculpted Luly. "You will," he breathed, and held Hollis's shoulders, held his eyes. "I'll send for you when it's safe."

"Safe! You can't even whisper your name here, to me, among the dead—you can't even tell me—"

"I can't," he said tightly. "Not yet. Please. I need to go alone. The bards were right about the hinterlands; the tales are true. You do not take the same path back out of them, nor do you find the world you knew. I crossed the sea again to Luly, but I have not left the hinterlands. They have become the world."

"I don't understand," Hollis said. He was silent a moment. Rook saw his eyes widen suddenly, as if he had glimpsed his own heritage, his own name. He added reluctantly, "I'll go to the provinces. For now. Be careful."

"I'll be safe. No one knows my name."

They gave the dead to the waves and the gardens of Luly. As they rowed from rock to land the bard Caladrius heard the singing of the whales accompany them across the sea.

PART TWO

Griffin's Aria

One

In the noisome tavern on Tanner's Street, Giulia Dulcet lifted her picochet bow and began a ballad just as Caladrius walked out of the forest at the edge of the Tormalyne Bridge.

The sky was smoky blue with twilight. The moon hung in it like a misshapen pearl. Beneath the moon, two griffins of jade and yellow marble crouched and glared across the massive lintel of the gate that opened, at the end of the bridge, into Berylon. As Caladrius caught sight of them other memories took wing: the griffin on a seal ring, on a gold banner, white griffins guarding a fireplace. His eyes filled with wings; his steps slowed. Between him and the griffin gate, a fat, overladen trapper's wagon lumbered, pulled by oxen. The creak of wheel and idle crack of the trapper's whip were muted by the boom and echo of water raging far beneath them. Caladrius, on the threshold of Berylon, heard the word of warning in the water.

Something moved between the griffins; fire swarmed suddenly across the gate. He saw the basilisks then, coiling black, with flat, smoldering eyes, on the tunics of the guards on the balustrade between the griffins. The wagon, at a snail's pace, swayed toward one wall of the bridge, then the other. Caladrius, following patiently, watched a gold-haired boy wearing the basilisk run down the bridge to light other torches along the low walls. He slid like a minnow between wall and wagon to reach torches on both sides, making for Caladrius, unnoticed behind the wagon, a bridge of fire into Berylon.

He had brought nothing with him from Luly. He had walked alone out of the north, down the long road through the forest, where the birds sang of gentler seasons, warmer light. Dressed in rough homespun and cracked boots, carrying a leather pack, he might have come from the provinces to look for work, having failed, with the picochet he had left behind, to inspire life in his fields.

He took another slow step on the span of marble stained and runneled by centuries. Stone flowers twined in and out of the graceful pattern of arches along the bridge walls. Some had been crushed or snapped off, as if under the weight of hurtled objects. What he remembered of the city's history was passionate and tumultuous. Roses and lilies bloomed, he guessed, green with moss among bones at the bottom of the river.

The wagon shuddered oddly. The trapper cursed, snapping his whip. A back wheel had begun to wobble. Behind Caladrius, the forest spoke. A raven called his name, disturbed. The guards on the balustrade turned their backs abruptly, alerted by something happening within the walls. Caladrius glanced behind him. The great, dark trees were motionless. An owl swiveled its head to look at him from a high branch. Silent as moonlight and as white, it spread its wings and floated into shadow.

He heard then, what the forest heard above the lion roar of water: voices among the trees, a slow but steady march of hooves following night to the Tormalyne Bridge.

In the Griffin's Egg, Giulia, sweating in stagnant summer heat, her hair collecting smells of stew and smoke from the tavern kitchen, scarcely heard the picochet wailing and yearning under her hands. Her thoughts veered erratically back through the day, lighting in a room full of students baffled by her desire for them to invent a musical instrument. Anything, she had assured them. Teacups. Plumbing pipes. Paper. Then she saw the messenger from Pellior House coming toward her down the hall. Tomorrow, the note had said. Pellior Palace. To speak of the autumn festival. Veris Legere's signature, in dove-gray ink, above the basilisk's seal. She saw the sun-gold face of the Prince of Berylon, his lizard's eyes smiling down at her.

He wants my music, she thought, amazed. She wondered how those eyes would look if they saw her with her frilly skirts hiked above her knees, her fingers stiff with heat, laboring up and down the picochet string like a handful of sausages.

She ended the ballad with a tooth-stabbing shriek; a burly docker inhaled beer and choked. A few northerners pounded on tables with their mugs. Everyone else ignored them.

"Thank you," Iona said sweetly into the din. "My mother thanks you. My father thanks you. Without your support they would have to pay astonishing fees to the Tormalyne School of

Music, which you are all helping me to escape. This brass bowl accepts gold, silver, copper, jeweled buttons, anything you can spare in gratitude for our efforts. Look closely at our picochet player. She is a genuine magister, freed from captivity for the evening. But not dangerous, unless you trifle with her picochet. If you drop a coin into the bowl, she will smile for you. Next I will sing—when Justin gets the spit out of his pipe—my own rendering of the old, sweet ballad 'The Brawl on the Tormalyne Bridge.' "

Yacinthe patted a roll of hoofbeats out of her drums. Giulia raised her bow.

A horseman rode out of the trees, the basilisk on the banner he carried crying its cock's crow challenge to the night.

Caladrius, his face taut, looked away from it quickly. He felt its baleful stare boring into his back as he followed the plodding oxen. Their pace had grown suddenly exasperating. More riders came out of the forest; he heard hooves strike marble, horses snorting at the scents of oxen and furs, their harness jangling as they jostled one another, crowding onto the bridge, and were sharply reined. A guard shouted at the trapper; he shouted back. Water roared over their words, swept them away. The voices behind Caladrius came more clearly.

"What's in it?"

"Skins, by the smell."

"What is it?" another voice demanded, sharp, querulous. "What's that on the bridge?"

"A trapper's wagon, my lord."

"Why is it going so slowly? Have it make way!"

"The only way it can make, my lord, is down."

"Then we'll ride to the Pellior Bridge."

"Patience, my lord. The wagon will be across before we get ourselves turned around."

"Patience! Where exactly do you think I have any left to spare? I've just spent six weeks smelling barns and eating sheep and listening to something that makes my teeth ache, and the last days blinding myself with dust and interminable trees. Either get that wagon out of my way, or I will ride alone to the Pellior Bridge!"

Caladrius slipped to one side of the bridge, found a shadow between two torches. He paused a step to look back. Riders still spilled out of the trees, adding more basilisks, more brightly colored silks, more weary, annoyed faces to the backwash at the bridge. They were pressing closer to him, easing around the balking rider, who seemed willing to toss the trapper's wagon into the gorge with his hands. He had a fretful, imperious face, dark, thinning hair, eyes that saw little beyond his own desire. They did not see the man in the shadows, only the wagon. One of the guards had better eyesight.

"You!" he called to Caladrius. "Are you traveling with this wagon?"

"No," Caladrius said, and added, "your lordship. I just walked down myself. From the north."

"Another mutton eater," the fuming rider muttered. He pulled abruptly at his reins, trying to turn his horse in the crush. "I'm crossing the Pellior Bridge. Make way!"

"Go with him," the standard-bearer ordered swiftly, to the guards nearest them.

"Might as well all go," one grunted. "That wheel is about to cross without the wagon."

It fell off as he spoke, wandered away, and crashed into the wall beside Caladrius. The dark-haired lord paused, blinking at the wagon. One corner sagged, as if under the weight of their stares, slumping lower and lower. The trapper, bewildered, shouted at the oxen. The end lurched suddenly, boards parted, and an entire hillock of furs, not entirely cleaned, reeled onto the bridge. The wagon lurched again as the oxen, goaded by the whip, pulled forward.

Swords spilled in a silver cascade onto the furs.

"You're inspired tonight," Justin said to Giulia, wandering over at the end of the ballad to help her tune. He blew a note. "You sound like all the wildlife in Berylon in spring."

She twisted the peg on the picochet, plucked the string. "I wasn't paying attention," she confessed. "My hands feel like wood in this heat." She paused, pulling up the loose neck of her blouse, which had slid halfway to one elbow. "Justin—"

"What?"

She looked at him, drew breath. "Justin," she said again.

A brow quirked. "Well, what?" he asked, amused and mystified.

"I may have to—I may not be able to play here for a while."

Both brows went up; a line formed between them. She put her hand on his arm. "Why not?" He was no longer almost smiling. "Are you tired of us?"

"No—that's not—Justin, of course not. It's just that—"

"Just tell me."

"I received a message from Veris Legere, the Master of Music for Pellior House. I am to see him in the morning."

"For what?" he asked bewilderedly. "To teach Her Pruneface the picochet?"

"To discuss the autumn festival, he said. I'm not sure what he will want me to do. There is always an opera—"

"Opera." He said the word cautiously, as if it could crack a tooth. "You mean he wants—"

"I don't know yet, but he might, and this might be my last night here."

His face flushed suddenly. "You'd leave us?" he demanded incredulously. "To play opera for that malignant warlock's birthday?"

The loathing in his voice startled her; it ran far deeper, she realized, than Hexel's, who could set aside his aversion long enough to play the prince's music. She said, distressed, "I'm sorry. I would miss playing here. With you. But I am responsible to the school—I can't always choose the music I play."

"Any begger in the street can choose the song he sings." His face was suddenly grim, the face of the stranger who lived life in a different Berylon, who heard music she did not know. "Say no."

"I can't. I can't offend Pellior House. The Tormalyne School exists because Arioso Pellior permits it to exist."

He was silent, studying her, still unfamiliar. "You want this," he said. "This festival."

"I want—" She paused, then simply nodded. "I want its music." She met his eyes. "And I want you. And I want the music I play here, in the smoke and heat and noise. Is that wrong? If I can only play this music here, is it wrong to love it? Or if I can only play the lavandre under the Basilisk's eyes—is that wrong? Should I not play at all? Should you not love me because I play it?"

"No," he said, startled. "Don't go that far."

"But it can go that far. If we let it."

He was silent again, his head bowed, his eyes hidden. Behind them, Yacinthe and Iona waited, impatient and curious, for them to finish their lovers' squabble. He said finally, carefully, "I do understand. More than you think. Be careful in the Basilisk's house."

"I'll do what I'm told. In matters of music. I don't see what trouble I could get into."

"That's how the basilisk kills. You don't see it until it looks at you."

She gazed at him, puzzled, troubled by what he did not say. He sighed, his face loosening, and touched her cheek. "We'll miss playing with you."

She kissed him quickly. "I'll see you when I can. No matter what. Give me that note again."

Justin lifted his pipe. Yacinthe's hands danced over her drums. " 'The Ballad,' " she announced, " 'of the Trapper Who Trapped Himself.' "

On the bridge, the trapper abandoned his wagon and began to run. Caladrius, cornered by torch fire and the broken edge of the wagon, with a pile of reeking furs at his feet, saw the trapper's choices: the guards at the gate, or a quick leap into the gorge. The guards might show more mercy; they had not yet seen why the trapper was running, only that he had left a mess in the middle of the bridge. He was a soft, heavy man; the three guards caught him easily, dragged him through the wagon and out the back. Faced with a firelit pool of weapons and the basilisk rampant everywhere he looked, his quivering face drained the color of suet.

The guards silently questioned the lord of the House, who said with extreme irritation, "Kill him."

The standard-bearer ventured a protest. "My lord, it might be better—"

"Kill him! Get him out of my sight! Now!"

They dragged him, struggling and incoherent, to the bridge wall; a couple of riders dismounted to catch his legs. Caladrius, breathless, his heart hammering, saw the trapper's face just before they rolled him over the wall and into the gorge: his eyes, protruding in terror and astonishment, pleaded senselessly with the moon beyond the fire. Then he dropped, transfixing them all with his scream echoing up from the sides of the gorge before rock and water swallowed him.

Caladrius seized the torch at his back. The movement broke the gorge's spell; guards, turning, remembered him. He leaped into the wagon as they began shouting. He left the torch on the wagon floor. Fire swarmed over the remaining furs, found fat, and blazed a bright gate across the back of the wagon. It began to pick at the wagon's bones as Caladrius slid out the front. The oxen, shifting uneasily at the smoke, began to drag the burning wagon. They caught his eyes with their protruding, senseless gazes. He heard himself make a sound, an inarticulate protest at their demand for life. But he paused to fumble with their harness; freed, they managed a quicker pace.

Water swallowed all but the most furious voice behind the wagon. He would, he thought, remember that voice: it followed him as he walked, trailed by fire and oxen, through the Tormalyne Gate into Berylon.

The narrow, winding streets were quiet for the moment, except for the tavern beside the bridge, its thick windows smoldering with smoky light. Amid the muted, chaotic noise that seeped out of it, came the last sound he expected to hear.

It reached into his heart, stunned once more by death and memory, and pulled him like a hand into the Griffin's Egg.

Giulia, stroking long, husky notes of lament for the trapper, was remembering her grandfather on the farm. Taciturn even for a northerner through an entire winter after her grandmother died, he mourned through his picochet. So he had taught Giulia the inarticulate phrases of the heart. Engrossed in memory, hearing him speak in her playing, she thought at first that his fingers loosened the bow in her hands, his fingers coaxed the instrument from her. Then she heard the stranger's voice.

"Please," he breathed. "Just this one. Please."

He was, Giulia realized with astonishment, begging to play her picochet. Some drunken, homesick farmer, she thought at first, and then, still astonished: Why not? No one had ever asked before. She relinquished it and rose. He sat quickly, his head bowed against the long neck, the way her grandfather had played it. She moved to one side, leaned against the wall, listening. He seemed tentative at first; his hands were shaking badly; he did not drive the bow hard enough. Someone tossed an empty tankard at the squeals he made. And then he found the strength he needed, and struck fire from the picochet.

She listened, her eyes on the floor, until a sudden disturbance blew through the door. Raising her head, she saw basilisks in the shadows. She watched, surprised. They had not come to drink. They pushed through the crowd, searching. Voices flared; a pitcher was broken. Through it, the cold north winds sang out of the picochet, the ghost of someone looking back on his life, singing beyond his death. Giulia dropped her eyes again, found the bottom of the picochet and the stranger's boots. The picochet was patched there; so were his boots. She lifted her eyes slowly along the line of light running down the dark wood, polished by the hands that had held it. Her eyes stopped at his hands, lingered, then rose more quickly to his face.

It was half-hidden behind the picochet. But it seemed oddly familiar, a face out of the past, though whose past she could not remember. Some composer carved in white marble, some painting, hanging in a practice hall, of that lean face, with its clean wolf's jaw and broad, strongly molded bones. She could not see his eyes; the shadow of the picochet cut across them. His short, silver-gold hair looked as if he chopped at it haphazardly with a pruning knife.

The tavern door slammed behind the last basilisk. The ballad came to an end. The stranger rested his face against the long neck of the picochet a moment, as her grandfather had done, as she herself did, as against a lover's face.

Then his eyes flicked through the tavern. He rose, still searching, and turned swiftly. He leaned the picochet carefully against the stool and brought Giulia her bow.

"Thank you," he said. She saw his eyes then, so dark they held no color, powerful in their directness. The guards, she realized, had come looking for him; he had hidden himself within his playing. He had stopped trembling, but his haunting face was harrowed, colorless.

"Who are you?" she asked in wonder. He only gave her the memory of a smile and disappeared into smoke and shadows before she could ask another question.

Two

Giulia made her way backward down the marble corridors of the Tormalyne School of Music. Busts of composers, musicians, patrons of the art watched her out of white, pupilless eyes from their niches. Doors opened and closed between the busts, loosing delicate sighs of music, energetic outbursts, sudden collisions between instruments. Someone sang a scale; flute notes leaped up broken chords. A phrase was repeated over and over, pure and liquid, on a glass harmonica. "Magister Dulcet," she kept hearing. "Just one moment. Giulia!"

"I have to go," she said desperately to Hexel Barr, who had sprung like a clockwork figure out of his workroom. He ignored that, calling her stubbornly until she turned again, still walking, students laden with books and instruments dancing out of her way.

"I need your help," he insisted. "Now, Giulia. For just

one moment. I have one idea, one puny, weak, starveling idea for this opera, and if it is worthless, I can't go on. Someone else will have to be found."

"Hexel, you always say this — every year — and then you — "

"This year I mean it. I am a desert. A wasteland. Barren."

"And then you produce something wonderful — "

"Because of you," he said adamantly. "Because of you. My muse."

Behind her a young student snickered. "Not now," she said tersely. "Find another muse until tonight. I must go."

"Giulia." A viol player, passing, touched her arm. "Don't forget, we are rehearsing this afternoon before supper."

"I won't." She gazed at the graceful, limpid-eyed woman, who was holding her viol in both arms like a lover. "Why," Giulia pleaded, "can't you be Hexel's muse instead?"

She only laughed. Giulia, moving, heard her name again, saw her youngest students through an open doorway, surrounded by copper pipes, nails, plant pots, upended buckets, vases, beer mugs.

"Come and listen," they begged. "Is this what you wanted?"

"Try glass," she suggested, "Something light. And you have no reeds. Remember: even grass sings."

She escaped finally into the street, to be confronted by a small, exquisite carriage with basilisks painted on the doors. She hesitated. A page swung open the door, bowing deeply.

"Magister Dulcet?"

She entered, speechless.

The Master of Music for Pellior House met her in one of

the appointment chambers within the palace. It was a small room, striped with white and crimson marble. Lily and rose lay underfoot, on the marble floors; they grew in the patterned marble hearth, up striped pillars, along the walls. Only the ceiling, painted gold, and the crimson velvet curtains and chairs, were not made of stone. It was as cold and quiet as a tomb.

"I know your reputation and your work," Veris Legere said. "And you know the needs of the house. Something elegant, traditional, elaborate but not lengthy, sumptuous but never gaudy, a touch of drama for the singers to display their skills, and of course a happy ending." He paused a moment, expressionless; beneath his silver hair, his face seemed ageless and devoid of humor. But Giulia knew that his lack of expression could express a great deal. "One stipulation. The Lady Damiet will sing an appropriate role, as a birthday present for her father."

Her Pruneface. Giulia kept her face still. "I see."

"I'm sure you do."

"I don't know the Lady Damiet's voice. The appropriate role would be—?"

"The maiden, the princess, the virtuous young woman—in short, the heroine."

"I see."

"She has a vigorous but untrained voice. Her range is limited, but it will be adequate."

"And her ear?" Giulia asked cautiously.

"She has two," the Master of Music said with precision. "Beyond that I cannot speculate. You ask me why we have a sudden need for a music director for the festival."

"I didn't. I do." She paused, guessing. "I don't."

"Berone Sidero was advised of Lady Damiet's determination to sing. Within a day or two he decided to become afflicted with some elusive malady curable only by several months of peace and quiet in the provinces."

"Oh."

"Your health is good?"

She hesitated; he lifted one silver brow. "Yes," she said finally, and the brow descended. He smiled unexpectedly.

"Good. The prince has mentioned your name once or twice. I thought that someone who plays the picochet in a tavern on Tanners Street and the prince's music in a consort from the Tormalyne School might be capable of dealing with the unusual demands of this festival."

She felt her face warm with horror, thinking of her piecemeal costumes, the beer-drenched floor. "How did he—"

"The prince's interest in music is broad and not always formal. He pays attention to detail; he encourages me to do so. You mentioned the picochet to him. He grew curious. When he cannot see and hear for himself, he uses others' eyes and ears. Sit down." He opened the door, spoke to someone. She sank onto a hard oval of crimson velvet, seeing Justin suddenly, with her in the Griffin's Egg, hearing his acrid, pithy comments about the Basilisk. No one could have understood him in that din, she decided. And if she were not in trouble for listening, he would not be for speaking. . . .

"Now that I have persuaded you," Veris said, rejoining her, "let us begin to deal with practical matters. I have sent for chocolate, cakes, and the director's' notes for the last decade."

Two hours later Giulia left him, her arms full of notes,

her head cluttered with names and dates, one of which demanded that instead of playing with Justin in the Griffin's Egg the following week, she teach Lady Damiet to sing.

"And of course," Veris had said, "we must have the music. The drama itself. As soon as possible. How is Hexel faring? As usual?"

"Hexel has no ideas, he is uninspired, he tears his hair, he is surrounded by crumpled paper, his music is trifling, he can't think of a plot, and he is a barren wasteland."

"As usual."

She met Justin in the tavern across the street from the school, where he waited, hunched over ale, to hear how she fared in Pellior Palace. She told him, eating hastily before her afternoon classes. He listened silently, picking at a splinter in the table, his brows twitching together now and then.

He said only, to the splinter, "Then I won't see very much of you for a while."

She put her hand on his wrist, feeling heartbeat and bone, holding him as if for balance between two worlds. "Only for a while. I'll come to you when I can." He raised his eyes finally; she read the question in them. Her hand tightened. "Yes. I need you. I need to know you will be there. Or will you be too angry with me?"

"No," he breathed, turning their hands to find the milky skin beneath her wrist, that never held the southern light. He kissed a vein. As he raised his head she still saw silent questions in his eyes; these she could not answer yet. She linked their fingers, raised his hand to her mouth, wondering eerily who around them watched the magister and the tavern musician out of the Basilisk's eyes.

Returning to the school, she taught lessons on the harpsichord and the lavandre, then listened to her young students beat on their plant pots and copper pipes with stones, shoe heels, and strands of glass beads. She rehearsed a duet for a performance at Marcasia Palace. She ate supper quickly, then hid herself in a practice room with the lavandre and her picochet, which she played softly, caressing the notes out of it, thinking of Justin. Her thoughts wandered, after a time, to the stranger who had hidden from the Basilisk's guard within its music. He knew its voices, those that sang, those that wailed, those that whispered and threatened and cajoled. But he had finished her ballad for her and vanished, without explaining, into the night. Perhaps he will return, she thought, and then: But I will not be there.

"Giulia!" Hexel flung open the door of the tiny practice room. Her bow jumped; the picochet screeched. He winced. "How can you bear to share the world with that demented instrument?"

"Hexel," she exclaimed, returning from the tavern to the school. "I am to direct music for the autumn festival. Go away and finish your opera and bring it to me immediately—we have no time to waste."

Pleased, he caught her hand and kissed it, nearly blinding himself with her bow. "That's wonderful. You will appreciate my work in ways that Berone Sidero never did. He refused to let me choose singers for my own songs. His taste was never quite disastrous, but—" Attuned as he was to every tremolo of mood around him, he stopped. His hand tightened on hers; he searched her eyes. "But why you? Where is Berone Sidero?

He fusses over this festival like a goose with a string of goslings. He is jealous of every flea. Did he drop dead or something?"

"He became ill," Giulia said temperately. "Hexel. About the singers—"

"Illness was not in his schedule a week ago. He was hounding me for music." He loosed her to fling up his hands. "How can I write music? I have no—but listen to this." He took the picochet impulsively, found a note, and played a simple, haunting melody. The picochet whined fretfully in his hands; Giulia, lifting the lavandre, repeated it in dulcet tones and smiled.

"It's lovely."

"It's a song to an absent lover." He put the picochet down and tried to pace around it. "Or perhaps a lost love, one mysteriously vanished. I can't decide. How can I? I have done everything already; there is nothing left to hold my interest. Everything bores me. Lovers, lovers parting, lovers reconciled. That is the only plot in the world and I have exhausted it."

"But it becomes new with every pair of lovers who have never loved like this before—"

"And never will again. I know. The Prince of Berylon wants a bauble for his birthday. An airy pastry stuffed with pastel cream. I am starving on all this sweetness. This year, I am going to kill someone."

"Not on his birthday!"

"Why not? He did."

She rapped his shoulder sharply with her bow. "He did not. Which is the reason for the autumn festival."

"That he stopped killing people."

"That Berylon was at peace again. Which is saying the

same thing," she added as he opened his mouth. "I know. But in language he would wish to hear. And which will not get the music school closed. You may rant at me about the Prince of Berylon, but you will write a confection for him."

He sighed, leaning over her, his hands on the arms of her chair, his head bowed. "Then help me."

She thought, silent. He straightened, picked up her lavandre, and blew softly, playing his love melody. She set the bow to the picochet, whispered a duet.

She saw the stranger's face again, an odd echo of the past, as if a dusty painting had come to life. Hexel, watching, lowered the lavandre. "What are you thinking?"

"Nothing. I mean something out of the ordinary. But not extraordinary. Just—"

"What?"

"Just a man who came into the Griffin's Egg and played my picochet and left. That's all."

He leaned back against the door, still watching her beneath half-lowered lids. "That's not all."

"He played like my grandfather."

"Did he look like your grandfather?"

"No."

"What did he look like?"

"No one I have ever met, but somehow familiar . . . He barely spoke. He interrupted my ballad, finished it for me, and was gone. That's all. Yet I've never heard anyone play like that except my grandfather."

"And you."

"And me."

Hexel made a soft sound; his eyes grew opaque. "The stranger who is not a stranger, returning . . ."

"Returning from where? He looked as if he had been born in the provinces and had just walked down from them. He played like it."

"Perhaps," he said softly. "But you like him mysterious."

"Well, so he seemed. . . ." She paused, and decided not to invite the Basilisk's guards into Hexel's imagination. "He wouldn't tell me his name. His eyes were—"

"His eyes?"

"He looked—" She stopped, inarticulate again, and met Hexel's curious gaze. "His eyes didn't look," she said finally, "as if he had spent his days watching corn grow. But he probably did."

"I," Hexel said, "prefer him mysterious." She lifted a brow; he did not see. He had focused on the shining coils of the lavandre. "I see him returning from somewhere, some ordeal. . . . Returning perhaps to Berylon, where he was born. And where once he loved."

She raised the bow, pressed it meditively to her lips. "And he wonders now—"

"If she still loves him. If she is still free. If she will recognize him."

"Why wouldn't she recognize him? He can't be that old."

"We must have some dramatic tension."

"She pretends not to recognize him," Giulia suggested, inspired. "She dares not."

"She's married."

"No," she said hastily, remembering Damiet. "She must

be virginal for the prince's opera. You may not raise moral issues."

"She's engaged, then." He sat straight suddenly. "No. I know. She doesn't know him. They have never met. Upon meeting, by chance, love flares between them, their hearts are lost to one another. But they must love in secret because their families are bitter enemies. Which is why he was forced to leave the city."

She stirred, hearing overtones of history in his plot. "Hexel, you are treading too closely to truth. Love must have been thwarted like that during the Basilisk's War, and in the lives and memory of some who will be watching this. They'll find only bitterness in your happy ending."

"And, returning, he is still in danger. . . ."

"You're not listening to me."

"Yes, I am. How can you say that?" He caught her shoulders, kissed her exuberantly. "I hang on your every word. You are my muse."

Three

Caladrius found lodgings, a tiny room above a tavern across from the one place he knew that held no sorrow. Some inner compass had led him there, through vast currents of strangers moving ceaselessly between stone and light that could, he learned, be merciless. Its fierce warmth had hatched basilisks in that city, griffins; the phoenix of Marcasia House shriveled in it like paper and was reborn; the chimera of Iridia House could be glimpsed in the hot, shrunken shadows and the shimmering glare of noon. In the cool pale marble of the music school he finally saw beyond the fiery light, to the child who had walked fearlessly through the city and knew his name.

From his room, he could look down at the griffins still intact on their egg-shaped shields on either side of the front doors. The Basilisk had destroyed the House, but had let the stones survive. A gesture for history, Caladrius guessed. A token to the dead. Watching the students, the black-robed magisters coming and going, their arms cradling instruments, music, books, he remembered his teacher's face, her luminous, powerful eyes. She had played an instrument for him that he had not heard again until he walked into a village in the hinterlands.

Perhaps, he mused, she had other strange instruments. She was of Iridia House; she would have no love for the Prince of Berylon. He could ask at the music school; they would tell him where to find her. If she had survived.

He descended to the tavern, noisy with students and laborers, and already stifling at midday. He ate roast beef and brown bread, drank bitter ale, his head lowered, taciturn as the farmer he seemed. He longed with sudden intensity for Hollis's company, and put the longing aside ruthlessly to think. The young man who had called himself Griffin Tormalyne had had a secret; perhaps it was that secret which had tried, so ineptly, to bring arms into the city. The name had not been forgotten; it had become dangerous. To whom? he wondered. Perhaps she would know, his old magister, with her seeing eyes. He was startled out of his musings by the young man sitting down opposite him at the broad, scarred plank.

"You're Giulia's picochet player!" he exclaimed. Caladrius gazed blankly at the good-humored, blue-eyed face under a tangle of pale gold. "Do you remember?" he persisted. "You played with us in the Griffin's Egg. Giulia wondered who you were."

"Giulia." He took a bite, chewed silently, and found, beneath the terrors and chaos of the bridge, calm hazel eyes within a limp, sweat-streaked fall of dark hair. "Is that her name."

"Giulia Dulcet." He added mysteriously, "We lost her to Pellior House. To the Basilisk's birthday party. My name is Justin Tabor. I play the bass pipe."

"Yes." He stretched a hand across the table, noticing then that the blue eyes were reddened with late hours, smoke, beer; the wild hair looked permanently tangled. He felt his own face ease slightly. "I remember the hair."

"Can you play with us again?" the young man asked impulsively. "We've gotten accustomed to the picochet; it's the only thing louder than the tavern. We're at the Griffin's Egg nearly every night. We can pay, if you're looking for work."

"I am," Caladrius said, after another bite. "But I left my instrument behind me. In the north. I'm a stranger here. I don't understand. Why you lost Giulia."

The rakish gentleness on Justin's face slipped like a mask; someone older, harder, inhabited that face. "She went to play music for the Basilisk. Arioso Pellior. Every year on his birthday, he gives us all a present. A feast. Music. The streets are dressed in ribbons and banners; Berylon turns into a festival. He bribes us to forget, and shows us at the same time that we have no power in remembering."

"You're too young to remember," Caladrius commented, and the untroubled musician reappeared, hiding his private face.

"The House remembers," he said briefly, and bit into the meat pie cooling in his hand.

"Perhaps when I'm settled," Caladrius said, intrigued by the hints of bitterness, of secrecy. "When I find another instrument."

"What kind of work are you looking for?"

"Almost anything. I've done many things."

"Can you read music?"

"Why?" Caladrius asked, arrested mid-bite.

"They're looking for a music librarian at Pellior Palace. To catalog the music collection from Tormalyne Palace that strangely refused to burn. My cousin Nicol was trying to persuade me." He brooded a moment at his pie, then looked up to catch the expression that had glanced through Caladrius's eyes. "I don't blame you, I don't want it either. Most likely," he added with his mouth full, "for entirely different reasons. You must be used to mortaring stones together. Tossing seeds around. Watching things grow."

"Or not."

"Well, they must have grown once, the way you play. Isn't that what they say? It brings up the crops? Giulia told me that. If you do get work and your instrument back, come and find us again. You can find Giulia across the street at the music school. You left before she could talk to you. You're the only other picochet player she's heard in Berylon."

Caladrius, making a sudden decision, replied absently, "It's not an instrument for the city."

"No. She grew up in the provinces on her grandfather's farm."

"Did she? So did I. Grow up north."

"Maybe you knew each other."

"No." He dropped a coin on the table and rose, looking down at Justin. "Which way is it?"

"What?"

"Pellior Palace."

Justin swallowed too quickly. "That way," he said when

he could. "Four streets over and then down Tigore Way. Half a mile or so past Tormalyne Palace. You'll recognize that. It's been dead for thirty-seven years."

"Thank you. You've been kind. I'll find you again. When I have a picochet."

He was nearly out the door when Justin got to his feet and shouted, "Wait! I don't know your name."

The familiar midday din in the tavern fell to a sudden hush. Caladrius, turning, faced inquisitive eyes all over the room, attention focused on him for no reason at all except that a young man, crying out a question, held them suspended in his curiosity.

He said to the city of Berylon, "My name is Caladrius."

The tavern resumed its noisy flow, burying his name beneath words like a stone beneath water. Only Justin, caught in Caladrius's glance as the door swung shut, hesitating before he sat, seemed puzzled as by a song he had once heard that had just haunted him again.

Tormalyne Palace lay in the bright, drenching light like the immense, blinded, sun-bleached corpse of some fabled animal. Caladrius tried to pass without looking at it, afraid he might stop in the middle of the jostling crowds and howl like a dog, tear cobbles from the street to wring sorrow out of stone. It loomed beyond his lowered eyes, insisting, until he finally looked, and was stopped. Memories swarmed through him; he could not see beyond the ghosts haunting him. Something struck him lightly: a passing lute angled across the back of a magister's black robe. The red-haired lute player, lost in his own furious thoughts, did not notice the man he had brought back from the dead. Caladrius lowered his head, took one step, and then another, and felt the fingers of fire and bone slowly loosen their hold around his heart.

He did not remember Pellior Palace. It was likely that he had never seen it: the rulers of Pellior House had paid court, for four centuries, to Tormalyne House. It rose white as bone above its placid gardens, banners spilling out of its windows, its turrets painted gold. Basilisks prowled the front gate. They demanded his business brusquely, laughed at his worn boots, his unkempt hair. Then, with nothing better to do than swelter in the sun, one walked through the cool trees into the palace.

Sometime later he returned, and opened the gate.

Veris Legere, he was told, would see him.

Veris Legere saw him in a small room of green-and-cream marble. He was a slight, aging man, unperturbed, it seemed by his complete lack of expression, at the sight of a farmer in Arioso Pellior's palace. He did, for a moment, search for appropriate words.

Caladrius said, while he looked, "Forgive my appearance. I just walked down. From the north. I'm looking for work. I studied awhile with the bards. On Luly."

Veris Legere found his voice, a hint of expression. "The bards of Luly," he said slowly. "I forget, sometimes, that they are more than a legend."

"They may be, by now," Caladrius said steadily. "No more than a legend. It was many years ago. But they teach in ways to make you remember."

"Yes. So I've heard." If he heard more than that, of fire on the rock, nothing in his cool eyes suggested it. "What did they teach you?"

"Various instruments. Poetry and songs. To read and write words and notes."

"Did you compose?"

"A few things."

"Who told you that the House needed a librarian?"

"A young man in a tavern." Veris Legere raised a questioning brow. "A musician. I mentioned that I need work. He remembered this. He did not expect me to be interested."

"The musicians of the Tormalyne School would rather play it than catalog it. The collection to be cataloged is quite large and very old. It was taken from Tormalyne Palace after the fall of the House."

"The palace burned." He found reason then to be grateful for the provincial abruptness. "The music did not?"

"I believe it must have been moved. To the dungeons, perhaps. It was moved here with equal haste, that I can tell from the disorder. Whoever brought it here forgot it, or was unable to tell anyone who thought it important. The prince's daughter Luna discovered it in various old chests and cupboards. Much of the music was written by members of Tormalyne House. Their names told us where the collection had come from. Some of the music is so old it flakes under the brush of air. It must be put in order, as far as possible, by composer and date. You would need to learn something of the history of the House."

"May I see it?" The passion he could not hide in his voice, Veris took for a music lover's; a faint smile surfaced in his eyes.

"Some of it has been moved into the music room. It is usually empty, at this time of day. Come."

"I'm not—I can't—" He gestured at his dust.

"You made it this far, Master Caladrius, in those clothes. Arioso Pellior does not question my judgment in matters of music."

The music room, as he had predicted, was empty. It was a vast cave of filigreed marble, all shades of white but for the solemn black strip that ran along the base of the walls. Cases of wood and glass stood back-to-back in ranks along one side of the room; they held instruments and music. Veris led him to the line of cases along the wall, opened one. Scrolls and flat manuscripts filled it in a disorderly pile. Veris lifted a brown scroll gently and handed it to Caladrius.

"Tell me what you see."

"It's old." He unrolled it carefully, his hands trembling slightly. "Song," it was titled simply at the top. At the bottom it was signed "Aurelia Tormalyne." "Someone of the House wrote it. There is no date. I would have to know when she lived. It is written for a single instrument in the middle ranges. Possibly to be sung. Perhaps there are words, somewhere." The scroll was shaking badly; he felt Veris's eyes move from it to his face. He let the scroll roll itself. "I'm sorry," he told the cold marble floor. "It's a thing that happens. When I want something very badly."

He heard Veris draw breath. The door opened then; he looked up and saw the Basilisk.

Arioso Pellior was speaking to someone, his face half-turned; Caladrius remembered his voice. His gold hair had lightened; beyond that he seemed to have changed little. Veris bowed when the prince glanced across the room. Caladrius, frozen, did not. The reptile eyes met the raven's, had begun to narrow when Caladrius bent his head stiffly, belatedly. Still he felt the Basilisk's glance, as if those eyes had scored his bones.

"My lord," he heard Veris say. "I believe I have found our librarian."

A woman laughed lightly. Caladrius kept his eyes lowered, listening to their footsteps, which continued to cross the room. Fingers touched stray notes in passing from the harpsichord. She said, "He dresses like a farmer, and has no manners."

"He is a northerner, my lady."

"Taur will not be pleased. Fortunately, he never comes here." Their footsteps seemed to be aimed at the doors in the opposite wall.

"See that he is suitably attired," the prince said briefly.

"Yes, my lord."

He murmured something; the woman laughed again. Caladrius let his eyes flicker upward; their backs were to him; they had nearly reached the open doors. The woman's hair was the rich gold that the Basilisk's had been once. Her voice, he thought, could melt gold with its charms; her mockery seemed light as air.

She turned, before she followed the prince through the door, looked back at him as if she heard his thoughts.

She was gone before he remembered how to breathe. Veris Legere took the scroll out of his hands and replaced it in the case. "The Lady Luna Pellior," he said dryly, before Caladrius remembered how to speak. "The prince's older daughter. Very like her father in all ways. Before you leave, I will give you money. When you return in the morning you will be dressed discreetly in black and your hair will be trimmed. Your boots will not be seen here again. You will become familiar, in time, with the need to bow your head upon occasion, Master Caladrius."

"Yes," he breathed. "That's not a gaze I'd want to offend twice."

Veris dropped a hand on Caladrius's shoulder. "You've seen the Basilisk's eyes and lived, Master Caladrius. It may not happen twice."

It has, he thought starkly. But never again. I will not live to survive him. She would see to that. His child. His mirror.

"Master Caladrius."

He bowed his head to the music of Tormalyne House in its glass prison. He thought he left the palace alone, but he found the image of Luna Pellior burned, like a quick glimpse of the sun, behind his eyes.

Four

Giulia stood in the music room at Pellior Palace, studying the four broad oval paintings on the ceiling as she listened to Damiet Pellior sing. The paintings depicted the Birth of Music, the Meeting of Voice and Song, the Marriage of Time and Harmony, the Children of Music Playing the Twenty-seven Courtly Instruments. Casting her eyes up frequently to the charming roil of pink flesh, discreetly draped linen, coy glances, rapt, well-fed faces, she was able to maintain an expression suitable to her task, which, she decided grimly, must be to introduce both Time and Harmony to the Lady Damiet, who did not seem to recognize either one of them.

"Good," she said briskly as Damiet finished a scale: which, Giulia was not certain. "You have a range adequate for—well, adequate. Very adequate."

Damiet gazed at her, already not listening, having forgotten, possibly, why Giulia was there. She herself might have stepped down from one of the paintings: Voice, perhaps, or Harmony descending to earth, picking more appropriate clothing out of the small, fat hands of the Children of Music along the way. She was tall, plump, and quite fair, big yet graceful; she watched Giulia out of blue-gray, slow-blinking eyes when Giulia spoke. So far she produced a bewildering impression that the words that came out of Giulia's mouth had not the remotest relationship to anything Giulia thought she had put into it.

"Do you know," Damiet asked, "what I am to wear? I think I should change my costume for every song, and I want one of them to be yellow. Please tell Magister Barr he must write a yellow song for me."

"Magister Barr is not a dressmaker. He is a composer and a dramatist. He won't care what color you wear, as long as you sing it well."

"So far he has given me nothing at all to sing."

"You have a scale. Many scales—"

"Yes, but he didn't write them. I don't think. Not for me."

"For you," Giulia lied extravagantly. "If you would sing another—"

"I just did; they're all alike." She blinked again at Giulia, her heavy, creamy face not so much obstinate as oblivious. Giulia went to the spinet, a black so lacquered it glowed like satin, inlaid with flowers of wood and ivory.

"Please. Listen." She touched a note. "Sing."

"Sing what?"

"This note."

"Just that?"

"Is it too difficult?"

"Oh, I doubt it," the Lady Damiet said. "There is only one."

Giulia struck the note again. It spun itself out with amazing purity in that cold room. She waited. The note parted into overtones and died away. She lifted her head, incredulous, and caught the fixed, blue stare.

"Do you think you will be finished soon?" Damiet asked. "I have never liked this room; it is too pale. You do well in it, though, with your dark hair."

Giulia sat down on the spinet stool. The first evening, she thought. The first hour. And I want to claw my hair over my face and wail to wake the dead. Hexel will be furious. He will flee Berylon to join Berone Sidero in the provinces. . . .

"Lady Damiet," she said desperately, "perhaps you might sing what you would call a yellow song for me. So that I can explain to Magister Barr. I can't think of one myself."

The blue eyes became faintly surprised. "Can't you?"

"Not one."

"But then," Damiet said, inspired, "you always wear black." She stopped, swallowed; her eyes grew fixed, slightly crossed. She opened her mouth. A page, entering the room with his arms full of scrolls, stopped dead at her first note. He shivered, hunched over the scrolls, and backed out, making small, birdlike noises. Giulia bit her lip and stared pleadingly at the beautiful, benevolent, androgynous face of Song, who extended a loving hand to the opening lips of Voice, whose eyes, like Damiet's, seemed faintly crossed in concentration. Giulia closed her own eyes quickly, and clenched her fists.

"Perhaps," she said carefully, "if I play it with you, I will understand yellow better."

Damiet sighed. "I do hope, Magister Dulcet, we will not have to go through this for every color."

"I'm very sorry, but I'm afraid we will."

They progressed after a fashion from yellow to blue, which Damiet expressed as an innocent version of a raw ballad Giulia had played at the Griffin's Egg. A blue to match my eyes, Damiet had explained. Giulia, not quite envisioning the shade, had her repeat phrases so that, she told Damiet, she could play them back to Magister Barr. She accompanied Damiet with one finger and a chord now and then, and tried to keep Yacinthe's raucous voice out of her head.

"One more verse," she said. "I've almost got it. Light blue."

"A smoky blue," Damiet corrected, sighing. "With cream lace. You will remember the smoke? You see it in my eyes? Magister Dulcet, I hope you won't confuse the colors."

"I'll write them down," Giulia promised. " 'The Shepherd's Dawn' for your yellow costume, and 'Pass the Pot' for the blue. Smoke."

The blue eyes fixed her once again, their marble gaze becoming slightly glassier, as if Giulia had hit an impossible note and caused a swath of linen to crack and drift down from one of the rosy figures overhead.

"Magister Dulcet, the song is called 'Sweet Bird Awaken.' Not 'Pass the Pot.' "

"Of course," Giulia said quickly, and was caught again, by the eye of Veris Legere as he stood quietly listening across the room. She felt herself flush richly. How long he had been there, she had no idea. He nodded slightly to her, his face impassive. He stood among the long ebony shelves and glass cases that held music and courtly instruments; someone knelt behind him, gently placing an armful of manuscripts onto a shelf.

"Do you think," Damiet asked, "we might go on to mauve? It is one of my best colors, and it will do for the sad scene—there is always one—just before everything resolves itself by chance and ends happily. Of course I will wear white, with pink rosettes, for the final song."

"A mauve song, then," Giulia said, her hands poised on the spinet keys. "And then the white, and then I'll leave you."

"But Magister Dulcet, there are other colors."

"I'll come for them soon. Perhaps you could practice them."

"Why?"

"It is considered good for the voice. You'll want to sing your best for the prince's birthday."

The Lady Damiet pondered this. "I always sing my best."

"It is like dancing. The more you practice, the easier the steps—"

"Dancing," Damiet said inarguably, "is done with the feet. Not the voice. Singing is far easier; there is nothing to trip over. Do you know 'The Dying Swan'? It is a mauve song."

She opened her mouth. A swan, shot out of the air by a hunter's arrow, thudded heavily onto the marble floor, shedding blood and feathers. It sang its death throes. Veris Legere coughed dryly. A scroll flipped and rolled, was caught and shelved. The man behind Veris Legere rose; Giulia caught a fleeting glimpse of his face as he turned. Her eyes widened. The swan shrieked and died.

"Mauve," Damiet said.

They were romping through white festooned with rosettes

when the man returned with more scrolls and a stack of manuscript paper so fragile it scattered a litter of brown flakes in the wake of air. Giulia, absently playing a child's song, studied his back. It looked sturdy enough, under the discreet black he wore, to have wrestled music out of the picochet. The height seemed right; the light hair was far tidier than she remembered. The boots looked too new. Anyway, what would a picochet player last seen in patched boots in a tavern be doing shelving manuscripts in the music room at Pellior Palace? Then he moved behind a case to put the music down and she saw his face, with its harsh, elegant lines, and his eyes as dark as the bottom of a well. She felt a sudden chill of horror. You were just in the Griffin's Egg hiding from basilisks, she protested silently. And now you are in the Basilisk's house. . . .

Damiet had stopped singing. Giulia looked at her, still playing. Damiet's mouth opened and closed a couple of times, but nothing came out. She had just seen her audience; perhaps, in surprise, she had forgotten the words.

" 'Merry in the break of day,' " Giulia prompted. Damiet looked at her blankly, then brought her attention to bear across the room again, where the men stood, caught and waiting.

"I am sorry, my lady," Veris said gravely, "for disturbing your song. Your white song."

Damiet neither moved not spoke; Giulia wondered starkly if she were about to throw a Pellior-sized tantrum. Then she gestured, a flick of fingers within the folds of her skirt.

"Bring the stranger to me. If he is going to listen to me, I want to know his name."

"Of course, my lady," Veris said, and led the stranger to Damiet. He must have seen Giulia before she had noticed him;

his eyes, flicking to her, held no surprise. "Lady Damiet, may I present Master Caladrius. He will be assisting me, as librarian, with the music from Tormalyne Palace which was rescued from it, and somehow forgotten."

Damiet extended a languid hand. A beat too late for exact courtesy, the librarian touched the air beneath her fingers, bowed unskillfully over them.

"Lady Damiet," he said. "You must pardon my manners. I never learned many. In the north."

You learned to read music, Giulia thought. In the north.

"My brother Taur says there are no manners at all in the provinces," Damiet said, with unexpected civility. Her eyes, unblinking and still faintly unfocused, glistened slightly. "I will teach you, Master Caladrius."

"And this," Veris Legere said in the silence while Master Caladrius seemed to grapple with responses, "is Magister Giulia Dulcet, who is directing music for the autumn festival."

"We have met," the librarian said swiftly as Giulia wondered. He took her hand, held it a moment, warmly, in provincial fashion. "You let me play your picochet."

Veris lifted an eyebrow. "You have surprising talents, Master Caladrius."

"I learned it from my father. To play for the crops."

"To play for the crops," Giulia said slowly. "That's how my grandfather put it. On the farm." She smiled suddenly. "You have me speaking that way again. In fits and starts."

Damiet made a rare, graceless movement beside her, a rustling fidget of skirts. "What," she asked frostily, "is a picochet?"

"It is an ancient instrument," Master Caladrius explained. "Much loved by farmers. My lady."

"So you are a land baron's son, Master Caladrius."

"I'm hardly that, my lady."

"Well, you are hardly a peasant. I will ask my father to find me a picochet. You will teach me to play it, Master Caladrius." The idea left Giulia groping; there was not a flicker in the librarian's opaque eyes. Damiet continued, "Now I am learning to sing opera. I will not be singing these songs, of course. Magister Barr is writing music for me. Tonight we are simply choosing the colors of my costumes."

"So I gathered," Veris murmured, a pinprick of amusement in his eyes.

"I am to be the heroine," Damiet continued, holding the librarian's attention with her unblinking gaze, her deliberate voice. "I will sing the most important songs, as a present to my father on his sixty-fifth birthday."

"He will be pleased. I'm sure," the librarian said a trifle shortly. Unaccountably, Damiet did not take offense.

"You must come and hear me sing again. I still have other colors to explain to Magister Barr. Perhaps you would have suggestions for me. As to color." She paused; they gazed at her wordlessly, transfixed in varying degrees of bewilderment. Above her, the Children of Music played sweetly in unheard realms; Song awakened the music in Voice; she turned her eyes to him, opened her lips, and brought him out of herself. Damiet's white fingers linked; her lashes descended, rose. "Veris Legere will see that you are here, the next time I sing with Magister Dulcet."

They all shifted then, still transfixed, making small movements, discreet noises, to struggle free.

"We still have white to get through," Giulia said breathlessly.

"I will be pleased to help in any way that inspires you to sing," Veris murmured. "Master Caladrius will be sorting scrolls here for some time."

Damiet extended her hand once again, her full lips parting slightly as she watched the fair, trimmed head bend over it. Giulia searched his face as he straightened, found neither humor nor calculation in it, nor any interest whatsoever. There seemed only the expressionless darkness. Damiet folded her hands again, and breathed more audibly, her eyes following the librarian as he returned to his manuscripts. She loosed him finally, looked at Giulia. Her fine, pale skin was flushed, Giulia saw; her eyes held a brighter sheen; in the depths, expression struggled to form.

"I will sing the white song again," she said. "From the beginning. You must tell Magister Barr that the white will be a very special song. Very special. There must, beyond doubt, be a happy ending."

Giulia sank down on the spinet stool, barely seeing the keys her fingers touched, barely hearing Damiet as she envisioned scenes of the impending disaster: the furious father, the obstinate daughter refusing to sing until she is promised her happy ending, no one able to provide one, Hexel in despair, the music director in disgrace, the festival in ruins, the librarian counting his bribe and leaving the city, or, more probably, languishing in a torture chamber beneath the palace until he is finally forgotten and the prince's daughter finds her ending far too late for anyone except herself. Giulia thought, torn between laughter and despair: I had better tell Hexel to put a librarian in the plot.

But, she thought more coldly a moment later. He is not a librarian. He is still a stranger. A farmer who studied with bards. A man hiding from basilisks behind my picochet. Who exactly has Damiet Pellior fallen in love with?

Damiet finished her song and reminded Giulia: "White."

Above her the courtly instruments played a final flourish.

Five

Reve Iridia received Caladrius coldly at first, not knowing him: the stranger in black at her door. She turned away disinterestedly, leaving Kira to shut him out.

"I take few students," she said, letting her voice drift back to him. "Most of them are children."

"I know," he said. "I was one of them." She turned then, slowly, circling her jeweled walking stick. He remembered her eyes: they had not changed, except possibly to grow more human with age. They fascinated him as a child, their gray so pale they looked luminous, sometimes seeing with alarming clarity, at other times blinded, it seemed, with light. He still found them startling.

"I no longer remember names," she said, frowning slightly. "There were so many of you."

"It doesn't matter. I only came to pay my respects, Magister Iridia. If that would please you."

She turned again, still slender, upright, in gray silk much darker than her eyes. Her hair, which he remembered as pale gold, had grown ivory. She kept it drawn back, coiled and pinned; he remembered her pins, an array of them that changed constantly. She had smiled in those days. Now her face had settled into grave and bitter lines, the expression she found least need to change.

"You have a pleasing voice," she answered, making her stiff and regal way toward her favorite chair. "Tea, Kira."

Seated, she pointed with her stick at a second chair. The dark-eyed Kira, who, a decade or two younger than her mistress, still remembered how to smile, nodded encouragement at him. He glanced around the room as he sat. It was small and quiet, with heavy draperies and carpets. Its furnishings were good but sparse; she kept no signs of her profession in that room except a small brass gong engraved with the chimera of Iridia House breathing fire at a flock of birds. Some of the flock were fleeing the firestorm; others fell, burning and unrecognizable, like bright leaves. A black-lacquered hammer lay beside the gong.

She caught him gazing at the scene on the gong. She said dryly, "A memory. Now, of course, the chimera is just that: a dream of power. Or perhaps I should not say such things to you. But I do not think Pellior House would come to me."

"I have no relatives in Pellior House," he assured her. "I barely have a connection to Berylon itself. I have been away for many years."

"But you were here as a child."

"I was born here," he said. "I came to the Tormalyne School to study with you when I was very young. Until—" He gestured toward the gong, a movement which seemed to arouse both memory and curiosity in her. Her eyes changed, saw past and present at once.

"So you remember the Basilisk's War." He was silent, waiting. Kira came in, set a tray between them: cracked porcelain cups as delicate as old bones, a pot that seemed nearly transparent with age. Reve poured, handed him a cup, and a lemon wafer that was slowly petrifying. "I had to leave the school because of that," she added, growing unexpectedly reminiscent, trusting him with her past. "For some years I stopped teaching. I hid with one relative or another. Iridia House on the whole fared much better than Tormalyne House, though a decade passed before the family ventured back into Iridia Palace. But I was afraid. . . ."

"Of what?" he asked gently. She lifted her astonishing eyes to his face.

"I had been in love with Arioso Pellior's cousin Demi. We had planned to marry. Then Pellior House tore Berylon apart, and Iridia House chose to fight for Tormalyne House. It was a disastrous alliance. Demi played the lavandre." She took a sip of tea. "We played duets. Until he came to me secretly one night, furious, weeping, cursing my House, cursing his love for me, promising to run away with me in one breath, then swearing fealty to his House in the next. He made me promise to wait for him, until Berylon was peaceful again. He left me his lavandre. I did not see him again for six years, until his wedding day, when he rode in procession through the streets to Marcasia Palace to claim his bride. Then I realized it was safe for me to come out of hiding; no one of Pellior House had any interest in me at all. So I began to teach again."

"Do you still have his lavandre?" he asked after a moment. Again expression changed in her eyes; he glimpsed the ghost of a smile.

"He came for it one day, years after his wedding." She sipped tea. "Now tell me what took you away from Berylon, and what brings you back. Perhaps," she added, musing, "you are Mistas? His hair was dark, I remember."

"No."

"A delicate boy with such big, dark eyes . . . Talented, too. I don't know what became of him. Did you leave because of the war?"

"During the war, yes. I barely knew what war was, or that there was a world beyond Berylon." He paused; his eyes strayed back to the chimera, the fire, the fleeing birds. "We went north, to a place where no one knew us. This is the first I have seen of Berylon since then."

"And you came back because . . . ?"

He set his cup down carefully on a small table. "I came to seek my fortune. I know that is a younger man's work. But I have nothing to lose. I came to see you because you are among the few things that still remain of my early life here."

"What," she asked curiously, "do you remember?"

"Of you? I remember the pins you wore in your hair. One in particular, shaped like a dragonfly with blue filigreed wings."

She stirred slightly; he heard her frail breath. "Demi gave me that. What else?"

"The room at the Tormalyne School where you taught. The walls were butter-colored marble, and always cold."

"Yes."

"And there were two niches in the walls beside the window. One held flowers, the other a man's head carved of white marble. I have forgotten his name."

She opened her mouth, hesitated. He saw her blink, and then her eyes held his again, too clear for expression, blind, he thought, with light. "His name was Auber Tormalyne." She lifted her cup an inch, set it down without drinking, still gazing at him.

"I used to imagine that his eyes moved when I wasn't looking at him. That he watched me play, having nothing else to do but use his eyes and his ears and his mind."

He heard her breath again, a long sigh; she put cup and saucer on the table, blinking again. "Yes. I remember his face now. Tell me what I taught you. What instrument."

"You taught me several."

"Yes. Which one do you remember most clearly?"

"The bone pipes. You taught me how to hear beyond what is familiar to us. Just because we hear silence, you said, does not mean there is no music. You taught me to play within the registers of silence." She was silent, absolutely still, as he remembered she could be. He added after a moment, "In the north, I learned to play the picochet."

"Ah." She moved slightly, a sigh of silk. "The peasant's voice."

"I learned to love it."

"It became your voice." She stirred again, leaning back

in her chair, her tea ignored. She watched him, her eyes half-closed now, hooded. "What will you do in Berylon?"

"I will do what I must. Perhaps you know someone who will help me. Or something."

"Perhaps. Iridia House has recovered from its struggles, but not easily; as you see, I do not live in luxury. You must not expect too much from us."

"I expect nothing," he answered. "But I have learned to do many things. In the north. I learned that if you pick up a stone and lay it on another stone, and lay another stone on that, you will have a wall, and then a room, and then a house. If you have enough strength and enough stones."

"If your stones do not slip and crush you."

"There is always that risk."

"And you came to me — "

"Because you listen to silence. Perhaps you hear what others pay no attention to."

"How could I, living as I do, in these simple rooms, with few but children and Kira to speak with?"

"I came to you," he reminded her. "I don't believe anyone who ever learned from you has forgotten you."

She straightened, reached for her walking stick. The jewel in its knob, catching light as it moved, left a streak of fire in his eyes before her hand closed over it. She pushed herself to her feet.

"Come," she said. "I will show you what I have."

He followed her to a closed door on the other side of the room, half-hidden behind a dark fall of drapery. She opened it. Again he was surprised by light. The velvet over the long windows had been drawn aside; light burned and winked and slid like satin across the instruments that lay across tables and chairs, hung along the walls, leaned within the window seats. Scrolls and sheets of music were piled in untidy stacks on shelves, on the floor. Some of the instruments were very old, he saw: the horn made out of a massive ivory tusk, patterned with painted eyes around its finger holes; the set of pipes made out of human bones; the gourd rattle with the big-bellied, dreaming woman embracing it, becoming it, nearly smudged away.

He saw the picochet leaning against a little, elegant spinet inlaid with scenes of courtly dances. The picochet looked worn. It had been painted once, probably during endless winter evenings; shadowy wolves leaped across the soundboard, vanished into darker wood.

She closed the door behind them, and then slowly, curtain by curtain, shut out the light and muffled the noises from the street below, until they stood in twilight, within the silence of unplayed instruments. She did not bother to light candles. He wondered if she saw catlike in the dark, or if she saw more now with other senses.

She said, "Auber Tormalyne spent some years in the hinterlands; he brought back a collection of very strange instruments, which he gave to the school. Like the picochet, they were viewed as curiosities, generally offensive to the ear, and relegated, at his death, to a storage room, where, after a hundred years, they grew cracked, dusty, and even more difficult to listen to."

"But you listened to them."

"Demi and I found them, once when we were looking for a place where no one would be likely to disturb us. I could not keep my hands off them. Demi grew impatient with me, and left me there, screeching, whistling, drumming—they were like neglected children to me, all crying out for human touch, human breath, crying out silently to be heard. I became all their voices. . . ." He drew breath, soundlessly, he thought, but she heard even that; he felt her regard like a touch. "I taught myself to play them, alone in a musty storage room, stumbling my way through their hearts. They began to speak slowly; I was clumsy with them, I hardly knew what I was doing. . . . There was no one in the school to tell me about them. What I learned, I taught. Not to all of my students, surely. But to a few, a very few. Most of them did not survive the war between the Houses."

"I did."

"Yes . . . And what did you learn in the north, besides the picochet?"

He picked up a wooden flute, cracked with age, very plain, without a carving or a stain of color on it. "I learned that this flute is played only among women, and only at childbirth or to the dead. Its outward simplicity suggests the humility which the player brings to the playing. The seam of gold hidden within it honors the beauty of its voice."

"Will you play it?"

He shook his head. "I may touch it, but if I play it, I will be haunted by all the dead women who heard it played for them."

She was silent; he could not see the expression on her face. "I didn't know," she said at last, "that it is a woman's instrument. That explains why I have glimpsed only women's faces."

"When?"

"Sometimes when I play it in a dim quiet place, like this. What else?"

He touched the glazed clay drum painted with flowers and with eyes out of his nightmares. "That the spirits of the dead become trapped within this drum. To free them, you must play it until it shatters."

She stood very still, so still that he would not have known she was there but for her voice. "Have you played it?"

"Yes."

"I never knew what to drum with. Wood and metal sounded wrong, glass is too fragile, my hands made no sound—"

"It is played with bone."

"Have I confused the dead with my playing?"

"Very likely."

She moved then, made her frail but unerring way through instruments and ghosts, to find something lying behind the closed curtains on a window seat. In the sudden flick of light, he glimpsed one she did not pick up: a small pipe whose finger holes glowed sullenly in the shadows, from the fires within the bone. He made no sound, he knew, but still she glanced toward him, before she let the curtain fall, as if she heard his thoughts within his silence.

"Can you play these?" She handed him a small set of pipes bound together, the smallest no bigger than his finger and stained red, the others gold. He lifted them to his lips; sounds bloomed out of them, fell gently, like tossed flowers. "No," she said patiently, as if he were still her student. "Not like that."

He gazed at her, wondering at what she had discovered

in that forgotten storage room. "Yes," he said finally. "I can play them not like that."

"I played them once for Demi, in the storage room. I stumbled then into their true voice. It was like being very drunk, he said, on music. We dreamed awake, and had the same dreams. The city disappeared around us, the wood swallowed it, the moon rose in the storage room. We swam naked in a river flowing through the floorboards. Strange people or talking animals joined us. . . . We found ourselves back in the storage room at dawn; we were still naked and our heads were wet. We could not find our clothes. We stole magisters' robes out of a closet; Demi ran home barefoot through the waking streets. . . . That was the last time I played them for anyone. Our spirits were trapped in it by war, and he and I did not survive."

"It is ancient. Its voices change with every player, and it is very susceptible to suggestion."

"And if you played it like that?" she asked. "Now?"

He laid it down, very gently, on the spinet; he did not answer. Instead he asked her, "Do you always play these in the dark?"

"Is it?" she asked surprisedly. "I scarcely notice shadows. I can't bear too much light. I see more with my hands and my ears and my memory, these days, than my eyes. I hear the power and the ambiguities in your voice. I saw your face very clearly, when you sat in that chair. In here, in the dark, I can see it even better. I can see it best in your voice."

"Then should I ask you for the instrument I want," he said steadily, "or should I just take it so that you will not know?"

She found his eyes, held them so long he thought she saw

through dark and blood and bone into his future. She turned to the spinet, stood with her back to him, pressing one key down softly, again and again, while he walked to the window where what he wanted lay among some yellowing scrolls. He slipped it carefully into his shirt. He could feel it against his heartbeat: a small, warm, deadly secret.

She said then, her head still bowed over the spinet, "That will be the one I could never play. I heard the scrolls shift as you lifted it. Why could I never get one note out of it?"

"Because it only plays one song," he answered. "And in your graceful and courageous life, you have never heard it." She turned then; he caught her fragile hand, lifted it to his lips. "Thank you, Reve Iridia."

"Will I see you again?"

"I hope so. If I play this right."

"Or not at all," she whispered, her hand pushing down across the keys, again and again, as he left. Their jangled protest followed him out, reached him, still warning him as he passed beneath the window, as if her spirit, caught within the notes, would struggle there until he freed them both.

Six

Luna Pellior stood on a high tower in Pellior Palace, watching the moon rise over Berylon. It drenched the ancient city with a pearly light; it gazed, with an austere and bone-white eye, down the stone streets, into windows open to catch the faintest brush of night air. In the gardens below, a bird sang to the moon among the orange trees. She waited for Brio Hood. He came silently, but she heard him before he wanted her to. His shadow, she might have told him, brushed too carelessly across stone. Still, she did not move before he spoke. Then she turned, smiling at him, the brittle collection of bone and cold shriveled thought that no one ever noticed, even after it was too late.

He bowed, then raised his head, his eyes steady as a hunting animal's on her face. He seemed not quite human; she wondered, now and then, if her father had made him in his secret chamber. But there were those who wondered that about her: her father's golden other, the self he had fashioned to take his place when he tired of his own body. His apprentice, his mistress of mysterious arts, his muse.

"She is nowhere," Brio said.

"Then my rose killed her."

"No one dead came in or out of the tavern. No weeping, no black ribbons at the door. Nothing. She is gone. There is some wizened creature who hardly speaks, to serve there in her place."

"How strange. Maybe I accidently turned her into something else. I need to know, Brio, if I did as my father told me. Or if I made mistakes. He won't be pleased with me if she is still alive. And Taur won't say. He holds yes and no in his mouth like jewels; he won't swallow one or spit out the other."

"He stopped there, on his way into the city, when they crossed at the Pellior Bridge. So I heard. I never saw him go there again."

"Very strange . . . And the matter of the arms?"

But his mistrust of everything living except her father overcame him. He said only, "About the matter of the arms on the Tormalyne Bridge, I have spoken to the prince."

She turned back to the night. "Thank you, Brio." She felt him leave, a spill of shadowy air down the tower steps, the faint rustle of dead leaves. She rested her chin on her hand, gazing at the moon again, as if it mirrored her, or she mirrored it, and they both took pleasure in their reflections.

After a while, Taur came up, looking vague, as if he did not know what had brought him up there, but found it as good a place as any at the moment. Luna had let him feel her desire to see him; her silent wish compelled him, in restless and aimless fashion, to search the house until he found peace on top of a tower he barely knew existed.

He said absently, "You come up here, too."

"Sometimes." He had been drinking, she saw. His shirt was loose; there was a wine stain on his sleeve. He was carrying something: a wooden puppet on strings. She added, "You've been with your children."

He looked blankly down at the toy. "It's safe, with them," he said. He wove his fingers through the strings, set the puppet dancing on the parapet. She watched him.

"Safe?"

"Our father has been furious with me ever since I came back."

"He doesn't seem angry."

"I can hear it in his voice, see it in his smile. He did lose his temper when he heard how I had the trapper killed on the Tormalyne Bridge before he could be questioned. He asked me how he could possibly have sired an heir with a coddled egg for a brain."

"You were tired," Luna said temperately. "You were hurrying to get home. He exiled you for six weeks among sheep—"

"Don't remind me."

"You're with your children more now. You used to be out all night. Did you have a lover?"

"Well." He let the puppet collapse on the stones. "It was a madness that passed."

"Who was she?"

"No one you knew."

"Was she angry, when you stopped?"

He shrugged a little, jerking the puppet limbs again; he would not let her see his eyes. "How would I know? I gave her no choice."

"Will you see her again?"

He met her eyes then, his tired eyes holding no bitterness, only a stunned wonder, a secret. She drew a long breath; the scent of oranges mingled with the distant, moonlit water. "I don't know," he said abruptly. "It seems like a dream. There was another man on the Tormalyne Bridge that night. He set the wagon on fire and ran, after the trapper was killed. Maybe if they find him, my father will stop being so angry with me."

"Was he a trapper?"

"He said he had walked down. From the north. You know how they talk. Or maybe you don't. He must have known something, though, the way he ran."

"What did he look like?"

"I don't know," Taur said impatiently. "Like a farmer."

Luna turned her head, questioned the moon with wide eyes. "A farmer," she said. "From the north. Why would he know anything?"

"Why did he run? He behaved suspiciously."

She picked up the puppet lying forgotten on the stones, tossed it lightly over the edge of the tower. "That's why."

"Luna! I made that!"

"That's why he ran."

Taur breathed heavily for a moment. "I still say he was—" He stopped, began again. "I wouldn't have thrown him over the bridge."

"It's too pleasant to argue."

"I'm not arguing. I'm trying to be reasonable, and you throw my children's toys into the trees."

She smiled at him. "Make another. It's only a toy."

"You are getting as impossible as our father. He should find you a husband. Or doesn't he want you to leave him? Or can't you leave him? Are you really something he conjured up in secret?"

"You should know."

"I wasn't paying attention when you were born. I was busy growing my first beard. I don't remember noticing you for years. For aii I know, he might have made you."

She leaned over the parapet, listening to the night bird. "Maybe he did," she said equably. "So then?"

"Then it doesn't matter. You'll die when he dies. And my children will never have to fear yours."

"And if I don't die?" She looked at him, her eyes still smiling, full of moonlight, cold and white as bone. His breath caught. Then he laughed a little, searching the moon-frosted leaves below for his puppet.

"Then I'll find you a husband, to keep you out of trouble. You can throw your own children's toys off the towers."

She laughed, too, softly, and slid her fingers into the crook of his arm. "Let's go down. I promised our father I would play his new compositions with him. Come and listen?"

"No, thank you. I would rather stay out of his way. Music makes me tired. That interminable opera on his birthday. It sounds like people being tortured. Maybe that's why he likes it."

They wound down the tower steps together, and parted company, Taur to his family's chambers, and she to a small alcove beside the music room. There, on a marble table, beneath a bust of Duke Drago Pellior, who watched her with her father's cold lizard's eyes, she played with an odd assortment of mirrors, lenses and prisms, copper rods and weights. She balanced a lens and a small mirror on rods set across from one another, and at a level with one of her ancestor's eyes. The eye within the lens, enlarged, gazed at itself within the mirror. A prism, dangling from a higher rod, neatly caught the reflected eye and trapped it in its facets. Footsteps passed her now and then, growing fainter with discretion, as if those who made them tried to walk on air behind her. She left such playthings here and there within the palace. No one dared touch them except her father, who toyed with them curiously, and found them pretty but inexplicable. She recognized his step and lowered the mirror. She turned, smiling, and felt the alteration of his inner world, its dark solitary businesses suspended in a sweet, momentary calm. He had been with his mistress; he wore her perfume and the expression she had given him.

He sensed something too, as he stopped to flick the prism and watch candlelight glitter in it. He said, "You have been with Taur."

"How can you tell?"

"He scatters his frustrations around him like an odor. Has he spoken of that woman again?"

"A word or two. No more. He is afraid you are angry with him."

"I am," the prince said mildly. "He should be afraid. He left a pile of arms on the Tormalyne Bridge and me with nothing to question except some solitary traveller who panicked and ran, who probably knows nothing at all. Brio is looking for him."

"Brio will find him. Brio finds everyone."

"Except that woman. He found a mystery instead. A rheumy hag whom everyone addressed by his lover's name. What did you send her?"

"I thought," she said ruefully, "what I was told. A glass rose, with a poisoned thorn. Maybe Brio gave it to the wrong woman."

"Brio does not make mistakes."

"Then I do. I am sorry, father. Anyway, she is gone and Taur spends his evenings with his children."

"A novel experience for them all. I must be content with that," he said. But she heard his leashed discontent. Someone of Tormalyne House had troubled him and, somehow, eluded him. Or perhaps not; he could not tell; Brio could not tell him. She felt his hidden exasperation turn to wonder as they approached the music room: Strange noises were coming out of it. A page bowed too elaborately, before opening the door too slowly. On the far side of the room, doors closed behind a rustle of smoke-blue skirts. The prince glanced around, bemused, found Veris Legere beside a trio of gilt chairs, bowing to him. He asked incredulously,

"Damiet?"

"Yes, my lord."

"In the music room?"

"Yes, my lord."

"That noise. Like a cat on fire—"

"It is a surprise for your birthday," Veris explained.

"But what was she doing?"

"Singing, my lord."

"Singing!" Arioso stared at him. "Damiet has no interest in music. She can't wear it."

"I believe Magister Dulcet found a way to persuade her that she can." He opened a cupboard, took out the prince's flute and some manuscripts. Then he drew his own instrument, an antique viol, from its case. Luna moved to the harpsichord, loosened her fingers with some broken chords.

"You must pretend to be surprised," she told her father.

"Surprised! I'm stupefied."

"You must be kind."

"Impossible."

She smiled, taking the composition pages that Veris handed her. "She wants to please you. Is that difficult to understand?"

"She never wanted to before. I would sooner have expected Taur in here singing arias."

"She's growing up. Maybe she's becoming more complex." Her father's chair creaked noisily under him like a comment. She played a few chords of his accompaniment, pressed a note for Veris to tune his viol. Poised, they consulted the prince with their eyes. The air sang tenderly to Veris's viol, and, somewhat more hesitantly, to the prince's flute.

They stopped and started, stopped again, as Arioso lowered his instrument impatiently. "It's wrong. I don't like it. It's a dance—it sounds leaden."

"Perhaps the harpsichord should be more fluid, my lord," Veris suggested gently.

They began to play again. The door opened softly, closed behind them. Luna, playing chords laid together like bricks, neat but dense, listened to the quiet steps, the slide and catch of glass doors, scrolls unrolled and rolled again. The door opened; she glimpsed a stranger in unadorned black, faultless as to hair and boots, discreet in his movements as he stepped through the door and closed it quietly behind him. The farmer has vanished, she thought curiously. He no longer exists. She remembered his eyes, catching hers across the room: the darkness in them, as if he had seen far more than crops die. Perhaps he had, so he had turned his back on everything he had loved, and come south.

Arioso, looking at her, lifted his flute abruptly from his lips. "Who was that?" he asked her. "Who is that in your eyes?"

"No one," she answered indifferently. "The librarian."

He waited for more, hearing overtones in her voice. "You remember him, my lord," Veris said, mistaking his silence for perplexity. "Master Caladrius. The farmer. He has been staying late to finish moving the music manuscripts."

"Farmers don't read music."

"This one studied at Luly."

"Did he." Luna saw the basilisk's face suddenly, beneath his smile.

"Many years ago. He remembers enough to be very helpful, though he knows nothing of history, and almost nothing of Berylon."

"Does he play music?"

"Very little, beyond the picochet. And that, not well enough, apparently, to save his crops."

The shadow of hollowed bone and darkness was easing behind the prince's face. "The peasant's instrument," he said, enlightened. "Giulia Dulcet mentioned that she once appalled the magisters with it. He does not play it here."

"No, my lord." Veris hesitated. "Not yet, at least. Lady Damiet expressed an interest in it."

"Damiet would not know a picochet from a pitchfork."

"You should encourage her," Luna said lightly, "if she is beginning to think."

"Children who think are dangerous. Not that Damiet would recognize a thought if she had one. But perhaps she is not so hopelessly like her mother. If she continues to express an interest, then teach her the picochet."

"My lord, I can't play it myself."

"Then have the librarian teach her."

"My lord—"

A flurry of notes checked him. "Enough of librarians and picochets. Do you want me to finish this without you?"

Veris raised his bow; Luna found her chords. Flute, viol, and harpsichord danced in the room, uninterrupted by the librarian, who returned, that evening, only to the memory of the Basilisk's daughter.

Seven

Caladrius stood in the gardens of Tormalyne Palace.

He had made tiny pipes of feathers he had found along the streets; birds answered him here as they had in the hinterlands. A night-bird, singing back to his playing, showed him the loose bar in the iron fence, the furrowed earth along which the bar swung sideways, that told him, as the bird did, that others came here secretly. Around him, the sleeping city dreamed, tossed fretfully, muttered, dreamed again. He wore the librarian's black; not even the moon, drawing stars like sheep across the meadows to the west, could see him there.

On a chain around his neck, beneath his shirt, he wore the fire-bone pipe he had taken from Reve Iridia.

In the hinterlands he had dreamed the pipe; in Berylon he had found it, an answer to his need, as if a monstrous head of mist and cold had loomed out of the hinterlands to lay that carved bone under his eyes. He remembered the warning: the words of the ancient tale all students were taught that had woven themselves into his dream. Fire burned within the pipe; it would strike where he willed it. And then it would strike him, find its way into his own heart and twist him into its deadly song of fire and ice. So the tale said.

He thought: There is no other song.

But he could not risk learning the truth of the tale at the moment he played the pipe for the Basilisk. He had been taught early on Luly that each tale had its grain of truth; the pearl that formed around it was layered by time and the bright, shifting words of the teller. A shy, unusual beast might have grown monstrous over many tellings through the centuries. The power in the bone might once have been no more than an enraged bard's wish.

Or every word might say exactly what it said, a clear and unambiguous warning to those who travelled past the boundaries of the human world to look for such a monster, such music.

The birds in the Tormalyne Gardens led him along a hidden path to the tiny barred window behind a weedy sprawl of juniper. The bars had been forced apart. He thanked the birds and, blind now, dropped down into darkness.

Stone caught him, a clumsy pile of steps that led down into a puddle. He stood a moment, felt the cool air, smelling of moss and standing water, flow into the shape of something vast and hollow around him. He moved away from the window, found a stone wall to follow with his hands, that became, within a few steps, a massive slab of wood and iron. He pulled at an iron ring; the rotting wood had begun to sag on its hinges, crumble against the stone floor. He heaved the door level, opened and shut it as gently as he could.

Dark and stone closed around him, formed a small, windowless room. Listening, he heard the sounds within the register of its silence: the forgotten screams of pain and despair that had seeped into the stones through centuries of Tormalyne history. As a child, he had never known such a place existed beneath his feet. Now, he would have assumed it, if he had thought. The fire-bone pipe, it seemed, hearing its own music, had led him unerringly there. He felt his skin constrict, his blood quicken, as if he had trapped himself there, in that place where names and past meant nothing, and time stopped.

He drew the pipe out of his shirt. It was warm, porous like bone; in the dark, its carved holes glowed. Studying it, alone with the broken ghosts that Tormalyne House had made, he heard his own heartbeat again. The truth of the tale, he sensed, was in the tale.

He raised the pipe to his lips and heard a step outside the door.

He lowered the pipe again, with infinite care, as if the sound of thread shifting against thread might travel through the stones. Then he waited, motionless, breathless. The steps passed the door. Others followed quickly, a patter of rain on the stones, many of them, trying to be quiet, all passing the door closely, as if they too followed the wall in the dark with their hands. They trespassed, he thought, breathing again, shallowly. The night watch would have brought torches; they would have found no need for silence.

He stood still for a very long time; nothing else, no voices, no other steps, broke the silence. Finally he slipped the pipe back under his shirt, and pulled the door open, one grain of wood at a time. He heard the faintest of sounds, a moth beating against glass, a distant word. He followed it.

He found them all finally, in a huge chamber with groined arches of wood and stone, dimly lit by a couple of oil lamps. He recognized racks for bottles and kegs, though they were empty. Pellior House must have appropriated the wine cellar along with the music. They sat among spider webs on kegs and barrels, fifty of them maybe, all of them young, many of them younger than Hollis. He recognized the cob-haired piper from the tavern, who was arguing with a lean, red-haired young man with a thin, inflexible mouth.

Arms, they were discussing. The inept trapper who had spilled them all over the Tormalyne Bridge. Whom to trust. Whether to trust.

"We must wait, Nicol," Justin insisted. However passionate, they kept their voices low, barely above a whisper. "He must be watching for us now."

"He'll be watching the Tormalyne Bridge. The Pellior Bridge is always crowded with people and wagons crossing to and from the countryside."

"He'll be watching all the bridges."

"Then what possessed the trapper," someone wondered, "to cross the Tormalyne Bridge when he would have been safer crossing farther down river?"

"It's natural for someone coming in with a wagon load of furs from the forest."

"How much did it cost us," someone else asked dourly, "to be betrayed to the Basilisk?"

"He didn't betray us. He didn't have time," Nicol said.

"Why would the prince suspect Tormalyne House? He destroyed it. He left some life in Iridia House. He wouldn't trust Marcasia House just because it allied itself with Pellior House during the war. Either of those Houses could be suspect. His own heir could be."

There was a small silence. A young woman said somberly, "What about Luly? Griffin Libra called himself Griffin Tormalyne and went up there, as far as you can get from the Basilisk without vanishing into the hinterlands. And he is dead. From fire on a rock in the middle of the sea. Justin is right. He suspects Tormalyne House."

"The House no longer exists," Nicol said stubbornly. "A few poor scattered scions. No one bearing the name was left alive. Why should he suspect us?"

"Because he is who he is," Justin said. "That's why Griffin went to Luly. Because he had some vague idea that Arioso Pellior has secret powers. I think he was right. And I think that it was no accident that Griffin Tormalyne was killed again by fire. Arioso Pellior has a long memory and he sees with killing eyes."

"But with all that power," a young man in the shadow of empty ale kegs asked perplexedly, "why would he fear a House he destroyed? Why make such a gesture across such a distance? What did he think Griffin Libra could do to him.? Or even Griffin Tormalyne?"

"What would a basilisk fear?" Justin asked, and answered himself, "His own eyes."

Nicol sighed. "Metaphysics aside, we can't afford to wait, if we want to strike during the autumn festival. That's the time he'll be off-guard. If he ever is. We should bring arms across the Pellior Bridge. And we need to find the witness who ran before the Basilisk does. If he knows anything at all—if he speaks—"

"We're searching, Nicol."

"Well, search discreetly. We can't let the prince know that anyone else has any interest in him at all."

"It's hard to look and not look—"

"Don't speak. Just listen. And trust no one. No one."

Caladrius eased back into the darkness. They would have set a watch somewhere: just outside the window, most likely, since no one had stopped him inside. He must wait until they left before he could. He found another open doorway, another room, that held moonlit windows and no secrets. There he slid to the stone floor and stared into the night, contemplating the unsettling image of the heirs of the ruined House raising what arms they could manage to get across a bridge against the Basilisk's guard. They would be slaughtered. He quelled a sudden, futile urge to appear among them, name himself. He would not dissuade them; he would only give them something more to fight for: an illusion of the future. He turned the pipe in his fingers absently, feeling the subtle intensity of heat above its finger holes. A live thing waited within it to be set free, to sing. He thought of Justin's question: What would a basilisk fear?

Its own eyes. Its own power. So a claw of fire had ripped across Luly, where the great bards were taught to find their own power within the hinterlands. The young man calling himself Griffin Tormalyne had come to Luly in a search for such power. Caladrius had considered him misguided then; now, holding such a song in his hands, he realized it was he himself who had been misguided. The Basilisk saw far more clearly the dangers in the hinterlands, and what he feared was the meeting of his enemy and all the ancient powers of the north.

We have met, Caladrius thought. Still now, he watched the silver rim around the window slowly darken as the moon set. They had gathered so carelessly under a full moon. At least they would not disperse under it. He would wait, he decided, and fight with them, when they fought the Prince of Berylon. He would play a song for every basilisk he saw.

They left finally, with as little noise as they had made entering. He watched for the darkest hour. Then he followed shadows through side streets and alleys. He sensed no turmoil in the streets: the children of the House had scattered like the stars before the dawn.

At his window above the tavern, he watched the music school until its doors were opened to morning by a yawning magister. He crossed the street, walked between the griffins into the halls. Even that early, someone played a harpsichord. He remembered the smells of flowers, resin, lamp oil. He lingered there in the hall, trying to put names to the various white-eyed heads who studied him, until someone living, dressed in black, came along.

They recognized one another; she smiled, surprised.

"Master Caladrius."

"Magister Dulcet," he said, relieved at the sight of her calm face after a damp night underground. "I have come to borrow books."

"Veris Legere must have books on everything you need."

"For the history of Pellior House," he explained. "Not Tormalyne House. Where the music came from."

"Of course," she breathed. "I wasn't thinking. Come in

here. Take whatever you need." She opened a door. Within the room, a young man kneeling to see a book on a shelf, flashed a look at him and rose abruptly. They stared at one another, while Giulia introduced them.

"We have never seen a bard this far south before," she added, as if the bard were a migrating bird. "He is visiting for a while. The students are fascinated. Master Caladrius has come to borrow books on the history of Tormalyne House, to help him catalogue a collection of music."

The bard murmured politely, got out of their way. Giulia moved along the shelves, choosing appropriate tomes and manuscripts, while Caladrius, blinking, gripped the edge of a table to keep himself from following his son out the door.

Eight

"Which is interesting as far as it goes," Hexel said, "but I can't get it farther than that. She is in love. He is in love. Lovers are only interesting to one another. He sings of love. She sings of love. What else is there to sing about?"

"Clothes."

"Giulia, are you paying attention?"

Giulia stopped roaming Hexel's cluttered study. She stooped to pick up a stray sheet of music on the floor. "Now I am," she said firmly, trying to convince herself. She had not seen Justin for days, except very briefly, for moments snatched away from her duties. He did not complain; he, too, seemed preoccupied, but by what she could not guess. Another woman seemed most probable. But, she thought, I would guess that.

"What are you thinking about?" Hexel demanded. "You are not listening to me."

"I was thinking of Damiet," Giulia answered, which was another perplexing worry: Hexel knew her only by Giulia's tales; he had not yet heard her. He grimaced.

"Bad enough she must sing my music, must she also occupy my study?"

"She wants me to find her a picochet, so that the librarian can teach her to play it."

"Is she still in love with him?" Hexel asked promptly, on the scent of a plot.

"She watches him come and go while she sings. She sulks when she doesn't see him. She asks his advice about her singing, as if I am only there to turn pages. She dresses for him, and is offended when he doesn't notice."

"And he?"

"He doesn't notice." She frowned, gazing absently at the manuscript sheet, which had a dusty footprint across it, and a message, not written in Hexel's hand, in the margin. "He is polite."

"He loves someone else."

"I don't think love is on his mind at all. He seems oblivious of Damiet's state. He should be careful. Damiet Pellior rejected by the music librarian could be dangerous."

"Her father will put an end to it soon enough."

"Her father hardly seems to notice her state, either. He told Veris to have Master Caladrius give her lessons."

Hexel, seated at his desk with a scribble of notes in front of him, rapped his pen impatiently on the paper. "What kind of a plot is this? It is completely useless. A love unrequited, a beloved who pays no attention, a father who does not care—Give me something to sing about."

Giulia was silent, trying to think. The message on the music sheet resolved itself under her gaze: *Magister Barr, I no longer find it possible to hide my feelings for you. My heart is in tumult. Only you can give me peace. Meet me . . .* "Hexel—"

"I've finished a duet about their perilous and passionate love. They meet at night, in secret. They sing, they part. Now what?"

"Someone sees them."

"His family or hers?"

"How much singing to you want Damiet to do? Hexel, did you?"

"Did I what?"

"Meet Cressida under the orange tree at midnight?"

"What Cressida? What orange tree? Giulia, try to keep your mind on my work. The families are feuding, the lovers must hide their love—How can it end happily?"

"Someone must help them," Giulia suggested. "Him. Damiet does not need to sing much, but she must have scenes to wear her dresses in. They part after their duet, he climbs her wall and falls into the path of—No. Better yet, someone discovers them in her father's garden. That way he can sing, and Damiet can be seen."

"Who discovers them?"

"Her sister, who, being in love herself, takes pity on them."

"Do we have someone who can sing the part?"

Giulia sighed. "Yes. But she'll make Damiet sound like a goose with its tail feathers caught in a door. They can't be in the same scene together. Perhaps a brother would be better. Or some wise servant."

"What's the point of their families being bitter enemies if all they do is skulk around in the dark? Where is the dramatic tension in a wise old servant? Giulia, you're trying to keep this too safe."

"I'm not—"

"The father sees them."

"He'd toss her lover in the dungeon. How are we supposed to get him out? This has to have a happy ending."

"You'll think of something," Hexel said briskly. "And I can write a sad, bitter, despairing aria for him to sing about love, life, loss and death, just before he is set free."

"How?" Giulia demanded. "How will he be freed?"

"I don't know—the families reconcile or something. That way we could have everyone sing at once, and drown Damiet."

"But, Hexel, it would be easier if he is never in the dungeons in the first place."

"I must have some drama!"

"I'll let you figure out the rehearsal schedule. But we must know where this plot is going, so that I can tell the scene painters."

Someone tapped on the door. Hexel, pacing, called peremptorily, "Come." The visiting bard stepped hesitantly into his path and was seized. "Just what we need—the poet and storyteller. Sit. Listen."

"I was looking for Magister Dulcet. I don't mean to interrupt."

"Then don't."

"Hexel, let him speak," Giulia protested. "I'm your muse; you can be rude to me. How can I help you, Master Hollis?"

He glanced warily at Hexel. "I wanted to ask you—Perhaps later—"

"No—"

Hexel sat down on the desk beside Giulia. "Please," he said with unexpected mildness. "We need help. Perhaps you will inspire the muse herself. Living among the arias of seals, trumpeting storms, choruses of barnacles—"

"We are trying to work out the opera plot," Giulia explained succinctly. "Are you familiar—"

"With opera? No. But with plots . . ." He paused. Hexel, intrigued, perhaps, by the odd, guarded expression in the bard's eyes, became suddenly patient. "The librarian," Hollis said finally. "Master Caladrius. I wondered where I could find him. He is a northerner. Isn't he? I think we may have met before."

"Yes," Giulia exclaimed, enlightened. "He studied on Luly. But years ago, he said."

"Oh."

"But maybe you've met him since?"

"Do you know where he lives?"

She thought. "He never said . . . I can ask him easily enough. I see him often, in the music room at Pellior Palace."

The bard opened his mouth, closed it. He produced words finally. "Pellior Palace."

"He is cataloguing the music of Tormalyne House."

"In Pellior Palace."

"It must sound strange," Giulia said, "if you knew him as a farmer."

"A farm—" He bit off the echo, leaned back in his chair, his brows drawn. Giulia, waiting, found her eyes lingering on his long raven hair, that looked wind-swept even within the tranquil walls of the school. His face, abandoning its smile, became oddly grave. She felt Hexel's eyes on her and shifted.

"He plays the picochet very well. Does that sound like the man you know? He played mine when we first met, in a tavern."

"It sounds—" He nodded, his thoughts returning to them. "Yes. It does sound like him. I believe I met him on Luly." He spoke carefully, as if the meanings of words he knew were apt to change unexpectedly within the city. "I think my mother knew him. She was there, too. On Luly."

Hexel, smelling drama, asked abruptly, "Is he your father?"

"Hexel!"

"This plot is far more intriguing than the one you are giving me, Giulia. We could set the opera on that rock, among the bards. Master Hollis could help us with the music—it can't be that different. The young bard returns there, searching for his father. No. A stranger comes to the rock, spends one night with a woman there—"

"Damiet?" Giulia interrupted drily. The bard had not taken offense. His face had flushed, but he was smiling again.

"I do know my own father, Magister Barr."

"Well, it was a thought . . . I should leave such business to my muse. But both you and my muse seem to find some mystery in this man. This farmer who is a librarian who studied to be a bard. I don't suppose we can get all that into one act."

"No," Giulia said flatly. The memory of the picochet player's eyes haunted her a moment, stripped of all expression and unfathomably dark. Her eyes flicked to Hollis, questioning now, and found strength in his face, a kindliness. She could trust him, she decided, with the enigmatic northerner. "When I see him next in Pellior Palace," she said, "I'll ask him where he lives."

The tension left the bard's face. "Thank you. He wouldn't be staying there?"

"No. We both come and go. I'm giving the prince's daughter voice lessons so that she can sing in the autumn festival."

Hollis, about to rise, hesitated. "I don't quite understand the autumn festival. At Luly, we are taught poetry rather than history. I have some idea that it celebrates a victory?"

Hexel snorted. "If you call the slaughter of Tormalyne House a victory."

Hollis's hands closed again on his chair arms; beyond that he did not move. "Slaughter?"

"Berylon had four centuries of comparative peace under the rule of Tormalyne House," Hexel explained. "By peace, I mean that none of the uprisings of the other Houses were permitted to last long. Then the Basilisk of Pellior House opened his eyes, and members of Tormalyne House began to die in mysterious ways. Raven Berylon suspected Arioso Pellior, and fought back. But by the time there was peace again in Berylon, no one bearing the name Tormalyne was left alive."

"No one."

"Raven Tormalyne, his wife and children had been slain like animals in Tormalyne Palace. A few scattered scions lived to remember, but no one carries the name."

"I see." His voice was oddly stiff. So was his face, Giulia saw; its expression, brittle as glass, might have broken at a touch. He stared at something in the air between them. "This—Arioso Pellior. It's his birthday feast?"

"And his victory feast. He has ruled for thirty-seven years, since he had Raven Berylon put to death with his wife in Tormalyne Palace. Their children had already burned."

"Hexel," Giulia breathed. The bard loosened his grip on the chair, drawing breath.

"And you write music for him."

Even Hexel was silent a moment. "We keep the peace," he said simply. "He is an aging basilisk, but still astute and very dangerous. He keeps Berylon's mind out of its memories by providing distraction in the form of a feast, processions, music, a sweet and silly drama—"

"What would happen if you made a drama out of what happened in Tormalyne Palace?"

"It would not have a happy ending," Giulia said soberly. "He is as capable of destroying the Tormalyne School as he was of destroying the House."

"I see." He shifted, looking at her without seeing. "At Luly, such violence becomes transformed into poetry. Time and the traditional order of words makes it unreal. Past. Until the end. When words made themselves real again." He stopped abruptly.

"It must be very peaceful," Giulia said gently, puzzled.

"Yes. It is. Very quiet." He got to his feet slowly, with an effort. Giulia, distressed by the vague, stunned expression in his eyes, rose with him. She rounded Hexel's writing table, stopped Hollis with a touch as he drifted toward the door.

"Please stay," she said abruptly. "Hexel has been telling

you nightmares. But that's all they are now. Ancient history. I'm sorry we disturbed you."

"I asked," he said. His eyes cleared a little, as if he finally saw her again. "I don't understand opera at all," he added. "I would stay to learn more. But I promised I would find some old instruments that were brought down from the north. There is a storage room, someone said."

"I'll take you there," Giulia said promptly, and ignored Hexel's exasperated protest. "I need to get a picochet for Damiet. Hexel, I won't be a moment."

The bard was silent as she led him down the corridors, still noisy with the fitful evening tides of students and magisters. She said slowly, tossing pebbles into his silence, to see what might surface, "While Master Caladrius played my picochet that night, the basilisk's guards crowded into the tavern, looking for someone. He did not stop playing until they left. He kept his face hidden behind the picochet. I didn't see it clearly until he stopped. His playing seemed very powerful and very—sad. He reminded me of someone . . ."

She saw his mouth tighten. But he did not speak until they stood at the storage room door. He said only, to the door, "I tried to explain the hinterlands to the students. I have never been there. I thought some of the instruments might explain it more clearly than I can."

She reached for a lamp in the hall and opened the door. Light spilled across tables heaped with odd, dusty shapes. Hollis stepped into the room, his eyes wandering from shape to shape. Giulia watched him move among them, touching a carving, plucking a string, stroking a skin pulled taut across a split, painted gourd. He looked at her incredulously.

"Most of these I've never seen. Some I recognize only from tales . . ." He continued roaming, playing them in his head, she guessed, as she watched curiously. He made a sudden sound, picked up a pipe. "This one," he breathed, inarticulate with wonder. "Look at this."

She came to his side. The pipe was small, dark, the ovals of its finger holes painted a dull red. "What is it?" she asked. It did not seem extraordinary.

"I've seen it . . . In a tale . . ."

"Play it."

He shook his head slowly, still gazing at it. "Not here," he said inexplicably. "May I stay a while?"

She set the lamp on a table; shadow shifted across the pipe in his hand. The painted holes in it seemed to glow. She blinked; his hand closed around it.

"Of course," she said. "Shut the door when you leave. And be prepared for complaints."

"Thank you," he said again, smiling. The smile did not quite reach his eyes. She lifted a picochet in its dusty case, oddly reluctant to leave him there, among the silent music of the past. But he gave her no reason to stay.

Returning to the study, she found Hexel seated at his desk, writing furiously. He threw the pen down as she entered, leaving grace-notes of ink between his lines. "I have it! Listen to this, Giulia. A stranger comes to Berylon, the prince's daughter falls in love with him, not knowing that his family and hers are bitter enemies, and that he has sworn to kill her father."

"Hexel—" Giulia said doubtfully. He held up a hand.

"Hush. Listen. Let me tell you what happens next . . ."

Nine

In the music room in Pellior Palace, Caladrius played the picochet to Lady Damiet. He did not hear what he played; neither did she. Her eyes, pale and moist, clung to his face with an expression of rapture unlikely in anyone actually listening. She spoke now and then. Her words wove themselves somehow into the fitful, eerie cadences of his music, so that he felt them, rather them heard them, and answered her absently without words. Behind him, Veris Legere sorted music discreetly in the cupboards; Magister Dulcet sat quietly on the harpsichord stool, both, by their presence, warding away any hint of impropriety. Caladrius finished an ancient ballad about a cornstalk turning into a woman in the fullness of summer, and withering into a dying stalk in autumn, to the amazement and consternation of the farmer who had found her in the field. It was not, he suspected, a song that had ever been heard by the rosy, smiling faces above them on the ceiling. He wondered, lifting his bow, if they were still smiling.

"Now. You try it, my lady. Your fingers there. And there."

"Master Caladrius, it will not fit among my skirts. Perhaps you could adjust them for me."

"Perhaps you could rest it against your knees. For now. It is a peasant's instrument. It is more used to flax and wool than showers of lace."

"Do you like my dress, Master Caladrius? I chose it to match the color of the picochet. Gold-brown. Do you think it matches well?"

"Very well."

"You have not looked," she said reproachfully. "Your eyes are on my fingers."

"Take the bow. Curve your fingers, lift them away from it. The power is in the wrist, in the shoulders. Draw the bow across the string slowly. Feel the tension in the string. Press harder. Harder."

"Master Caladrius—"

"Listen to yourself."

"I am listening. Next time I will wear silk instead of lace. I have a pale gold which matches the color of my hair." She drew the bow with a flourish, produced a singing wail that brought his attention momentarily back to the room, to her. It reminded him, he realized, of her voice: energetic, untuned, and oblivious of art. "Master Caladrius." She played another with vigor. "Or I might wear the thinnest of linens . . . Which would you suggest?"

His thoughts drifted again; he only answered, "Good.

Spread your fingers like this on the strings. Now lift them one at a time as you bow. Good."

"I shall wear the linen, then. The picochet will rest better among my skirts."

"Again . . . Good."

She progressed, in peculiar fashion, somehow transforming clothes into music, along with whatever else was on her mind. That something distracted her, he was made vaguely aware by her fixed gaze, by her long, slow sighs when his hand rested near hers on the bow or the string. His own thoughts were acrid with past, disturbed by the glimpse of Hollis in this basilisk's nest; he could not spare a guess at hers. She was Arioso Pellior's daughter, milky and bland as unlit tallow; she was, like the paintings and marble pillars, a background detail in the house of the Basilisk. Only her bowing, the unexpected, enthusiastic shrieks she got out of the peasant's instrument, made her incongruous, and therefore real.

He was aware, after a time, that the astonishing sounds echoing off the cold white marble had conjured, like a spell, an improbable vision. Luna Pellior appeared out of nowhere, like sunlight falling into a windowless room. For a moment he simply looked at her smiling, secret eyes, the various warm and charming golds of hair and brows and skin. And then, belatedly, he remembered whose gaze held his.

He rose quickly, interrupting Damiet in mid-screech. He bowed his head, startled at the ease with which she rendered him thoughtless, powerless.

She said, "Master Caladrius. What strange instrument are you teaching my sister? And what a rare assortment of noises."

"It is a picochet," Damiet answered complacently. "They

play it in the north. The color of my dress matches it exactly, have you noticed, Luna?"

"Indeed it does. How clever of you, Damiet. I won't disturb you if I listen."

Caladrius stepped away from his chair. "Please—" She sat next to Damiet, studied the instrument with interest.

"It looks old."

"Magister Dulcet brought it from the music school for me." She applied the bow, sent a note careening off the ceiling. "Magister Dulcet also plays the picochet. But I wanted Master Caladrius to teach me."

"Did you?" Caladrius, his eyes still lowered, felt her brilliant gaze again, or the sudden touch of her thoughts. "And why is that?"

But Damiet, her father's daughter, became unexpectedly evasive. "Because he once studied in the north, as a bard. That seems to be important."

"Yes," Luna said softly; Caladrius felt her gaze burn into his mind. "It is important."

"It was long ago," he said, chilled. "My lady."

"Was it so long ago?" She did not let him reply. "My father has many odd instruments that, if coaxed, do unusual things. Perhaps you learned to play some of them?"

"Not there, my lady."

"But somewhere?"

"No. My lady."

"He has one, a very small harp, with a high, sweet voice, whose strings break if someone playing it has told the listener a lie. My father has found it useful. Have you ever played such a thing?"

He was spared answer by Damiet, who became suddenly restless. "I think we should continue with the lesson, Master Caladrius. I do not want to learn about harps. They bore me. They all sound alike. Master Caladrius must sit beside me to teach me the position of my fingers."

"It is not necessary—"

"It is," Damiet said firmly. "Very necessary." She countered her sister's disarming warmth with blue frost. "Bring another chair, Master Caladrius, if my sister wishes to stay. Put it here beside me." She patted the air next to her. Luna showed no signs of rising, merely watched as Caladrius settled a gilt chair opposite Damiet.

"It's easier," he said, answering Damiet's wide stare, "for me to see. What you're doing."

"Master Caladrius—"

"Your skirts distract me." She smiled faintly then, and straightened her bow. He paused, unsettled by the sight of both pairs of eyes, intense and unblinking, on his face. He cleared his throat. "Now. Where were we?"

"Where, indeed, Master Caladrius?"

"Here," Damiet said, and produced a sound that might have cracked marble, but did nothing at all to disturb her sister's smile.

He walked home wearily that night, troubled by Luna. She was the Basilisk's heir, he guessed, in power if not in name. She was his mirror. If he played the fire-bone pipe for one, he must play for the other, or she would kill whatever harmed her father. He seemed to trouble her as well. She would bring him that small harp, if it existed, and watch, smiling, as he broke strings with his lies. What he had done to make her suspicious of him, and what she suspected him of, he could not imagine. And there was Hollis, not safe in the north with Sirina, but living in Berylon as a bard after the Basilisk had shown so clearly, at Luly, how far he could reach to destroy a name, and all who might have spoken it.

The night watch saw Caladrius but did not stop him; they recognized him now as one who came and went in the Basilisk's house. He ate in the tavern, silent and alone, as always. It was late; the place was full of students, and one other solitary man at his supper. This one drew Caladrius's attention. He seemed, like the woman in the hinterlands, to be made of bird bones or twigs, someone not quite real, who might speak the language of crows. He ate slowly, never looking up from his meal; he was still there when Caladrius took the narrow shadowy stairs to his room.

He lay awake for a long time, reading the books he had borrowed from the school, learning the history of Tormalyne House through its music. The night was so hot the air itself seemed to sweat. It was full of restless noises: broken words and objects, a cry perhaps human, perhaps not, drunken singing from the students below. He could even hear faint music from within the school, a frail butterfly of sound blown aside by ruder noises. The moon, shrinking now, peered with an old woman's hooded eye through the window, then passed on. Engrossed in Auber Tormalyne's account of his impulsive journey into the hinterlands, and his collection of divers strange instruments, he realized only slowly that the sound intruding on his attention was not from the street but at his door.

He glanced up and, frozen, watched it open.

He breathed again at the sight of Hollis. He rose without

speaking, embraced his son tightly, feeling a moment's simple joy because he was no longer alone in a city of strangers.

Hollis said softly, "I followed you back from Pellior House. I waited hours before I came up." His face looked patchy in the candlelight; he seemed close to tears. "I don't think anyone but the tavern keeper saw me."

"What are you doing here? You told me you would to go to Sirina."

"I did. Long enough to give you time to get here. I told her what happened to Luly."

"You didn't tell her why."

He sighed, his hands falling heavily onto Caladrius's shoulders. "How could I? I'm barely piecing things together now."

"Do you realize what danger you're in?"

"I'm beginning to." His hands tightened briefly; he loosed Caladrius then, and went to the bed, studied the books on it. "Tormalyne House. I've been learning some history, too. Where were you when your father was killed?"

"I had crawled into a marble fireplace to escape the fire. I was covered with ash. Too terrified to breathe. Arioso Pellior never saw me."

Hollis looked at him sharply. "You saw—"

Caladrius started to answer, shook his head. "It's nothing to talk about now. It's what drives me. I don't want it driving you."

"I can guess." He gazed at Caladrius, his face hard, white. "You saw what would make you run from the sight for nearly forty years. What are you going to do here? You're working under the prince's roof. If you kill him, they'll kill you."

"It's not what I want," Caladrius said tersely. "But it's hard to see a way around it. That's why I wanted you to stay north. If Arioso Pellior names me before he dies, they will search for anyone remotely connected with the House. I may kill him, but he has a daughter with his face and his eyes. Above everything, I wanted you safe. Ignorant, in the north, and safe."

"Well, I'm not," Hollis said simply. "Ignorant, in the north, or safe. I won't leave you. I suppose you would not consider coming back with me to the provinces?"

"No."

Hollis sat down on the bed. "Then you might as well tell me what lost dreams I will inherit."

Caladrius moved after a moment, sat beside him. "A charred, empty palace, a name that's barely more than a memory, and four hundred years' worth of ancestral ghosts who ruled Berylon. If you live long enough. But I want your promise." He caught Hollis's eyes, held them. "My vengeance dies with me. If I'm killed, you forget you ever heard the name Tormalyne." He gripped Hollis's wrist as he stirred. "Promise me. Or you won't see me again after tonight. This is my burden. Not yours."

"I promise," Hollis said, too easily. Caladrius's hold eased after a moment; he sighed.

"I'm being unreasonable."

"You can't ask me to do what you won't. You can't give me such a heritage and then ask me to go back and sing on a rock."

"If there's no hope?"

"Even if there's no hope." He paused, then smiled a little, tightly. "There's Berylon itself. City of stone circled by water.

I'm not sure I would want to leave it, to go back to the provinces. It sings, like Luly. Not with wind and sea, but with the living. I want to stay."

"I wish I could see it out of your eyes. Without bitterness."

"Maybe—" Hollis said doubtfully.

"Maybe," he said, with no hope whatsoever. "It's enough now, just to see you. Tell me what you want to know."

"I want to know what you ran from, all those years. Why you hid yourself from yourself. Why you woke us all with your dreaming at Luiy. What you saw when you harped. Will you tell me?"

Caladrius told him. Hollis stayed with him until dawn, when the tavern filled with students and laborers, and he could slip away among them without notice. From his window, Caladrius watched him cross the street, with his long, free stride, open doors between the rampant griffins, and enter. For a moment he wondered if leaving Arioso Pellior alive, unrepentant and unjudged, would be worth the freedom Hollis had, to move through the singing city beyond the Basilisk's regard. But it was only an illusion of freedom, he knew; the city was not ringed by stone, but by the Basilisk's eye. And ridding it of one monster would only crown the monster's daughter with power. She would, he suspected, deal with her father's heir as subtly and easily as her father would have done. And Hollis himself would inherit only Caladrius's city of bitterness and fear.

At the moment it was all Caladrius had to give him. He left finally, to return to the Basilisk's house.

Ten

Justin sat in the tavern across from the music school, eating supper with Nicol. They shared a bench beside the cold hearth, holding meat pies in one hand, ale in the other. All the tables were filled, which suited them; the noisy crowd gave them far more privacy than a few morose tipplers would have done. Nicol, his head lowered, picked at his food like a bird, talking all the while. He had to hurry to rehearse music, paint a tree, something; Giulia had appropriated half the school for the festival.

"They are crossing the Marcasia Bridge," he said, his voice almost too low to be heard. "Tomorrow. I want you there watching in the morning."

"All morning? What am I supposed to do there? Set out a cup and pipe for coins?"

Nicol paused, a brow cocked. "Yes," he said. "Why not? If you can think of nothing better to do."

Justin, who couldn't, grumbled mildly, "I'm barely awake by noon."

"Gaudi will take your watch at noon. She couldn't come earlier. She works."

"Thank you. You know they've been searching wagons since the trapper's disaster."

"Not every wagon. Harvest is beginning. How do you search a wagon full of potatoes? Anyway—" He stopped to smile as a student greeted him. "Anyway, the wagon you will watch for is carrying stone."

"What—"

"Marble. From the southern quarries. One of the stones will be hollow."

Justin grunted through a bite, impressed. "Who is paying for the marble?"

"The sculptor who ordered it. Of course he doesn't know."

"About—"

"No."

"If they're discovered—"

"Nothing," Nicol said firmly, "is going to happen to this one. We've spent all we have. The stone we want will be delivered to Evera's uncle, who carves grave markers and monuments. His yard is full of odd pieces of marble. He won't notice one more."

Justin drew a long breath. For a moment the mellow sunlight in the tavern grew dazzling; the amber of his ale seemed a rare and astonishing hue. "And then we fight."

Nicol's voice grew thin as thread. "Once he is dead, the other houses will rebel with us. They won't let us take power, but at least we'll be free."

"What about—"

"Taur?" He shook his head. "He's not a fighter. And the daughters will be easily subdued."

"It sounds like a dream."

"It is," Nicol said simply. "And we've been dreaming it for years. It's time to act. Don't be afraid." He finished his ale, missing Justin's glare. "Tomorrow. Early. Don't do anything to make yourself suspicious." He rose, brushed a crumb off his robe, and picked up his lute, which he wore everywhere like a disguise. Justin, annoyed, emptied his own tankard, wondering, not for the first time, what Nicol thought he carried around in his skull. A tall, gaunt man slipped onto the bench beside him, carrying a bowl of stew. Justin, rising with a friendly nod, got a vague impression of a hand composed of twigs and knobs, a thin, seamed neck stretched like a tortoise's toward the bowl. The man did not look up. Justin picked up his pipe and headed for the Griffin's Egg.

The next morning, he sat with his back to a stone wall, watching the sun, climbing above the city, throw a glittering largesse of light ahead of itself that turned water into gold. He had settled himself on the street that ran along the water. The city wall was breached on both sides of the wide bridge by steps leading down to the docks. Piping without enthusiasm, he could watch the bridge and the fishing boats with their bright sails that had caught the breeze at an hour he didn't know existed. The guards, already stopping wagons, ignored him. A fisherman, whistling that early, had dropped a copper into his battered cup out of pity, Justin suspected, for the demented young man with raw eyes and matted hair making lugubrious noises in the street.

The wagon hadn't come by noon; neither had Gaudi. Justin, cursing Nicol, took his handful of coppers down to the docks and bought bread and smoked fish in a tavern. Through its tiny, grimy windows he could see the tops of wagons pass above him along the marble balustrade. It was, as Nicol said, harvest. Corn passed. Onions. Squash. He yawned. Then he turned abruptly, before he fell asleep, to go back up to the street and look for Gaudi. He nearly bumped into someone behind him: a thin, spidery man carrying a bowl of fish soup. He apologized hastily; the man muttered something to his soup. Walking out, he found the sun blazing like a phoenix overhead, consuming shadow until the streets shimmered with light, and on the bright water the barges seemed to float into fire.

He saw no sign of Gaudi. He sank down against burning stone, sweated there a few moments until his still, limp body caught the guards' attention. He moved down the street, found shallow shade within a doorway, and fell asleep for a moment.

When he opened his eyes he saw a wagon full of blocks of marble lumbering up to the guards at the end of the bridge. He watched, not moving. The wagon stopped. In the heat, the horses' dark flanks glowed like satin with sweat. The white marble stood ranked like tombstones behind them, unmarked against the glaring sky. Justin, stunned with the heat, half dreaming, watched a talon of light reach down from the sun, write names on a slab he could not read, yet knew he recognized. The stones lurched forward; the wagon passed the guards, whose attention already had turned to whatever followed it. The wagon rattled down the street away from Justin. He closed his eyes.

When he woke again, shadow spilled over him, stretched halfway across the street. He moved stiffly, carving himself, bone by bone, out of the stone around him. He was so thirsty he could have drunk stone. He picked up his pipe, found a coin left in his pocket, and stumbled back to the tavern for ale.

Midway through the tankard, he remembered the wagon, the white stones against the blazing sky, the letters waiting to be carved on them. He put the tankard down with a thump and a splash of ale, thinking coldly: We are armed. He left the tavern, began the long walk back to the heart of the city to find Nicol.

Passing Pellior Palace in the early dusk, he saw a fair man in black come out of the gate, walk quickly down the street. He blinked, puzzling a moment, then remembered him with longer hair, untidy clothes, looking up from his meal in a tavern. He quickened his own pace, caught up with the librarian.

"Master Caladrius?"

He turned, startled, and studied Justin out of eyes darker than Justin remembered, so still they seemed almost inhuman. Then his face eased a little. "Justin? Isn't it?"

"Justin Tabor. I sent you here."

"You sent me here." He added as Justin measured his lagging steps to the librarian's brisker pace, "As you see, the work suited me. You don't look well."

"I got up too early and walked across most of Berylon to the Marcasia Bridge. To meet a friend. I fell asleep on the stones, waiting."

"Did the friend find you?"

"I saw him, yes." He felt the librarian's eyes on him again, and added, "I had to come back to play tonight. On the other side of the city."

"The place near the Tormalyne Bridge."

"The Griffin's Egg. You never came back to play there."

"The only picochet I play belongs to the music school. Giulia found it for the Lady Damiet. I'm teaching her."

Justin lost a step. "Damiet? The goose girl?"

"She has a certain artless feel for it. It's an artless instrument."

"Why you and not Giulia?"

He shrugged slightly. "I don't know. She asked for me. I do what I'm told."

"Do you prefer that? Doing what you're told?"

"For now," Master Caladrius said briefly, and left it there. They walked awhile in silence, Justin in his stupor, the librarian apparently lost in his thoughts. Reminded, perhaps, by the massive, silent structure they approached, he spoke again. "I'm learning the history of Tormalyne House. By all accounts, the House was creative, vigorous, and very powerful for centuries. There's nothing left of it now. It vanished quite suddenly."

Justin opened his mouth, closed it. He pushed his hands against his eyes, wondering if the sun had melted his brain like butter, so that he would announce to a man who worked in Pellior Palace that the death of the House was an illusion. Its heart still beat in the silent, charred husk ahead of them. Its eyes would open soon. It would arm itself and rise.

Tormalyne Palace, colorless as a skull in the dusk, loomed above its vine-tangled trees. The librarian's steps had slowed;

his face had turned away from Justin, as if he tried to find, within the shadowed gardens, the blind, blackened windows, some reason for its downfall. Swallows flickered through the trees; birds, invisible in the dense cascades of ivy, sang to the evening star.

Justin's thoughts wandered back to the wagon, with its incongruous load of arms and artist's marble. The librarian touched his arm, speaking, his voice oddly low.

"Walk ahead of me. Cross the street."

"Why?"

"Someone is following."

Justin, about to protest that when the streets were filled with people someone inevitably followed, swallowed his words suddenly. The librarian had shifted shape once again, and he had let Justin see. What he had become, Justin had no idea. He quickened his pace promptly, curious, while the librarian lingered beside the iron fence, studying the ruined palace, the monument to the dead, that those born in Berylon scarcely noticed when they passed.

Justin did not look back until he had crossed the street. He eased into a doorway on the crowded corner, and turned. There was no one behind Master Caladrius, except for a tall, bony man who looked frail enough to be toppled by a vicious picochet note. He passed the librarian without a glance, continued his solitary way along the fence.

There was a movement above his head. A shadow, a crumpled black cloth, dropped out of a tree. The man ducked suddenly, hunching; another shadow fell, danced above his head. The man beat at the air with one hand, tried to cover his sparse hair with the other, tried to look up. A shadow clung briefly to his eyes. Justin saw him cry out, but could not hear him, nor could he hear any sound from the ravens darting and tearing at him like a pair of street urchins guarding treasure with splinters of broken crockery.

The librarian was approaching to help him, but not swiftly. Justin, still idling, felt his sudden dark gaze across the street. He froze then, glimpsing pieces of the gaunt man in memory: in the tavern when he had spoken with Nicol, in the tavern beside the Marcasia Bridge, where he waited for arms. *Go,* the raven's eyes said, and Justin pulled himself out of the doorway, fled into the evening crowds, pursued by a noisy flock of questions.

He sent a message to Nicol at the music school, then waited for him in the tavern, sitting in a corner, drinking ale and watching, tense and edgy, for a glimpse of the bony man sitting alone with his bowl of soup and a bandage on his head. Nicol came finally, looking vaguely irritated.

"Where have you been?" he asked, making Justin shift across the bench. Justin studied him narrowly, noted the subtle complacency that smoothed his brow and made his tone suspect. He drew a breath, easing back against the bench. "I can't stay," he heard Nicol say to the tavern keeper, and then, to Justin: "Where were you? I got a message from Evera that the wagon stopped at her uncle's yard hours ago."

"I fell asleep," Justin said. Nicol made a sharp, exasperated noise. "Nicol—"

"So you never even saw the wagon cross?"

"I saw it, yes. It wasn't searched. The street was burning, and Gaudi never came. Nicol, I was followed."

Nicol stared at him, wordless for once. Then he took Justin's ale out of his hand, dropped a coin onto the table, and pulled him out of the tavern, across the street into the music school.

They settled again in a tiny room with nothing in it but a rosewood music stand. Someone sang scales incessantly to one side of their room; on the other side, he could hear a group of instruments doggedly trying to drag a piece of music in several directions at once.

"Followed by whom?" Nicol asked tersely. "When? Where?"

"He was in the tavern last night—"

"In the Griffin's Egg?"

Justin blinked. "I don't—if he was, I didn't see him there. He was across the street. He sat down beside me when you left. A bony, quiet man without much hair. I hardly noticed him. He was in a tavern at the Marcasia Bridge when I went there at noon. I didn't recognize him there. He followed me back—"

"What did you do when you saw the wagon? Think back. Carefully."

"I had fallen asleep in a doorway. I opened my eyes and saw the wagon just as the guards stopped it. They looked at the stone, and under the wagon, then waved it on. I watched it turn down the street."

"And then?"

"I went back to sleep."

Nicol's face smoothed. "Good," he said after a moment, unexpectedly. Justin sighed, wishing for his ale.

"When I woke again and walked back, I saw the librarian leaving Pellior Palace."

"Who?"

"Master Caladrius. The man cataloging the Tormalyne collection."

"He followed you?"

"No. He told me I was being followed." Nicol looked at him silently, his brows rising over his bright hawk's stare.

He asked, succinctly, the question that had plagued Justin all the way from Tormalyne Palace, "Who is this librarian?"

"I don't know. He told me to cross the street. I looked back when I had, and saw the thin man again, but I still didn't realize I had seen him before. He has that kind of face and bearing. Nothing your eyes want to stop at, nothing in particular to remember. The librarian was standing still, watching him, too. And then a pair of birds—ravens—flew down from the trees and started pecking at the bony man's head. The librarian looked at me and I left. That's the last I saw of either of them."

"How did—" Nicol stopped, started again. "How did he know? If you didn't?"

"I don't—"

"I want to know who he is."

"I'm not following him," Justin said. "I think he talks to birds."

Nicol ignored this. "He works for Pellior House."

"He works in Pellior Palace," Justin corrected him. "With the Tormalyne collection. He told me he was learning the history of Tormalyne House through its music."

Nicol paced a step or two, wheeled. "Don't trust him."

Justin sighed. "Of course not."

"They may have been working together."

"Which one of them do you suppose talked the birds out of the trees?"

"But find a reason to see him again. Let him talk to you. Ask him why he thought you were followed. Ask him anything. Was he born here?"

"He came from the provinces."

"How long has he lived in Berylon? Exactly when did he come here?"

"How should I— " He stopped, staring with rapt interest at a scene playing itself out on the music stand. "That night he asked Giulia for her picochet— "

"What?"

"In the Griffin's Egg. It's the only time I've ever seen the Basilisk's guards in there. Not just the night watch, the House guard. They were looking for someone while he played. It was that night— "

"What night?" Nicol demanded.

His eyes moved from the music stand to his cousin's face. "The night the trapper was killed on the Tormalyne Bridge. I think he is the missing witness. No wonder they can't find him. He's in Pellior Palace, under their noses. And he changes shape every time you look at him."

"Well, what shape is he now?" Nicol asked bewilderedly.

"Nothing I've ever come across. Not even the Basilisk can see him."

"You see him," Nicol said tersely. "He lets you. Be careful. He may be very dangerous."

Justin felt the black, still gaze again, across the city's noisy twilight. "To someone," he guessed soberly, and the librarian changed shape yet again in his head, to a farmer from the provinces, who played the picochet and talked to birds. He shrugged, baffled. "Or maybe not."

"Just be careful," Nicol said again, and passed out of Justin's evening without, Justin noticed surprisedly, leaving him annoyed. He even added, before he left, "You did well."

We must be about to die, Justin thought, and took himself and his pipe to the Griffin's Egg, where, to his relief, he saw no one made of kindling bending a raven-scarred head over his supper.

Eleven

Caladrius, carrying the history of Tormalyne House under his arm, crossed the cobblestones between tavern and school in an ocher haze of late-afternoon light and heard, like an echo of the city high in the sky, the bustle and gabble of birds arriving from the north. As he glanced up, someone shook a banner out of a high window in the school. A basilisk unfurled, black on red, in a silken cascade that did not quite touch the marble griffin crouched beside the door. Another banner drifted down on the other side of the door. A third, gold as wheat and covered with apples, fell to frame the top of the door. ARIOSO PELLIOR, it said in gold thread across red apples; beyond that it did not comment.

He recognized it little by little: the change of seasons in a city of stone. Light from the setting sun drew shadows of a different slant along the street. The light itself, warm and limpid, had loosened its burning grip on the city; its fiery brilliance had softened to harvest golds. In palace gardens, leaves turned the color of light. In the Tormalyne garden, ivy fanning across the marble walls had begun to flame.

Around Luly, the sea would turn pale green beneath gray cloud; the winds would already smell of the snow beyond the hinterlands. He felt a moment's helpless longing for the singing of the restless autumn seas, for the simplicity of fire, water, stone. In Berylon, the words had changed to mean complex things. On Luly he held stone, he held his hand to fire; waking and dreaming, he heard water. In Berylon, such words had lost their innocence; even fire belonged to the Basilisk.

He stepped between the griffins snarling at the basilisks and opened the doors. He was stopped at the threshold by a painted cloud carried down the hall, followed by a swath of sky filled with turtledoves. He could hear singing behind a broad pair of doors. A voice interrupted it, shouting in pain and despair; the singer noisily burst into tears. He heard Giulia's voice, alternately chiding and soothing. The doors opened, the cloud passed through. A dark-haired man strode out, nearly fell into the sky. He disappeared behind a slammed door. The singer began again.

Giulia came out, said to the dove-bearers, "They don't have eyes. You forgot to give them eyes."

The painters studied them. "Love is blind?" one suggested helpfully.

"Love may be," Giulia said, her phrases suddenly terse. "But the Basilisk is not. Give them eyes."

The doves retreated down the hall, the painters wondering audibly if a basilisk's look could kill what had no eyes. An intriguing question, Caladrius thought. Giulia's eyes fell on him and smiled.

"I came to return this," Caladrius said. "And to ask a question. If you can spare a moment."

The surprise on her face turned suddenly to calculation. "You were among the bards. You learned to sing."

"Not well," he lied hastily. "And very long ago."

"A pity. Perhaps," she added thoughtfully, "Hollis. I need more voices in the chorus. Did he find you? He asked about you."

"He found me, yes."

"Did you see which door slammed?"

He nodded to it. She took the book from him, and paused to listen to the love aria coming out of the closed doors, a simple melody that expressed inexpressible longing. "It's pretty," Caladrius said.

"Yes, it is. You can't tell by listening to it that the composer has no patience and no tact and no sense whatsoever."

"No."

She gripped the book like a weapon and headed briskly for the door in question. "What did you want to ask me?"

"Where the music will be performed. And if it is a public occasion."

"It's traditionally performed in the Hall of Mirrors in Pellior Palace. It's much bigger than the music room. It's attended by the prince and his family and guests from the three Houses, the magisters, various officials of the city, and whatever students are invited. Ask Veris Legere's permission to come. I'm sure Damiet will expect you."

"Why?" he asked absently. Her steps slowed. She regarded him silently a moment, her eyes as cool and unreadable as a hinterland mist.

"Damiet is in love with you," she said finally. "Why do you think she's learning the picochet?"

He considered the question blankly. Then he dismissed it, unable to equate love and Damiet. "I'm old enough to be her father. And out of the provinces. You must be mistaken."

"Perhaps. But, Master Caladrius, I would advise you to tread very carefully around the Basilisk's daughter. She may be without thoughts, but she is not without feelings."

He shook his head, his mouth tightening. Whatever vague feelings Damiet might have, he thought, would not survive the song he would play for her father. He said only, "It won't last. Whatever you see. I haven't noticed—"

"Yes, I know," Giulia said. "It's a thing men don't notice unless they're interested." She felt his glance and met his eyes, smiling again, wryly. "The subject makes me provincial."

"Because it goes to the heart of the matter," he said simply. "The place where you learned to feel. I will be careful with Damiet. But I can't believe it is important."

"Believe it," she said soberly. She paused in front of the door behind which the composer had flung himself. "Did you know each other?" she asked. "You and Hollis? He said you might."

He hesitated, not knowing what else Hollis might have told her. He said only, "Yes. We've met."

"I thought so. You look alike sometimes. Not your faces, but your expressions. Something left from Luly, maybe." She studied him a moment, silently, curiously, perhaps hearing things he wanted to say, but could not. Her eyes dropped finally; she remembered the book in her hand. "Did this help?"

"Oh, yes," he said. "Thank you."

"Perhaps it will help Hexel." She hoisted it in the air abruptly and opened the door.

Daily, the city transformed itself to suit the season. Walking to and from Pellior Palace, Caladrius saw stone softened and colored by banners, ribbons, pennants, bright scallops of cloth draped across the weather-stained faces of buildings. Wreaths of corn husks hung on doors; baskets of jesters' faces painted on guards rattling with last year's seed appeared on street corners, sold for luck, and to distract the basilisk's eye. The streets grew even more crowded with visitors from river towns and farming villages, who came to build stalls and sell their wares. Itinerant musicians lay their caps beside every tavern door; stall makers' hammers beat time to their ballads. Puppeteers threw up flimsy stages for the children; they enacted protracted battles between the Houses and other scenes from Berylon's history. Caladrius, leaving Pellior Palace one evening, was frozen mid-stride by a puppet with a raven's face pleading for its life while a red satin fire shook in the background and a crowing basilisk scythed its way methodically through a hapless army of griffins. Barefoot country children watched solemnly; some wore basilisk masks made of feathers and paper. They clapped when the basilisk slew the raven, promising peace at last to the convulsed city. Caladrius, turning away, was stunned again by a figure burning in the street. Something flew out of the flames. The crowd around it cheered and scattered, trying to catch it. It fell at Caladrius's feet. A phoenix, he realized, staring numbly. The phoenix of Marcasia House, made of metal and paint, built to spring out of the fire as the straw phoenix burned. He should have caught it, he was told; bad luck to let the phoenix fall to earth. He turned quickly, blindly, found his way to the only quiet place in the city: the ruined gardens of Tormalyne Palace.

But even that peace was marred by the seamed, unblinking face of Brio Hood, turning in slow, tortoise fashion to see who else walked the empty side of the street in festival time. He stood in front of the iron railing, as if he searched for the ravens that had tormented him. His eyes took in Caladrius, returned to study the railing. He reached out, touched a bar, and Caladrius, slowing, felt a sudden claw of pain behind his eyes.

Brio spoke, with some half-forgotten urge to exchange words with the man who had helped him. "It moves." He looked at Caladrius, and back at the bar. He touched it again, slid it an inch to one side. "Someone dug a groove for it." He looked at Caladrius silently, inviting comment. Caladrius shrugged slightly.

"For what?"

"Yes," Brio murmured. "For what?" He gazed, entranced, at the leaf-covered groove. "Someone goes in there."

"It's empty. Why would anyone bother?"

"Someone goes there in secret." He turned his back to the railing then, and leaned on a firmer bar, passing idle time with the music librarian while his eyes flicked at every passing face.

"It's old," Caladrius suggested. "It was made a long time ago." Brio did not bother taking up the question.

"It's secret," he repeated. "The prince doesn't like secrets.

Except his own." His face changed then, as if the prince were watching him; thought flowed out of it, left a shadow man, so frugal he gave away nothing even of himself. He did smooth a hand over his scant hair, where a jagged furrow was healing. "The birds left me when you came," he commented equivocally. "You always pass this way."

"I like trees," Caladrius said. "It's what I'm used to."

"Being a northerner."

"I'm not used to crowds, yet. Or the noise. It's worse, now."

"It's the prince's festival. His day to remember." His eyes touched Caladrius's face, slid away. He straightened. "I noticed this when the ravens came at me. How the bar gave when I fell against it. I didn't remember it then, only that something happened that shouldn't have. Besides the ravens, I mean. Something was out of place. I came back to look for it."

"You weren't afraid of the ravens?"

Expression glided across his face; he blinked once. "They're dead now," he said. He turned without another word, made his unremarkable way down the street toward Pellior Palace. Caladrius, motionless, watched him out of ravens' eyes until, past the Tormalyne gardens, the crowds swelled toward Brio and swallowed him.

Caladrius returned after midnight. The warm streets were still noisy; the night watch, its attention turned to drunken brawls, flaring tempers, burning phoenixes, had no time to patrol the haunted stillness around Tormalyne Palace. Brio would also return at night, Caladrius guessed. Dark held secrets, and the answers to secrets. He had found the loose bar. He would find the path: the broken stalk, the overturned stone, the place where weeds had stopped growing. He would make his careful, skilled way to the window with the bars bent apart. He would wait, knobbed and silent as a root underground, night after night, while the moon waxed and waned, until he heard a sound in the empty palace. A footstep. A whisper.

The children of the House would fare no better than the ravens in the trees.

Caladrius would leave something among the barrels in the old wine cellar: a word on the wall, a charred torch, a torn piece of cloth, to let them know that they had been discovered. He had no idea how often they gathered, but if they came later that night, they would all be warned. He dared not leave a warning at the window, or beside the rail for Brio to see. In the morning, he would send some crude message to the red-haired man Nicol, whom he had seen in his magister's robe at the music school, to stop the gatherings. He had thought of finding Justin, but Justin, playing at the Griffin's Egg, could do little that night, except demand some answers from Caladrius. Descending noiselessly from the barred window, he realized that Justin would not have been where Caladrius expected to find him. They had come before him; he sensed them instantly, as if their thoughts had left a trail.

He stood, trying to still his breathing, listening to the silence which held, like overtones, ripples of movement, warmth, spoken or unspoken words. He heard, very faintly, a sound that might have been a rat disturbing stagnant water, that might have been a word. Chilled, he moved quickly, found the wall, and followed it, to get them out before Brio gave them like a birthday present to the Prince of Berylon.

He saw them through the marble archway, sitting quietly

as they had before, dimly lit among the empty racks and barrels. This time only Nicol spoke; the others listened intently. Caladrius, on the shore of the dark, about to step into light, suddenly found himself unable to move. Something had formed near him, clinging like shadow to the wall on the other side of the arch. Caladrius, his skin constricting, turned his head slowly.

He met Brio's eyes.

Something struck him, flung him back into the shadows. against the wall. Desperately he shook away the raven's wing of dark pressing against his eyes. He tried to cry out; no words came. He felt blood slide through his hair, down his neck. He swayed suddenly, tried to keep his balance, wondering why he could not speak, why he could only watch while Brio made adjustments to the small thing in his hand. What it was Caladrius did not recognize, except as dangerous. It looked like a palm-sized crossbow with a tiny quarrel. Brio turned it at Nicol.

"This one is deadly," he breathed. "Poisoned. Yours will only keep you dazed and quiet. The prince makes them. Don't make a sound. I never miss what I must kill."

He reached out with his free hand, the quarrel tip never wavering, as if his bones worked independently of one another. He caught Caladrius with unexpected strength, pulled him so close that Caladrius could feel the metal and wood of weapons he hid in his clothes. A blade slid out between his fingers, angled upward beneath Caladrius's jaw. "If you do anything to warn them, I will kill you. And then them. All of them. Listen to them. . . ."

"During the opera," Nicol was saying. "Giulia Dulcet still needs singers in the chorus. Get yourselves into it. Do anything that will get you in to see the performance. I'll give those of you who aren't invited magisters' robes. Come late and stay in the back so that the real magisters won't see you. You will arm yourselves beforehand at Evena's uncle's yard. He'll be away at the festival. Anyone left outside will stay close to the palace gates, to overcome the guards if they are summoned, and open the gates to the people."

"Northerner," Brio whispered. "Farmer. You were the man on the Tormalyne Bridge, who set fire to the trapper's wagon." Caladrius tried to speak; his throat closed, trapping words. The blade moved abruptly, stung. "You're still alive because I don't know what you are. Your hands don't have years of earth worked into them. You don't speak of fields and crops, you speak of music. You read it. You play it. I think you came down from Luly when it burned. You're still alive because I don't know why you are in the prince's house." Caladrius, feeling a raven claw behind one eye, lurched suddenly; the relentless grip pushed him back, held him still. "Don't move. I know better than to kill you before he sees you. You set those ravens at me. I don't know how, but I know why. And then you pretended to help me. There's a power in you like his. He doesn't use birds; he would if he knew how. But he would know it might be possible. You will tell him how, before you die." He turned the tiny crossbow away from Nicol; it loomed at Caladrius until he shut his eyes. He felt the poisoned tip against one eyelid. "It takes nothing to set this off. A breath. A hair falling across it. Walk. Slowly. Slowly. Don't do anything to startle me. Don't try to open your eyes. If the point scratches, you'll die. It will take longer, though. Walk."

It took forever, it seemed to Caladrius, moving in the dark with a knife at his throat and an arrow at his eye, before he sensed a change in the air. It was stagnant now, and echoing with past. He felt the quarrel leave his eye, heard the soft drag of wood across earth. He recognized the sound, the closing door. Despair caught in his throat, tried to turn into words. The knife bit at him, warning. Brio backed him to the wall, guiding him with the quarrel tip; odd shapes of chains and leather hanging against the stones shifted and clanked behind Caladrius.

Brio gave a grunt of satisfaction.

"You'll stay here while I deal with the others. A fire among those old racks and barrels . . . There is only one door; I will be waiting for them there. The one with the red hair, I'll keep alive for the prince. There must be something here for your hands. . . . But first . . . You're too strong. . . ."

The dark exploded. Caladrius, gasping, fell into metal and stone, and then earth struck him. Waves of color broke over him, tried to drag him away into a vast ocean of darkness. Brio caught one of his arms; Caladrius heard him scrabbling among the chains. Cold metal wound around his wrist. He closed his eyes, fighting the merciless undertow of pain, the promise of peace beyond it, and pulled the fire-bone pipe out of his shirt.

He glimpsed an enormous eye smoldering with fire in the utter dark as he began to play.

He woke sometime later, falling piecemeal into pain, and then darkness, and then memory. He pushed himself up, felt the chain coiled around his wrist slide away. Trying to rise, he stumbled, fell against something. His hands shaped cloth, a face. Brio, memory reminded him; the fire-bone pipe. Brio did not seem to be breathing. Caladrius pushed the pipe back into his shirt, and fumbled through eerie shapes of leather, and wood, and metal before he finally found the door. He followed the wall until it turned from rough-hewn stone to marble. He saw nothing, and realized that his eyes were still closed. He opened them, still saw nothing but dark ahead of him. He stood in the silence, listening for breath, movement, thought. His eyes closed again. He caught himself trying to imagine what Brio had seen, what had killed him. Then, shocked into clarity, he realized that the tale had told the truth: he had played death with his music. The pipe, still warm, alive against his skin, would kill the Basilisk.

He made his way out of earth and stone back into the world, which was black with the last, chilly hour before dawn. The streets were as still as if the whole of Berylon had glimpsed what he had summoned. Even the moon had fled. Shivering and bloody, he walked the maze of side streets and quiet alleys to elude the watch, and managed, reaching the tavern at last, to elude even dawn.

He found Hollis, like a gift from the unpredictable night, waiting in his room.

Twelve

Giulia sat at the spinet in the music room at Pellior Palace, playing Damiet's costumes, one after another, in a final lesson before she put the rehearsals at the school, and the scenery, and Damiet together for the first time in the Hall of Mirrors. Damiet had learned Hexel's words and music to a degree that would make them at least recognizable to the composer. She kept time fairly well; occasionally she even wandered into tune. That day, however, she could not summon enthusiasm. Her usual vigorous tones were pallid; she forgot words. Giulia, listening absently, sorting details in her head as she played, was startled when Damiet stopped dead in the middle of her rose-and-silver love aria.

"Magister Dulcet."

Giulia's hands slid from the keys; she looked up to find

Damiet's frosty displeasure aimed at the cabinets on the other side of the room. "Lady Damiet?"

"Where is Master Caladrius?"

Giulia turned, found an unusual lack of a librarian among the manuscripts. "I don't know. He's late today."

"Where is Veris Legere? Master Caladrius must be summoned. How can I sing these songs without him? And there is my picochet lesson—"

"Perhaps he is ill," Giulia suggested temperately.

"He was not ill yesterday."

"Then he will come, I'm sure. Something must have delayed him. Shall we start from the beginning?"

Damiet, her lips thin, gazed at the cabinets as if a door might open under her eyes to reveal the missing librarian. Her foot tapped. Giulia played a chord, coaxing. Slowly Damiet's fingers loosened, her arms dropped, as nothing stirred among the cases.

"Perhaps, if I sing, he will come." She drew breath and began precipitously, leaving Giulia to plunge after her a half beat behind.

The door opened. The quality of the note Damiet sang changed perceptibly, becoming full and remarkably in tune. Veris Legere entered; the note flattened itself again. No one followed him. Damiet interrupted herself after a phrase or two.

"Master Legere," she said peremptorily. "Where is Master Caladrius? He is not here to listen to me sing."

"Master Caladrius may not be with us for a day or two, my lady," Veris said temperately. "He sent word that he has fallen somewhat ill."

Color swept again into Damiet's face; she took an impulsive step. "Then my father's physician must be sent to him. At once."

"It is not that serious, my lady; he says he needs only rest. He may return tomorrow."

Damiet considered. Giulia watched her motionlessly, wondering herself what ailed Master Caladrius, and what more Damiet might inflict upon him. Even Veris waited silently. Damiet's face cleared finally; she said, composed once more, "Then I will wear my autumn silk tomorrow."

"You will be rehearsing tomorrow in the Hall of Mirrors," Giulia reminded her.

"I will wear it for my picochet lesson," Damiet answered, and began, in the middle of the word and somewhere around the note where she had stopped.

They were nearing the end of the mauve song when Giulia became aware of someone near them, listening. She finished the song grimly, wondering if Hexel would be driven into seclusion, or if he could survive the force of Damiet's transmutations of his inspiration. She looked up into Luna's smile.

She rose hastily, and curtsied, feeling oddly that the Basilisk himself looked out of his older daughter's eyes. Luna moved to the spinet, studied Hexel's music.

"How lovely," she commented. "And how apt."

"It is my mauve song," Damiet said with dignity.

"Did you choose the color? So clever of you. Please sit, Magister Dulcet; go on with the lesson. I only came to listen."

"We have only the white song left," Damiet said. "The final song, where the lovers are united forever and sing their happiness to each other. After that, everyone else must sing, but we have nothing more to say. Magister Dulcet, of course

Master Caladrius will be there, will he not? If he is ill that long, my father's physician will attend to him. He must be there. I will wear white with pink rosebuds," she added to Luna.

"You will look like a birthday cake," Luna answered. "Everyone will feast their eyes on you." She turned over a page of music. "Is Master Caladrius ill?"

"He didn't come today," Damiet complained. "He told Veris that he needed to rest."

"Did he?" She turned another page, her bright eyes moving across the notes, Giulia noticed, without seeing them. They lifted, abruptly, to Giulia's face. "Magister Dulcet, is it serious?"

"I don't know, my lady," Giulia said. "I hardly know him. He was here yesterday; beyond that I can't guess."

"It was sudden, then, this illness."

"Apparently, my lady."

"Veris says he might be back as soon as tomorrow," Damiet said, "to give me my picochet lesson. If he is not—"

"If he is not, of course you will be patient," Luna said, shedding her radiant, random smile at her sister. "Things you want come sooner when they come in their own time. Like mice out of holes. Or love."

"I am not watching for a mouse," Damiet said disdainfully.

"No, of course not. You are waiting for the librarian who was unexpectedly taken ill and cannot come. At least you know what happened to him." She pressed a key, so softly it did not sound. "At least you know." She loosed the key and looked at them, her green eyes wide, still smiling, and, in their fashion, not smiling at all. "Perhaps I won't stay to listen. I will let you surprise me, Damiet. You do it so well."

Giulia curtsied deeply, relieved. Damiet waited until the door closed behind her sister before she spoke. "I think my sister is in love with Master Caladrius," she said calmly. "But she would not suit him at all. She is not very musical. We have one song left, Magister Dulcet, and then I must practice the picochet."

Returning to the school, Giulia found an unaccountable number of singers suddenly inspired to join the opera chorus. She set some students frantically copying music for them, bade them learn it overnight for the rehearsal, and sent them to be measured for robes. That accomplished, she approved a leafy bower, half paint, half potted ivy, within which the lovers were to sing, and sent it on its way to Pellior Palace. Walking briskly down the hall to listen to the enraged father practice his aria with Hexel, she found herself walking out the door instead, across the street with ribbons fluttering from every post, and into the tavern where Justin stopped sometimes, at that hour, to eat.

She stood in a crush of students and strangers, not seeing him, but still looking, as if wishing would call him there. In that moment she admitted the perplexing anxiety that, unable to get her attention in the school, had finally driven her out of it. Something had changed in Justin. He saw her only vaguely, through whatever compelled his own attention those days. He had made no attempts recently to find her at the school, and forgot to ask her to meet him, even in his bed. Her own constant work might have overwhelmed him, but he had retreated without a struggle, leaving her to wonder how far he had gone.

She was standing, she realized, in the wrong tavern. He would be at the Griffin's Egg later. She would find him there, even if she had to rehearse singers until midnight. She moved out of the path of a harried boy holding a tray of mugs over her head and turned to see the bard Hollis coming down from the rooms upstairs with a bowl in his hand.

He had not seen her. His brows were drawn above his eyes; a dark midnight blue, they looked in the shadows almost black. The expression on his face, grim and still, seemed familiar, but not, she thought suddenly, on his face. He wore it like a reflection of something he had seen, and in that moment he looked very like Caladrius.

Her brows rose. He noticed her then; she watched him assume a more appropriate expression, like a mask. It did not succeed very well, but she allowed him his privacy.

"Magister Dulcet," he said, dropping the bowl onto a passing tray. "What are you doing here?"

"Looking for a friend," she said tersely, and offered him secret for secret. "I have not seen him for days. I'm wondering if I have inadvertently sacrificed him to the prince's festival."

His face hardened, but he answered gently, "I doubt that."

"Have you been visiting Master Caladrius?"

"Yes."

"Is he very ill? Veris Legere said he only needed rest for a day or two."

"It's not too serious."

"What shall I tell Damiet? She expects him tomorrow for a lesson."

He shook his head doubtfully. "I don't know." He hesitated; she waited. "He became faint with a sudden fever, coming home last night in the dark. He fell down some stone steps. The fever is lessening, but he hit his head."

"Does he need a physician?"

"Just rest." Again he paused. "I can watch him."

"That's kind of you," she said, keeping the curiosity out of her voice so well that he looked at her closely.

"Magister Dulcet—"

"Giulia. Here, I am Giulia, looking for Justin. And finding you instead, taking care of Master Caladrius. He's fortunate to have such a friend."

He seemed on the verge of explaining, giving her the truth, or a more plausible lie. He said only, "Giulia. I'll tell you tomorrow if he will be able to return to Pellior Palace."

"Thank you."

She went back to the school, forced herself to concentrate so completely on her work, that when she left the rehearsal hall to find Hexel so that he could resolve a troublesome note for the tenor, she did not recognize Justin until she nearly walked into him.

She gathered her thoughts hastily out of painted stars and feverish duets and caught his wrist before he could escape. She pulled him into the nearest lesson room and shut the door. The room was empty but for a harpsichord, an enormous urn of flowers in a niche, and a man's head carved in white marble in another niche, his face angled curiously toward them. Justin pulled her against him as the door closed, held her tightly. She closed her eyes; her hands slid over skin and muscle beneath his shirt; she smelled a tavern weave of smoke and stew in his clothes, and his own familiar smell of sweat and cedar.

"I'm sorry," he said. He sounded sorry; his voice shook.

"I thought you thought I had forgotten you. And so you forgot me."

"No. It's just—" He shrugged, not explaining just what. "Things."

"Things."

"Happening." She felt him draw breath; he became articulate again. "Family matters. Nicol keeps me occupied. He pretends I have nothing better to do. I've missed you. So has the Griffin's Egg."

"I've been too busy to miss anything but you. I looked for you, today, across the street."

"You did." He drew a hand down her hair, snagging pins; she heard them drop onto the marble. She pulled his head down, kissed him. Behind her, someone opened the door, closed it quickly. She opened her eyes, pulling back, but reluctant to let go of him.

"I have to—"

"I know," he said. "So do I. Giulia—" He stopped.

"What?"

"I just—"

"What?"

"I'm just sorry. That's all."

"For what?" She frowned, searching his eyes, which met hers, then flicked away, then returned. "Justin," she said incredulously. "Did you take another lover? Is that it?"

"No," he said, astonished.

"Then why do you look so stricken? As if you've hurt me and I don't know it?"

He was silent; she gazed at the bust behind him, which

told her nothing either. Justin said finally, slowly, "I'm sorry we have so little time these days. I see you so much in memory, so little in life."

"This will be over very soon," she said, perplexed. "A few more days."

"Come with me tonight." They both shook their heads, then; she felt his exasperated sigh. "I have to help Nicol after I play."

"All night?" she asked, marveling at the prim, soft-spoken magister. "What is he doing?"

"Moving things," he said vaguely. "He has no time during the day. Do you know where Master Caladrius lives?"

She consulted the bust again, at the unexpected question. "Across the street. Why?"

"I need to speak to him."

"About what?" She took a handful of his hair, pulled his head down lightly to see his eyes. "Don't tell me 'things.' "

"Nicol asked me to. Ask him something." She raised her brows, at a loss to guess. Justin added inadequately, "Something about birds."

She pushed her head against him, bewildered. "Justin. You're making very little sense. Nicol will have to wait. Master Caladrius is ill."

"Ill?"

"A fever. It's passing, according to the bard Hollis, who for some secret reason is taking care of him. You are all getting mystifying. But I only have room for one plot in my head at a time, and Hexel's must take precedence."

"A fever?"

"He fell and hit his head. So Hollis says. He must rest."

"When?"

"Last night, sometime. Damiet is—" She felt his body stiffen and paused. "Justin," she said slowly. "What is going on that you aren't saying? What do you and Nicol and Master Caladrius and Hollis all have to do with one another?"

"I don't know Hollis," Justin said, eluding the question so promptly that she stared, wide-eyed, back at the marble head.

It began to change itself under her eyes. Then Justin came between them, distracting her from mysteries. Flushed, hair disheveled, she clung to him long past time for them to part.

"Be careful," she begged, not knowing exactly what she meant. He seemed to know.

"I will." He kissed her one last time, and left her standing there, gazing thoughtlessly at the head, which became, feature by feature, familiar: the broad, high bones, the lean wolf's jaw, the slanted brows, the clearly defined mouth. Even its white eyes held something of his direct, unflinching gaze upon the world.

It was the face of the stranger who had played her pi-cochet in the tavern beside the Tormalyne Bridge. She moved finally, as in a dream, to read the name carved into the base of the bust, though she knew it; she had known it since she had first been given lessons in that room.

"Auber Tormalyne."

She shivered suddenly, chilled to the heart, glimpsing beyond Hexel's sweet and trifling opera a darker, unpredictable drama. She whirled abruptly, flung the door open, and then the outer doors across the hall. She ran down the steps, looking for Justin. But he had disappeared into the night, and behind her a chorus of voices had begun to call her name.

Thirteen

Caladrius, returning to Pellior Palace the next morning, walked through a dream of Berylon, in which familiar objects had become scarcely recognizable. Doors were no longer made of wood but of flowers, corn husks, wheat stalks, braided and shaped into birds and animals. Ribbons and long streamers of grapevine grew out of windows. Huge, grotesque faces loomed at him unexpectedly; the phoenix, the basilisk, the chimera walked the streets on human legs, their fierce faces fashioned of glittering threads and feathers. He saw no griffins except those involved in colorful and gory battles along his way. The griffins always died.

Hollis had argued vehemently against his return. Caladrius, who still had some trouble speaking, simply pointed out that he and Brio should not both disappear at the same time. He could move easily enough by then, though through what world he was not always certain. A dull fever or something lingering from the quarrel tip exaggerated commonplace sounds, faces, words, until they took on the intensity and ambiguity of dreams.

The guards at the gate of Pellior Palace seemed to watch his approach with the hunger and ferocity of the mock basilisks fighting on the streets. But he passed unchallenged; they saw a librarian, not a griffin. As he entered the palace he heard, very faintly, a high, pure voice singing of some enchanted world that existed, like a bubble, only in that moment.

In the hall outside the music room, the basilisk's eyes found him, brought him to a stop. He bowed his head and waited, thinking the librarian's thoughts of manuscripts and dates, not the griffin's memories of violence in the night, a song played on the deadly instrument he wore beneath the librarian's discreet and modest black.

"Master Caladrius."

"My lady," he murmured.

She had turned away from him, to something small and elaborate she was building on a table of pale green, filigreed marble. It looked like a birdcage made of fine gold chains and slender rods. As he watched she shaped chain into a pentangle on a round mirror, and lifted the cage to stand on it. Then, smiling, she reached between the bars, swirled the chain around her finger, and the pentangle vanished.

"Master Caladrius. I hear you have been ill." She looked at him again, her eyes lucent, warm; he could not force himself to look away.

"For a day. My lady. I am well, now."

"You look very pale. Perhaps my father's physician should see you."

"It is a lingering headache. It will pass."

"It was sudden, this illness."

"The change of seasons," he suggested.

"I fear the change of seasons must have also stricken one of my cousins. Brio Hood. Do you know him?"

"Only slightly, my lady."

"He said you rescued him from an attack of ravens. Perhaps they wished to use his hair in a nest. Do you think so, Master Caladrius?"

"It's long past the nesting season."

"So it is. And my cousin did not have an extra hair on his head to give away. Does not. I spoke of him as if he were dead. Is dead. Words are imprecise, in this situation. Is he or isn't he? What do you think, Master Caladrius?"

He tried to answer; words caught, trapped in the strange, nightmarish spell left by the tiny quarrel. He forced them out finally. "Words fail me," he explained. "My lady."

"Yes," she agreed softly. "They do, Master Caladrius." She held his eyes a moment longer; he glimpsed a cooler temperament behind the warmth, and found it enticing, like shade in a bright garden. She turned abruptly, loosing him; he closed his eyes, regaining some lost inner balance. "Words fail my father also," she continued. "He calls for Brio; Brio does not appear. My father grows impatient and disturbed, for Brio has never failed my father in his life." She paused, attaching tiny circles of gold to the ends of two chains dangling from a rib of the cage wall. "It would be accurate to say that Brio would only fail my father in his death."

Caladrius watched the braided light run down the trembling chains. Memory intruded, tangled with sight; he felt chain, massive and cold, wind around his arm, the ring of gold clamp on his wrist. Cage, he thought, giving words to what he saw. Bird. Caladrius.

Her smile became brilliant, as if she had read his thoughts. "But, Master Caladrius, I am keeping you from your work. Which is so important to you that you have come, half-ill, to study the musical heritage of Tormalyne House. Though I suppose it cannot be called a heritage if there is no one left to inherit it. Do you agree?"

"We all inherit music," he answered evenly. "We are all fortunate that it was considered by Pellior House too valuable to burn."

She looked down, pushed the chain lying on the mirror into another shape. Horns, he thought. Or the crescent moon. "My sister is waiting for you," she said; it sounded like both warning and dismissal. "Perhaps the picochet will soothe your headache."

He bent his head, thinking: Your cage has no door. Lightning flickered behind his eyes, a dry, distant storm. He walked through it into the music room.

Veris Legere, among the music cabinets, greeted him without perceptible surprise, made courteous, perfunctory inquiries about his health. Damiet waited for him as usual on a gilt chair beside the spinet. She wore a gown the faded gold of autumn leaves; gold flashed here and there in her pale hair. A costume, he assumed, for the opera.

"Do you like it?" she asked as he tuned the picochet to

its simplest scale. Her own tunings were erratic and impulsive, done usually through a flurry of words.

"Very pretty," he answered absently, and handed her the instrument. "Which song is this one for?"

She turned her wide, surprised stare at him, that told him he had not pleased. "It is for you, Master Caladrius." He felt the lightning flicker again behind his eyes and touched them. She shifted on the chair, a rustle of satin and lace. "It is not very comfortable," she added. "And I cannot hold the picochet correctly. But I wanted to wear it for you today, since you have been ill."

"That was kind of you, my lady."

Mollified, she set the bow to the string and produced a stringent wail. Something hit the floor lightly among the cabinets. She continued in energetic, incoherent fashion; through jabs and streaks of sounds her bow seemed to drive into his head, he finally recognized the ballad. He said breathlessly, reaching for the bow and her hand, "Perhaps if you held it less tightly. Spread your fingers. So. The wrist does the work—"

"Master Legere," she called abruptly; Caladrius wondered wearily if he had offended again.

Veris turned, letting the scroll in his hands close gently around itself. "My lady?"

"You must go at once to the Hall of Mirrors and tell Magister Dulcet that I will be late for my rehearsal."

"There is no need," Caladrius said quickly. Veris also had murmured some demurral, that under Damiet's fixed gaze, faded into the marble silence.

"Master Legere."

"Lady Damiet," he said expressionlessly, and left them.

"I will not keep you long," Caladrius insisted, "if Magister Dulcet expects you. Your singing is far more important now than this."

She looked down at her fingers, where he had positioned them, one by one, on the bow. "Is it?" She struck a note, sent it flying with a squawk. "You are not well, Master Caladrius. You came to give me my lesson in spite of that."

"I did not realize that Magister Dulcet—"

"You misunderstand." She turned the bow and tapped it against the floor, a series of staccato notes. "Master Caladrius, we have no time for this."

He felt a warning snap behind his eyes; walls built around him, into a small room smelling of stagnant water; chains with cuffs of gold hung down the walls. "I am sorry," he heard himself say. "I have misunderstood."

"Master Caladrius."

He opened his eyes. She dropped the picochet with a hollow thump and rose impulsively, clasping her long, white fingers against her breasts. He watched emotion gather in her eyes, and the full fury of the storm flared and spat behind his eyes.

He fell against the spinet; keys jangled under his hands. He struggled for balance, panicked that she would summon help and help would ask too many questions, find too many incongruities. But she did not want their solitude interrupted so soon.

"Master Caladrius," she said as he missed the spinet stool and slid abruptly to the floor. "You must speak to my father."

She blurred, candle wax and gold, as he blinked up at her. "My lady?"

"Master Caladrius, I cannot bend in this dress." She tugged at his hands. "You must get up. You cannot declare your love to me sitting under the spinet."

"Lady Damiet," he said desperately, pulling himself up on a few demented chords. "I—"

"We are finally alone, so you can speak freely. I wore this dress for the occasion. Gold is appropriate for the season, and I wear it well, with my coloring. I know that my father may not seem pleased to have a librarian and music tutor fall in love with me. But you must be persuasive. After all, you have persuaded me to fall in love with you, and he must—"

"Damiet," he said, and for a moment she was speechless. The storm had passed, leaving only a raven picking at him. He pushed his hands against his eyes. "Please. Sit down."

"You sounded like my father."

"I beg your pardon."

"I am ready now."

He looked at her; she sat composed and attentive, waiting for him to speak. Words failed again; he wrestled with them while she watched curiously. He freed his voice finally.

"Damiet. I am a librarian."

"Yes."

"I am not even that. I am a farmer. Who, having failed at that, became for the moment, someone who—" He stopped, added grimly, "I am not even that."

"I know all of this," she said impatiently. "It cannot matter. I will refuse to let it matter. My father has always given me whatever I ask for."

"Please. Listen."

"I am listening, but you are saying nothing at all, Master

Caladrius. You bend over me, you touch my hand, you are in the air all around me, your voice falls through me like rain. I have given you leave, you may speak of more than music." She waited briefly, shifting on the chair; satin commented stiffly. He shook his head, overwhelmed. Blood pushed into her pale face; her eyes widened, glittered with frost or tears, fury or pain. "Master Caladrius," she said, with a logic that seemed inarguable, "how can I possibly sing if you do not speak?"

"My lady—"

"Do not call me that. You have called me Damiet." Her foot swung, struck the picochet. "You cannot call me lady now."

"Damiet. You are singing to your father—"

She held his eyes, her face still flushed, her expression frozen between love and hate. "Master Caladrius. I am singing to you."

He sat down on the spinet stool. "I did not hear," he said softly, carefully. "When you sing on your father's birthday, I will listen. I promise. Sing to me as long as you can. I'm sorry to be so clumsy now. I am still ill. I can scarcely think, let alone say the fine things you expect of me."

"And after?" she said. Her voice was cold, but the angry color had receded, leaving her face marble pale again, and calmer.

"And after you sing, I will speak."

She looked at him remotely, letting him guess, for a moment, whether she would accept his gift. Then expression flicked into her eyes, a vague confusion, surprise, as if she were finally seeing him without music. "I don't know your name," she said slowly. "Only Caladrius."

"I will tell you then."

"Master Caladrius—"

He bent to pick up the picochet; the raven clawed at him again. "Lady Damiet, for now that's all I am." He coaxed the picochet into her hand. "Play for me. You do well on this instrument."

"How can it matter?" she asked moodily, but accepted it. "Show me again how to place my fingers on the bow."

"Like this. And this," he said patiently. "It can be, at times, the only thing that matters. Try the ballad again."

Veris Legere returned a moment later, cast a glance over the music lesson. A flock of wild geese, honking and gabbling, flew past him, escaped into the hall as he closed the door. He said, when the last goose had clamored away and Damiet rested her bow, "My lady, Magister Dulcet sends her most urgent request for your presence at the rehearsal."

Damiet favored him with a chilly stare. "I wish to stay with Master Caladrius and finish my lesson."

"Lady Damiet, you must give Magister Dulcet your time now," Caladrius said gently. "You have worked very hard for her. The picochet will wait until you have sung." She turned her head, held his eyes obstinately, until he amended, "Until I have listened to you. Sing. Everything can wait until then."

"I will only sing if you are listening," she reminded him ominously.

"I will be there."

She rose, handed the picochet to Caladrius, and cut a glacial path past Veris Legere's bow. Caladrius had put the picochet back into its case, and was trying to knot the leather strings a fourth or fifth time when he felt a hand on his shoulder.

"Master Caladrius," Veris said with sympathy. "Go home."

In the hall, he paused to bow to Luna, who was still toying with her cage. Raising his head, he was trapped, birdlike, in her green gaze. The cold marble diffused into a summery mist; again he sensed cooler, darker realms beyond her smile.

"I will listen to you as well," she said softly, "on my father's birthday, Master Caladrius. Unlike my sister, I know your name. The caladrius is a beautiful bird, is it not, who sings at the deathbed of a king?"

He felt a sudden, blind twist of pain; the raven, scoring bone, stared out of his left eye. She did not wait for an answer; she left him there, alone in the hall with the golden, doorless cage, which now held prisoner a tiny, tantalizing object. But if he looked more closely at it, he knew, he would find only himself caught within the mirror within the cage.

Fourteen

The Basilisk's birthday began with a brilliant dawn that stained the clouds with fire above the Tormalyne School. Caladrius saw it standing sleepless and dressed at his window. Within the school, Giulia, her back to the fire in the window, began a hasty rehearsal with the piecemeal chorus, half of which had come out of nowhere at the last moment. The bard Hollis, and, to her astonishment, Justin, were among the latecomers. The chorus, ragged but energetic, achieved a veneer of polish as the flames burned out. The clouds faded into gold, and then into a seamless blue that unfurled like a banner over Berylon.

Under that banner, the prince made his triumphal procession through his city. Caladrius, still at the window, watched a blood-red current of guards flow through the crowds ahead of the procession, along its sides, and behind it. Trumpeters at the windows of the school saluted the Basilisk, creating a noisy skirmish with the prince's trumpeters. The prince's heir and daughters rode with him, dressed in the colors of the House. Luna carried a mask on a wand, a gaudy cock's face framed by a glittering snake. She lifted it now and then, to gaze through it at the crowds, which looked back at her out of a startling array of masks. Enormous puppet faces loomed among them. Flowers, rings of wheat and corn husk figures rained out of the windows. Once something heavier fell; Taur's horse shied. A scarlet thread of guards unraveled from the procession, wove through the crowds into various doorways. What they did inside was unclear; shutters snapped shut, floor by floor; the people they brought out with them wore masks and what they shouted could not be heard.

Hollis joined Caladrius briefly after the procession had passed. He wore a magister's robe and carried music for the opera. Why he had chosen to sing for the prince's birthday eluded Caladrius completely.

"This day of all days," he said tersely, "you pick to walk into the Basilisk's house."

"Magister Dulcet needed singers," Hollis answered. He would not meet Caladrius's eyes, and his voice sounded obstinate. He added, "You're going."

"Yes."

"Why?"

"I told Damiet I would listen to her sing." Even to his own ears, it sounded preposterous. Hollis only laughed sharply and without humor. Caladrius caught his eyes finally, added mildly, "Oddly enough, it's true."

"Well then, so am I. Going to hear her sing."

"Hollis. Do something I ask. Just this once. Stay out of Pellior Palace."

"I will," Hollis said grimly, "if you will. Master Caladrius."

Caladrius, his eyes going back to the griffins guarding the doors of the Tormalyne School, had no answer. Hollis gave up waiting for one.

"I must go," he said. He embraced Caladrius briefly, and left Caladrius watching him, moments later, striding through the crowds toward Pellior Palace.

In the Hall of Mirrors, Giulia stood with Hexel, rehearsing crucial parts of the opera with what singers had already arrived. The stage, with its walls and bower, its soaring doves, had been set. The nervous singers wore their costumes. Damiet, who had returned from the procession, had been summoned to no avail.

"Where is she?" Hexel muttered fretfully as the wrathful father on stage threatened to kill his daughter's suitor.

"Changing her clothes," Giulia said tensely.

"What is he doing to my music? Listen to that. A nutcracker could sing better."

"Hexel—"

"I want to hear her sing before she sings."

"You should have come last night."

"I had to rewrite the final chorus. You know that."

"I know it," Giulia said tautly. "I had to rehearse it at dawn. She'll be here. This is for her father. It's Master Caladrius you should worry about."

"Why?"

"If he's not here, she may refuse to sing. She told me this two days ago."

"How could she refuse to sing?" Hexel demanded so vehemently that on stage the singer leaped up to an unexpected note. "Because of a librarian?"

"She sings much better with him," Giulia said, and was troubled, suddenly, by the ghost of Tormalyne House she had seen in his face. How close, she wondered, would Hexel's plot cut toward the truth? A group in black entered. She scanned their faces for Justin's, but he had disappeared again after the morning's rehearsal.

"And what does she sing like without him?" Hexel asked suspiciously.

"She goes flat. She forgets words. She is liable to stop in the middle of a song and ask where he is."

"Where does he live?" Hexel asked tautly. "I'll pay him to come."

"He'll come. He promised." Her hands were clenched within the sleeves of her gown. She forced them open, and watched servants bring in huge urns of flowers that bloomed apparently in some land without seasons. They set them precisely in the center of the mirrors beneath the basilisks. On stage, the father ended his aria and stomped out. More musicians arrived, added themselves to the scattering among the gilt chairs in front of the stage.

"Why is everyone straggling in?" Hexel asked fretfully. "You told them noon."

"It's hard to get through the streets," a flute player explained. "There are basilisks everywhere. Forming processions, slaying griffins, burning phoenixes. The air is getting misty with smoke. They're beginning to gather already at the gate outside, waiting for the prince to come out and throw bread."

"He doesn't do that until dusk," the harpsichord player protested. "After his birthday feast."

"They're hungry for gold, I guess."

"I don't think he's put gold in the bread for years. He just pays people in the crowd to lie about it."

A horn player made a sharp noise, his eyes darting to the basilisks in every mirror. The harpsichord player sat down abruptly and ran lightly through a scale.

The basilisks watched.

Caladrius walked through the streets of Berylon. Basilisks shrieked and laughed, ran in circles around the burning straw figures, which writhed and twisted and sometimes showed a griffin's face among the flames. Smoke and smells of food hung in the still air, smudged the brilliant sky. The Basilisk's guards clustered everywhere, at the scenes of mock battles, bawdy dramas, dances, their human faces cold and humorless among the colorful, glinting masks of birds and animals. Pipes and drums, flutes and viols sounded constantly everywhere as if the music seeped upward from the ground, or drifted from trees with the dying leaves. Near Pellior Palace, the crowds grew thicker, forming shifting circles around jesters and musicians, the enormous painted puppet heads bending to watch as well. Caladrius saw musicians and singers in black robes fighting through the crush; he wondered how many of them were armed.

He passed with them through the palace gates. In the Hall of Mirrors, only the musicians held the stage, tuning, gliding through scales and arpeggios as guests in their autumn finery began to gather. Caladrius saw the red-haired magister Nicol among the musicians, looking austere, ethereal, carefully tuning a harp. A curtain of silk painted with delicate cascades of ivy hid the scenery. An eye appeared now and then among the ivy, surveyed the hall with bright, unwinking scrutiny, then vanished again.

Veris Legere moved through the brilliant company to greet Caladrius, and sent a page hurrying across the hall. "Lady Damiet wished to be told the moment you arrived," he explained to Caladrius. "So did Magister Dulcet. She'll be glad you came no later."

A lean, dark man with long, disheveled hair and an intense blue gaze appeared at Veris's side and applied his gaze to Caladrius. "Is this the librarian?"

"Master Caladrius," Veris said gravely. "Magister Hexel Barr, the composer and dramatist of today's opera."

"You're Giulia's mysterious stranger," Hexel said briskly. "I put you into my plot. Oddly enough, you are in love with Damiet. In art, that is. In life, you are the object of her passion. She refused to sing if you did not come. We are all grateful."

"She's young," Caladrius said briefly, searching the hall for the swirling eddy of courtiers around the prince. "Her feelings won't outlast the day."

"Perhaps," Hexel said dubiously. "But I think you underestimate her. Her feelings may change, but not as easily as a wayward breeze. More like a full-blown gale. Already they nearly destroyed my opera." He paused, still studying Caladrius curiously, seeking the object of passion in the quiet librarian. "You were also among the bards, Giulia said."

"Long ago."

"That would explain it." What, he did not say. "At least you will add incentive to Damiet's singing. Spice. Giulia said she tends to go flat."

Caladrius's attention veered sharply back to Hexel. Veris, staring at him, spoke. "You haven't heard her sing?"

Hexel stared back at them. "No," he said warily. "Why?"

Behind the curtain, Giulia positioned the chorus in its ranks within a broad trellis covered with silk leaves and flowers. The prince finally entered the Hall of Mirrors, bringing his family and the remainder of the guests. In a brief glimpse through the curtain, she also saw Veris and the librarian, Hexel, court and city officials, musicians and magisters from the school who had escaped working with her. Her hands chilled, her mouth dried. She turned, seeking Justin's irreverent eyes among the chorus. But even he looked grave, tense; his thoughts had strayed elsewhere. She held up her hands, quieting them. Then, from behind the bower, she signaled the musicians to begin.

The curtains parted. The chorus drew darkness over the hall, brought the evening stars out above a great city, and then, softly, lightly, sang its evening songs. A stranger entered the city, weary and alone. He had, he sang, come from far away, from a rock in the northern sea where ancient music was born and the great bards taught. He had returned to the city of his birth. His family had been destroyed in a war years before; he had come back to nothing except his memories. He had brought nothing with him, except a magical instrument with which he hoped to please the prince of the city, and gain employment at his court. . . .

Behind him, the chorus sang of the sea; Nicol's harp weltered through their soughing voices. The stranger passed into the night.

Dawn broke over the city. Light warmed the garden where the prince's daughter, in a pale yellow dress, lightly sang her dreams of love, and tried to choose between her suitors.

There was a rustling, a faint murmur through the hall as Damiet began to sing. Beside the prince, Taur coughed, and studied the floor. Giulia, her hands clenched again, saw someone turn trembling and scarlet-faced out the doors. Hexel, staring frozen at the stage, looked bludgeoned with each note. The prince, standing in his birthday silks near the front, listened without moving; his green eyes hooded, narrowed, he looked as if he did not even breathe, lest he miss a note. Not even Damiet shook expression into his face.

The princess did not sing long; her father came out to interrupt her, telling her he had chosen a husband for her. Then a chorus of dressmakers circled her with richly colored swathes of cloth for her wedding dress. She chose; they whirled away, and the favored suitor entered the garden to sing of his love for her. A curious piping wove through his singing, distracting her. In the middle of his protestation, she turned her back to him, followed the seductive, beckoning pipe, and left him singing to himself.

The prince and the piping stranger walked into the garden. The prince's daughter, now dressed in smoky blue, drifted after them. The stranger noticed her finally; his pipe song stopped mid-note. Their eyes met, clung. Or they should have: Damiet barely glanced at the stranger before she looked into the crowd to find the librarian. "Who are you?" she asked him in three notes so rounded and tuned that Giulia felt her throat tighten with wonder. Damiet seemed surprised when the stranger on stage, moving to reclaim her attention, sang his answer.

The prince's daughter teased her father into letting the stranger teach her to play his astonishing instrument. The fond father acquiesced. The stranger, piping again, left the garden with the prince's daughter beside him. The suitor followed, still singing of his love, but only the prince was listening to him.

The stranger, now in courtly black, appeared again, alone in the garden, to sing with passionate confusion of his love for the prince's daughter, and of his perilous heritage, for his family and the prince's had always been the bitterest of enemies. . . .

Giulia's attention, diffused through a hundred details of song and staging, and whether Damiet was changing quickly enough for her rose song, suddenly contracted to a single point. She felt a slow prickle glide over her skin; her eyes felt oddly hot, dry. She turned them reluctantly from the stage, to find the stranger in his discreet black, with his face out of Tormalyne history, standing with Hexel near the back of the hall. Like the prince, his face held very little expression. Hexel had buried his in his hand, a gesture usually preparatory to an explosion. She spoke to him anyway, the barest whisper through the song the stranger sang on the stage: "Hexel, what have we done?"

The stranger finished his song, and reached for his pipe again to call the prince's daughter into the moonlight with him.

He was not worthy of her, he tried to explain. He was of lowly background, he had been born a simple farmer's son, raised to be a bard; he must give her up. She refused to listen; she looked in all his pockets for his pipe; she repeated again and again, to beguile a more suitable past out of him, "Tell me who you are and I will tell you who I love." That the prince's daughter had no interest whatsoever in her piping suitor was becoming obvious; she refused to sing to him, but sang instead, earnestly and inflexibly, to some point toward the back of the hall.

A few people turned to look, Giulia noticed, among them Taur, wondering what his sister was singing at. His attention, lax until then, had at last found occupation; he stared so long at the librarian that his sister Luna put her hand on his arm and whispered to him. He whispered back; she shook her head, smiling sweetly, keeping a hand on him until he gazed again, blindly, at the stage, frowning so fiercely that the piper forgot where he was and repeated most of his song. Damiet, following his lead obliviously, continued to sing to the back of the room.

Giulia heard an audible groan from Hexel. The prince's guests were too polite or too bored to notice; a couple of magisters, trembling and biting their lips, seemed in pain from suppressed laughter. The reluctant stranger, tormented beyond caution by the charms of his beloved, finally confessed:

"I am your father's bitterest enemy."

The rejected suitor, who had been listening behind a bush, hurried away to tell the prince. The prince's daughter, unwilling to believe their plight, continued her teasing. They would run away together, she announced, flee to some kingdom where roses opened to the full moon, and swans sang love songs to one another. There was a faint sound from among the chorus, as if someone had sung a note too soon. Giulia, glancing at them, saw Justin staring across the hall, his face rigid, so white he might have been watching someone die.

Damiet finished her song methodically, as though she were wrapping up a fish, and went to change for her mauve song.

"I will never write another note," Hexel was whispering ceaselessly behind his hand. "Never. Not a single note. I am struck dumb. Betrayed by my muse. Mangled, crippled, flayed by my own music. I can never compose again. Never. I have laid down my pen; I will become a tanner. A common laborer. Living by the bitter sweat of my brow, since there is nothing of art left in me that has not been outraged. Defiled. How could Giulia let that idiot girl sing my music?"

Caladrius, stunned by Hexel's transformation of his past, could not speak. The prince seemed equally transfixed. He had not moved since the stranger from the north had wandered on stage to the city of his birth with his magical pipe and his bitter memories. Caladrius had slid the pipe out of his shirt; his fingers were locked around it. He waited for the prince to turn, waited for the Basilisk's eyes to seek him, recognize him, understand the fate shaping itself out of the stranger's music. He scarcely heard the singing or Hexel's whisperings; they seemed distant, fragmented by his own breathing, the wash of his blood. The room itself, with its mirrors endlessly reflecting the elegant gathering, seemed as transitory as candle fire; a breath would blow it away. Only the pipe in his hand and the motionless prince were real, and the song, cold as hoar, simple as bone, waiting to be played.

On stage, the furious father, flanked by a pair of guards, made his entrance and sang his rage. The guards locked chains of gold around the stranger's wrists and led him away. The melancholy piping from the dungeons flowed into the prince's song of triumph that he had rid himself of the last of the family that had plagued him. Under Caladrius's eyes, the Basilisk stirred at last, his head lifting slightly, beginning to turn. Caladrius raised the pipe to his lips.

An instant before he played, before the prince turned, another pipe sounded from the stage, adding its own strange, haunting melody to the prince's exultation. Candle fire fluttered as at a sudden wind; the reflections in the mirrors grew oddly vague. The prince's attention riveted itself to the stage again. Caladrius, not recognizing the instrument, cast a glance away from the Basilisk and saw, in the midst of the chorus, the faint, glowing holes of the fire-bone pipe flickering and darkening as the piper's fingers shaped his song.

He recognized Hollis.

He caught his breath; music waiting in the pipe at his mouth seemed to flow back into him. Hollis, his hands moving almost imperceptibly in the shadowed, silent chorus, loosed a sullen fire at every note. The prince's aria came to an end; for a moment the two pipes sang together, one sweet and despairing, the other wild, husky, tuned to some raging winter wind.

Then Arioso's shout of fury snapped across the room, and Caladrius turned his own horror into answering music. Hexel flung back his head, staring in bewilderment at Caladrius. Veris Legere had also turned in wonder to the librarian. The blood left his face as he saw the pipe. His eyes jerked from it to Caladrius. He closed them, whispering something. The prince wheeled incredulously, caught between pipers. Above them, shadows cast by nothing visible began to swirl; in the mirrors, the basilisks' eyes grew bright with fire.

"Stop them!" the prince commanded. The guests and the guards at the doors, hearing only more music, glanced about them perplexedly for the source of the prince's anger. Veris Legere looked at the prince across the room and then at Caladrius. Suddenly aged and very grim, he folded his arms and studied the floor. Among the musicians, the red-haired harper dropped his harp and rose abruptly.

"For Tormalyne House!" he shouted. From the chorus came another voice, shaken yet staunch,

"For Griffin Tormalyne!"

On stage and in the crowd, black robes fell like old skins; the mirrors glittered suddenly with upraised swords.

Caladrius barely heard his own name. He let the pipe fall, all his attention on Hollis, who could not seem to move. Hexel gripped him, talking again; he broke loose, moved into the frightened crush. The palace guard, pushing in, were struggling with guests pushing to get out. Damiet, appearing to sing her mauve song to her beloved, stared in amazement at the fleeing audience. She opened her mouth stubbornly; Giulia pulled her away from what had been the chorus spilling, armed and shouting, off the stage.

Damiet shrieked, struggling in Giulia's grip, then cried across the hall, "Master Caladrius!"

The prince, holding ground against the turmoil around

him, caught the raven's eyes and held them in a fierce, unblinking stare.

I will kill you, it promised.

Around them in every mirror, pieces of an enormous, winter-white beast began to form: a great, fiery eye here, there a claw that spanned the mirror, a haunch, a line of spurs along the scaled back, the fold of a wing. Caladrius fought against the shrilling, panicking crowd to reach Hollis, who had found his way off the abandoned stage, looking dazed, spellbound by his own spell. Some of the guards had struggled through to surround the prince and his children.

Watching a claw emerge from the mirror, one shouted, "Break the mirrors!"

They shattered instantly at an impatient gesture from the prince, thundering out of the massive frames to the floor. From every piece the beast looked out.

"Ignore it," the prince shouted above the screams. "Bring me Griffin Tormalyne!"

The guard, seeing griffins everywhere, attacked magisters and musicians; the unarmed librarian slipped past their notice. *Go,* Caladrius commanded his son silently, at every step. *Run.* But Hollis did not see him, only something flowing up all around them out of the shards broken mirrors. His face lifted, paper white, toward what was forming above their heads. Caladrius glanced up and froze.

So had the prince, looking up at the massive white coils of snake with its fierce cock's head, its lidless eyes. It held the prince in its mad, glowing gaze. The great wheels of its coils rippled and tightened as if it gripped some struggling, invisible thing. The prince, his face still and waxen as a death mask, began to take harsh, struggling breaths through his open mouth. He could not seem to move; he hung limply, like a puppet dangling from invisible strings in the basilisk's stare. A low, hollow piping came from it, as if it sang as it killed.

All fighting stopped. No one moved, lest a footstep, a flick of bright cloth, attract the fuming, deadly gaze. The prince groaned suddenly, his eyes closing, and Luna raised her hand.

It was a small gesture, a hand lifted, perhaps in horror, that caught Caladrius's eye because of the absolute calm in her face. She opened her fingers and in the empty frames of the mirrors, the stone basilisks came to life.

They killed a guard, two guests, and a magister before they found the object of her desire: crowing, they fixed their onyx gazes upon the white basilisk among them. By then, guards, guests, and rebels were all fleeing the hall. Caladrius, reaching Hollis at last, shook him out of his trance. He still played the fire-bone pipe, Caladrius realized, hearing the music within his silence; it came from his bones, his heart.

"Hollis," he said softly, and Hollis saw him finally. Caladrius loosened his magister's robe gently, let it drop. "Come."

Looking back once, he saw the prince fall, as if loosed from the massive coils of snake. Luna bent over him. In the hall, the confused guard, seeing only the librarian and an unarmed guest, let them pass.

The crowds had fled the fighting that had spilled beyond the gate; basilisk masks and puppets lay scattered like leaves on the stones. To the west, the sky was stained again with red. Like a satin banner in the wind, color folded over itself and fanned, glowing from roof to roof. Above the city, the sun burned like a basilisk's eye through the fire.

Part Three

The Basilisk's Egg

One

"Close the city gates," Arioso Pellior said when he could finally speak. "No one leaves Berylon. No one."

"There's fire, my lord," a guard reported tentatively. "Along Weaver's Street. Houses and warehouses are burning. The country folk are fleeing across the Iridia Bridge—"

"No one!" Arioso screamed, or tried to, his face turning purplish gray. His physician, kneeling at his side in the Hall of Mirrors, amid a wreckage of mirror shards, spilled flowers, bloody weapons, and magisters' robes, bent over him, murmuring. Arioso's fist came down on a lily washed across the floor. "I want him!"

"Yes, my lord."

"Alive. Still speaking. The rest of them, kill them as you find them. Before they find a place to hide. Empty the music school and seal it shut. Search Tormalyne Palace and guard it.

Take them out of their houses—all of them. Even if they're blind, crippled, hairless, and deaf—anyone bearing a shadow of that name in their past. Kill them. I will obliterate that name until no one dares even think it. And then I will crush the griffins in the city into dust."

Luna, standing next to Taur, felt him still trembling, whether in excitement or fear she couldn't tell. He asked her softly, confused, "But which was he? Griffin Tormalyne? What does he look like?"

"The music librarian. The man in black."

"Him?" His voice rose slightly. "But I recognized him! I tried to tell you. He was the man crossing the Tormalyne Bridge behind the trapper. The one everyone was looking for." Their father made a strange, incoherent sound, glaring at Taur as the physician loosened his clothes. Taur added defensively, "How was I to know he was in the music room all this time? I hate music."

"Pick him up," the physician ordered the pale, hovering servants. "Gently. Take him to his bed." He moved to turn over a guard who had fallen under a basilisk's gaze. Luna, following with Taur after their father, heard the physician catch his breath.

"How did he do that?" Taur asked, glancing back nervously into the hall. "Make that thing?"

"The white basilisk?" Luna mused. "I'm not sure. Our father knows. He recognized the pipe."

"And how did those tiny ones come alive?"

"Something he did, I suppose. He can do some very odd things."

"You're very calm about all this," Taur complained. "Raven

Tormalyne's heir appearing alive out of nowhere after all these years, in the middle of our father's birthday—I thought the entire family had been killed. Our father saw them all dead. How can he be so sure—"

"Weren't you listening to the opera? He was with the bards when our father had the school burned. He was never a farmer. They hid him on Luly. Which is where, I assume, he learned to play such music."

"But someone else was playing, too."

"I know." Her eyes narrowed slightly; she smiled, out of habit, at what she saw. "I wonder who."

"Anyway." Taur stopped, started again. "Anyway, it was an opera. A story. Who—how did it turn true?"

"I have no idea."

"Well." He mused silently, watching their father laid beneath black velvet and lace. Arioso's eyes fluttered. He caught sight of the blood-red basilisk woven across the canopy overhead and groaned, closing his eyes again. "Well," Taur murmured. "It was the most memorable birthday he's ever had."

Their father spoke, his voice as dry as snakeskin. "Luna. Stay with me. The rest of you, leave."

"Father," Taur said. "I'm here. I'll stay."

"Go away."

"Sleep if you can," the physician advised. "I will see to Lady Damiet."

"What's the matter with her?" the prince asked fretfully.

"An attack of nerves," the physician added temperately. "Most likely she needs only a sedative."

"I will kill that librarian with my hands."

"Rest, my lord."

He did, for a time, while Luna sat beside him, with a little jeweled book of poetry in her hands that she did not see. Her father stirred once or twice, crying out; she whispered, calming him. Then she gazed down at the book again, seeing the face of the farmer in the music room with Veris Legere, and then the face of the librarian, and then the face of Griffin Tormalyne, above his magical pipe. The face of the piper in the chorus she had not seen as clearly; it had been lowered, shadowed. What their music summoned awed her, but it had seemed curiously apt. She wondered if her father had a pipe like that, somewhere among his odd instruments. He had never shown her one, but he had recognized it. Perhaps he did not trust even her to know.

She considered that, her green eyes narrowed again, flecked with fire from the candlelight. She was aware of her father's gaze before he spoke; he might have heard the double-edged question in her mind.

She loosed her thoughts, let them scatter, hid them within the light in her eyes as she turned to him. She waited for him to speak.

"I want you to look for him," he said very softly. "They'll never find him. He's eluded me for thirty-seven years. You have your ways."

"I will find him," she said.

"I wonder how he survived me. . . . And why he waited so long to return." He paused, swallowing; his eyes found the basilisk again and he winced. "He'll tell me. I have my ways."

"Yes."

"I should have recognized that Tormalyne face. But it was the last thing I expected to see."

"Who was the other piper?"

"I don't know. A bard of Luly, bent on revenge after I burned the school, perhaps. Find him, too." He groped for her hands, still linked around the little book. "Now that Brio has vanished, I must use you. You must be my eyes. Remember all I have taught you. And never be afraid to use it. Be circumspect." He paused, still holding her hands with one hand, his eyes filmy with memory or dreams. "I did not realize how much you had learned until you saved my life. But he surprised us both. Remember that. Be very careful."

"I will."

He brought her hands to his mouth, kissed two fingers and a jewel. "You are my supreme creation." He turned the book to see the title. "Your great-grandmother's poetry." He loosed her hands wearily. "Read to me a little. It's full of birds and flowers; it will put me to sleep."

The physician came in again while the prince slept. Damiet, he whispered to Luna, refused to be sedated, refused to stop crying, and was tearing her dress into ribbons in her distress. She had driven her maids and ladies out of the room; she had flung the physician's sedative out a window. She would see no one, she cried, but Caladrius.

"Indeed," Luna said. She rose, left the physician to watch her father, and went to Damiet.

She found her sitting in a thundercloud of torn mauve silk, her face patched and swollen with anger and tears.

"I'm going to him," she announced defiantly as the door opened. "I will search the streets of Berylon." She recognized her sister then, and jerked a purple ribbon loose, threw it on the floor. "Don't try to stop me. You don't know what it's like—you have never loved anyone."

Luna contemplated her silently. Damiet stared back at her challengingly. Luna chose the path of least resistance through her sister's tantrum and shrugged lightly. "I suppose I haven't." She turned, toyed with a clutter of jewels and ribbons in a rosewood chest. "If," she added slowly, "I were truly in love, as you are, I would knock on every door in the city until I found this man. As you intend to."

"I do," Damiet stated. "I will."

"I suppose you had better do it quickly, then; our father is very angry. There won't be much left of him if the guards catch him first."

Damiet's face flushed; her eyes grew swollen. "How can you be so cruel?"

"I'm only being practical. It's my nature. But I am trying to help. This man did, after all, try to kill our father. Our father's anger is, if not justified by history, at least understandable."

"It was the other piper—the man in the chorus!"

"So. Caladrius is innocent."

"Yes! He must be!"

"Because you love him."

"Yes," Damiet said impatiently.

"Then if you are going into the streets to rescue him, I suppose torn mauve is the appropriate costume. You look distraught in it. Rent by love and fate."

Damiet blinked at her. "You are beginning to understand. You aren't so heartless after all."

"I'm trying." She sat down among the tumbled bedclothes beside her sister, fingered the mistreated mauve. "It's very pretty."

"I never got to sing my mauve song. The one where I am so frightened and unhappy because my beloved is taken from me, and being treated so unjustly by my father."

"I think you are singing it now."

"After that song, I change into my white, with the rosebuds." Her face crumpled again; she gripped Luna's arm. "He said that on the day I sang to my father, he would tell me his name."

"He did."

"At my last picochet lesson. When I sent Veris Legere away, and Magister Dulcet was rehearsing. We were alone in the music room."

"Yes."

"I tried—he—" She stopped, pulling at a mauve rosette at her waist. "I gave him permission to speak then."

"Of what?"

"Of his love for me."

"And what did he say?"

"Very little." A line ran across her brow; she tugged more fiercely at the rosette. "Except that he would speak after I had sung." Her frown vanished. "Perhaps he will send a message."

"Why did he wait? Why didn't he declare his love then? He did in the opera, very promptly, and with passion."

"I don't know. He was ill. He fell into the spinet." The rosette parted from its last thread; she threw it on the floor moodily and wiped her eyes with the back of her hand. "Still, he could have said something."

"Indeed."

"He did not even praise the color of my eyes. Or try to

touch me. He should have spoken then. Now he is in danger and has no time, unless I go to him."

"When you go, be careful of the fires near the Iridia Bridge. And you should change your dress to avoid notice. So that you won't lead the guards to him."

"I could wear my black," Damiet said with remarkable lack of interest. She picked at a lilac button, frowning again at the shreds and wisps on the floor. "He could have waited to play his pipe. Or not played at all—our father would never have noticed him then."

"But he promised to tell you his name."

"He didn't—" She paused, gave a sudden jerk at the button.

"He did."

Her mouth pinched angrily; her eyes filled again. "Our father," she said ominously, "killed his father."

"Yes."

"All this is our father's fault."

"So he knows," Luna said steadily. "Because he thought he had killed all the children and he was mistaken. One lived to remember him. He should have killed them all."

The threads snapped. Damiet threw the button across the room, watched it strike the marble hearth and fall, spinning on the floor. "And now he will."

"So he says."

Damiet said nothing. Luna, watching her, saw tears slide down her averted cheek. She picked another button loose, let this one fall. "So he could never have loved me," she said suddenly, very clearly. "He could never have loved anyone belonging to this House."

"In that way, he is somewhat like our father."

Damiet turned at her fiercely. "He is nothing like our father. Nothing."

"Well. You know him better than I do. You saw him daily."

Damiet jerked ribbon out of a sleeve band, frowning at nothing. "I did not," she said finally, crossly, and tore the ribbon loose. "I did not know him at all."

"No one did."

"He lied to us all and tried to kill our father. They might have killed us all, the magisters."

"Yes."

"So he deserves to die." She did not sound convinced. She pulled the sash out of its loops around her waist and tried to tear it. The stiff satin refused to part; her fingers, working restlessly, began to string knots along it instead. "I sang to him. Everyone saw. Even our father. He did not even wait to hear my final song. My white song, with the roses." Her face twisted again briefly, then smoothed into a glassy calm. "I will miss him." She wrenched another knot tight. "The librarian, who taught me the picochet. I will never play it again. And if our father kills him, I will never sing again."

"Before our father kills him," Luna said softly, "he must be found."

"Perhaps he left the city."

"I doubt that. He has not finished his own song. . . ."

"You mean he has not yet killed our father." Her hands stilled; she let the sash slip out of her fingers, fall, weighted with its knots, to the floor. She picked a likely shred of silk off the bed and blew her nose. She looked at Luna finally. "If he kills our father, I cannot love him; if he doesn't, our father will kill him. What kind of an ending is that?"

"One for a black song. And no ending at all for Berylon."

She left Damiet still sitting in her tattered mauve. A maid had ventured in, and was hunting for buttons beneath a chest; another had opened the wardrobe doors to lure Damiet's attention to the colors within. Luna heard another button spin across the floor as she gestured to the brilliant cluster of ladies-in-waiting starting back from the opening door. Their entrance did not elicit protesting shrieks, only a single sharp word. All but one scattered into the hall again, leaned against the walls to wait.

Returning to her father's room, Luna found the captain of the palace guard beside the door. He bowed; she paused, sensing trouble.

"My lady—" He hesitated.

"What is it?"

"Brio Hood has been found. Should I tell the prince, my lady?"

"He is sleeping now," she said swiftly. "Where was Brio? Besides dead?"

"In Tormalyne Palace." He cleared his throat. "In a torture chamber. We were searching for the rebel magisters there."

"Did you find them?"

"No. The place was empty, except for the body."

"How was he killed?"

He shook his head slightly, perplexed. "No one can guess. He was well armed and not injured in any way that we could see. There were some fresh bloodstains on the floor, but not from him."

"I see . . ." She did so in memory, seeing the librarian with his halting, spellbound speech, and the smoldering pipe around his neck. "Perhaps he died of fear in that place."

"He died, my lady. That's all we can tell the prince for certain."

"I will tell him," she said. He bowed again, relieved.

She sent the physician to examine the body and took his place beside her father's bed. He roused after a while, with a hoarse cry. She put her hand on his arm, let him see her smile. She opened the book of poetry and read to him again softly, calmly, until his fixed, terrified stare into the shadowy canopy above him eased, and the basilisk freed him once again to dreams.

Two

The heir of Tormalyne House hid with his son within the flimsy curtains of an abandoned puppet stage at the edge of a square near Pellior Palace. At a glance, the square, with its empty stalls and stages, looked like a small, ramshackle village in the aftermath of some peculiar battle that had littered the ground with dead puppets and glittering masks. Smoke from cooking fires and burning phoenixes still smoldered, acrid in the fuming air. The guards had already searched the square, overturning many of the stalls. Apples, nuts, wheels of cheese, pools of ale and milk, strips of smoked meat, crowns of wheat and dried flowers, ribbons, balls, wooden swords, painted cards, the paraphernalia of games lay scattered in a whirlwind's wake on the grass. When night came, so would the hungry, the country folk trapped within the burning city, with no place to live but in their stalls and wagons.

Hollis, dreaming awake, scarcely seemed to breathe. Caladrius, still, tense, listened to the voices of the city: the distant cries among the billowing flames, the imperious commands of guards, closer shouts and screams, sobs and curses cut ruthlessly into silence. "No," he heard a woman moan over and over. "No, no, no, no," until her cry rose and a bird caught it in its beak and flew away, echoing her over the city. He closed his eyes, breathed a memory of ash and smoke from the fires that blew again over Berylon.

Hollis, drifting in and out of the music he had wakened, reached beyond his dream, touched Caladrius. Then he straightened, shaking the narrow stage.

"Have I been sleeping?" he asked in wonder. He cracked the worn curtains carefully, looked out. Caladrius heard his breath catch. "What are they—" He began to move. Caladrius gripped him quickly.

"No."

"But they're—they just pulled some old blind man out of his house and stabbed him. They left him in the street to die—"

"So they will kill you, if they find you," Caladrius said grimly. "They will let me watch."

Hollis turned to him, his face blanched, startled. "Why is he killing old men?"

"He is obliterating Tormalyne House. Anyone with a ghost's connection to the House. Anyone who spoke the name once forty years ago. Anyone who thought it—"

"Even the magisters?" Hollis asked incredulously.

"Everyone."

Hollis was silent. He eased away from the curtains finally, leaned back against a stall leg. His eyes were hidden, but Caladrius felt his thoughts, heard them, a high, mad, distant piping like the keening of wind over a barren world. He felt it in himself, his own bones singing, trying to shape something other than bone. The raven looked out of his eyes, night black and still, called through his thoughts in its own harsh language to the dead.

"What do we do?" Hollis asked. His eyes, meeting Caladrius's finally, held an odd, brief reflection of fire, as if the music smoldering in him had flared. Caladrius swallowed a raven's word, feeling a claw of sorrow enclose his heart. "The music failed, in there. It was not strong enough against him."

"It would have killed him," Caladrius said succinctly. "It was not strong enough against Luna Pellior."

Hollis blinked. "Luna. She didn't—"

"She pulled those basilisks out of stone. And now she knows your face. Above everything, I wanted to keep you safe."

"You could have told me what you were going to do," Hollis protested. "What you were thinking. That you were planning to die in the middle of Giulia's opera."

"You could have told me."

Hollis shook his head, still amazed. "I didn't think it would work. I knew the tale. But I didn't know it was true. I thought if it didn't work, no one would notice another pipe in all the music. And if it did—"

"Then they would kill you instead of me. You thought I would stand there idly and let that happen."

"I didn't—I wasn't thinking, beyond that. I just saw the pipe and took it to kill a basilisk."

"Yes," Caladrius breathed. "So did I." He wished suddenly, intensely, for Hollis to be far, far away, bored and safe in some land baron's court. "I always thought you took after your mother instead."

"How could you think anything else?" Hollis asked reasonably. "You never knew my father before."

"Where did you find that pipe?" his father asked.

"In the music school. There's a storage room full of odd instruments somebody brought out of the hinterlands."

"Auber Tormalyne." Caladrius mused a moment. Hollis watched him, toying with a puppet with wings and a lion's face partially crushed under a fleeing boot.

He said tentatively, following Caladrius's thoughts, "It's a source of power, the hinterlands. So the tales say. But there's no time to learn. And they'll look for you in the music school."

"They'll look for me everywhere. I learned to play a few things. . . . With all the visitors roaming the streets and those of Tormalyne House fleeing their own houses, it will be easier to move among them. We should separate, though."

"No."

Caladrius yielded reluctantly. "No."

"We made a monster to kill a monster and that failed," Hollis pointed out. "What other kind of music is there to use against him?"

"I'll find out."

"According to the tale, there is no other music we can play now. No other song."

"Then that," Caladrius said evenly, "is the song that I will play."

"What about her? The basilisk's powerful daughter? Do we kill his children, too?"

Caladrius's mouth tightened; he looked away, evading the answer, evading memory. He did not evade Luna, who stood in his thoughts, building her tiny, golden cage to trap a bird in it, leaving the mirror for him to see himself. He spoke finally, softly. "She knew my name."

"Griffin Tormalyne?"

"That, too, very likely. She understood the name Caladrius. She knew why I had come there." He paused, seeing again her brilliant, ambiguous smile, her secret eyes. "She could have killed either of us," he said, struck, and oddly surprised. "She knew me and she let me leave. She attacked the basilisk instead."

He heard the guards then, gathering across the street. They waited, silent, motionless, but the guards did not sweep through the square again. They would wait for night, Caladrius guessed, and seize whatever prey the stalls lured into them. The guards scattered again, in groups down side streets and alleys. There was a low, wordless mutter, at once strange and familiar. And then light fingers tapped against the cloth.

"Rain," Caladrius said, amazed by it in that city of stone and light.

"We can't stay here," Hollis said tersely. "They'll search again and drag us out of here like caged hares. But where can we go?"

"Wait until dusk. I know someone. . . ."

She received them without surprise, out of the dark and grieving streets, her eyes silvery as the moon, and as opaque. "Reve Iridia," Caladrius said, dripping and weary at her threshold. "My son Hollis."

She gestured. They entered; Kira closed the door quickly

behind them. "I heard," she said, "you played a song for the Basilisk."

"They are searching for us everywhere," Caladrius warned her.

"I know that, too," she answered calmly. "You played my fire-bone pipe for Arioso Pellior. He did not die, but neither did you. And now Berylon is again at war with itself."

"Only with my House."

"But the other Houses watch for their moment. . . . Brandy, Kira. And supper for them." She turned her lucent gaze to Hollis suddenly. "You played, too," she breathed. "I hear it in you. So that is why you failed. You played for one another, for life instead of death." They were both silent, staring at her. She turned away, tapped herself to her chair. "That's what I hear," she added, seating herself. "Sit down."

"We dare not stay. For your sake."

"You can stay long enough to eat. And to tell me what you have come to borrow now, since you dare not stay."

"I must get into the music school."

She pondered, the jewel on her cane glittering restlessly like an eye. Kira brought them brandy in glass goblets so thin they seemed blown out of air, and fragile, seamed plates of cold roast fowl and bread.

"The school is locked and guarded," Reve said. "One of the magisters came here to tell me. The magisters have fled. Those still alive." She fell silent again, her eyes filmed with memory and moon cold. "The Basilisk is loose in Berylon. How can you get into the school without him seeing?"

"You told me how."

Her face shifted oddly, trying to remember, he realized, how to smile. "So I did. But can you play that well?"

"I'm desperate," he said simply.

"Despair might work, as well as love."

Hollis had stopped eating, "Play what?" he asked uncertainly. "And how well? What could possibly get us through stone?"

"Music travels," Reve Iridia said obscurely. They heard shouts, then, in the street, the crash of breaking glass. Caladrius touched Hollis, pulled him out of his confusion.

"We must go."

Hollis rose, still chewing. 'Yes," he said bewilderedly. "But where?"

"I'll listen in here," Reve said. "I have no desire to find myself in Auber Tormalyne's storage room. It's far too cold."

Caladrius paused, lifted one of her butterfly hands from the cane, and kissed it. "Thank you," he said.

She freed her hand, laid it against his face. "Play as I taught you," she said austerely. "You used to play to please me."

"I will."

He crossed the room, took a candle from a sconce, and pulled aside the hanging. Hollis, speechless, carrying a chicken wing, followed him into the dark. Caladrius shed light onto the silent, gleaming instruments, until he found what he looked for: the set of pipes bound with threads of brass, the smallest no bigger than his finger and stained red, the others, varied in size to span his hand and painted gold. Hollis looked at them, at him.

"Now what?" he asked tersely.

"Now hold this," Caladrius said, and gave him the candle.

The first notes fell like silver ribbons of rain, like blown petals, bright falling leaves. He played those things until his breath warmed the pipes, and they fit into his hand like another hand holding his. The room slowly darkened; Hollis's breathing wove into his piping, his heartbeat. The dark flowed around them, one fiery eye open, illumining Hollis's eyes. Velvet blurred, walls swirled, opened to the night. He heard the vastness of the hinterlands within the pipes and played that, a black plain beneath a dome of stars, the only colors in it the small, still flame, and Hollis's unblinking eyes. He heard Hollis's thoughts.

Where are we?

We are nowhere, he answered. *We are sound. We are within the pipes.*

He fashioned a path for them across the plain. Somewhere the earth was hard as stone, somewhere it rained; on this plain only stars fell, burning white, into the small red flame, into Hollis's unblinking eyes. The horned moon rose before they crossed the plain; it caught a tear of fire from the candle as it passed, let it streak, a burning star, across the plain, through Hollis's eyes. He blinked. Wind, like a long, exhaled breath, rolled across the plain. Caladrius smelled the sea.

He stopped playing, recognizing the place where he wanted most to be. In that small, still light, the walls took shape again: pale marble now, with no windows anywhere. Around him, on long tables, instruments, each with its own language, waited to speak.

Hollis murmured something. Caladrius listened for a long

time, no footfalls disturbed the silence within the school; nothing was played; no one spoke.

He put the pipes down, very carefully.

"Wait for me," he whispered. Hollis looked at him incredulously, as if Caladrius thought he might play himself back into the pipes and go elsewhere. He sat wordlessly on a bench, still holding the candle.

He was still there in the same position when Caladrius returned, though he had set the dwindling candle into its melted wax. "I went through it," Caladrius said softly. "There's no one here. Except—"

"Except."

"The dead."

"Is—" Hollis's voice caught.

"I couldn't see faces. We'll know in the morning." He stopped, blinking, feeling the gritty weariness like burned-out stars in his eyes.

"Where," Hollis breathed, "did you learn to play that?"

"Somewhere in the hinterlands. Where all the magic was trapped. By the first bard." He gave Hollis one of the blankets he had taken from a bedchamber. "You know the tale," he added, too tired to think any longer.

"I know the tale." Hollis moved finally, stumbling a little as he rose. 'It's the first one the bards teach. No one ever said it was true."

"Arioso Pellior knows."

He lay awake watching light and shadow flicker over the odd, silent shapes of music, until Hollis fell asleep. And then he rose and began to play.

Three

In the rainy dark, the city burned more slowly. Fire was a sullen red crescent to the west, eating into rooftops, warehouses, barges moored on the moat water. Giulia, watching from behind a basilisk's mask as she huddled beside Hexel in a group of stranded villagers, scarcely felt the rain now. It had fallen lightly but steadily since dusk. The dress she had worn for the basilisk's birthday, a fine dark silk, was torn and muddy. She had pulled garish, flimsy curtains off some stage to cover herself; they, too, were soaked.

She watched for Justin in every movement, every flicker of shadow. They were at the Pellior Bridge, not far from where he lived. Like the other magisters, she and Hexel had gone at first to the school, the one safe place they knew. The magisters and students who had not attended the festival had already been driven out of the music school. Instruments had been thrown into the streets, music scattered like leaves. Those who protested, who fought, had died in the street. A vision of an old magister in his black lying on the cobbles with one arm hugging his broken lute haunted Giulia. The doors of the school were chained shut; guards stood at every corner. Someone had pounded the faces of the stone griffins flanking the doors into dust.

For a long time she could not speak. She could only move at the sound of Hexel's voice, at his touch. He led her through streets she had never seen, through crowds of frightened villagers and weeping children, past crazed, yawning doors of wheat and ribbons out of which guards dragged astonished and fearful people: a plump woman with white hair whose hands were powdery with flour, a short, thin man still marking the page, with one finger, of the book he had been reading. What happened to them, she guessed; she could not watch.

Now they sat on the bank beside the Pellior Bridge. The gates of the bridge were closed and guarded. Wagons choked the streets, as farmers and villagers, trying to flee, waited for the gates to open. Others huddled beneath the bridge along the river. Some had tried to swim across; the guards' quarrels had found them unerringly. They floated now, pale stains in the billowing torchlight. The torches had been lighted along the city wall and on the bridge to mid-river, to illumine escape. The far half of the bridge was dark.

Hexel had been speaking for some time, she realized; she had not understood a word. Now she heard her own silence; she roused a little, turning her dark, plastered head to look at him behind the mask. He was staring at the deep water, its smooth, glassy flow lightly roiled now and then by powerful forces beneath the surface. She spoke his name. He looked at her, then back at the water suddenly, and spat. Startled, she felt the first harsh sting of tears. He took the mask from her, crushed it into a mass of thread and feathers, and tossed it into the water.

"I'm sorry," he said heavily; for what in particular she was uncertain. She wiped a fallen tear, left a streak of mud on her face.

"It wasn't your fault. Music doesn't kill."

He clutched his hair with both hands and pulled, then shook his head at the water. "It shouldn't," he answered bitterly. "I was careless. And now look at us. Locked out of the school, hiding in the mud. We threw a stone at the sleeping basilisk and it opened its eyes."

"Maybe he is dead," Giulia suggested without hope.

"His son is stupid, but no less ruthless. And he hates music." He paused. "I suppose the prince might, too, by now. What was that pipe they played?"

"I don't know. I think Hollis took one from the storage room. I can't guess where Caladrius got his. The hinterlands, maybe. They meant to kill, with that music. So music can. Kill." She pulled the light, frayed cloth tighter around her arms, shivering. "Justin warned me."

"About what?"

"Playing music for the Basilisk. I thought he was wrong. That no harm could come when no harm was intended."

"The harm was not in the music but in the tale. In the telling. I played with a life and exposed its secrets so carelessly. How was I to know that there was any truth at all to such a hackneyed tale? The stranger who returns to the city to reclaim his heritage, the lost heir . . . I pulled in the librarian's life only to make it less worn, something to inspire my music." He touched his eyes and groaned. "I probably killed him."

"He was alive when I last saw him. They both were. He and Hollis."

"Who is Hollis?"

"His son, I think."

"I knew it."

A child began to cry beneath the bridge, a thin, hopeless wail no soothing could quiet. Someone passed among them with a dogged, heavy tread, carrying a basket. A raw potato dropped into Giulia's lap, an onion into Hexel's. He held it up, studied it morosely.

"Where did they get the arms?"

"I don't know," Giulia said tersely. The sight of her demure chorus flinging off their robes and drawing swords in the middle of her work left her still stunned. "It must have been," she added, "what Justin was apologizing for."

"What?"

"The night I saw Caladrius in that marble bust of Auber Tormalyne."

"You recognized him?"

"I recognized Tormalyne House. But—" She lifted a hand helplessly, let it fall. "Justin had vanished, and I was so busy. . . . How could they?" she asked in disbelief, wringing the potato with both hands, and rocking a little in the mud. "How could they have been so senseless—"

"Desperate."

"That they would attack Arioso Pellior in his own palace?"

"It was brilliant. He was unprepared, nearly unguarded, surrounded by—"

"They could have dropped a cobble on his head when he paraded past the school."

"And if they had missed him? He would have destroyed the school."

"So they did. And so he did." She wiped angrily at another tear. "And now I don't know what any of us are going to do, or even if Justin is still alive."

"You could go back to the provinces," Hexel suggested. "They'll let you leave."

"After they finish their slaughter." She looked at him suddenly, trying to see his profile in the flickering light. "Hexel. Would they let you leave?"

"I would not be caught dead in the provinces."

"But can you leave? Or will they hunt you, too?"

"I have some vague connection to Iridia House." She breathed again until he added, "On one side."

"And on the other?"

"I believe the vague connection connected itself to Tormalyne House."

"Oh, Hexel."

"I had forgotten it," he said calmly. "It's obscure; my family fought for Iridia House during the Basilisk's War. It hardly matters. How long would Arioso Pellior let the teller of that particular tale live anyway?"

"What will we do?" she whispered numbly.

He shrugged. "Change the ending of the tale. I never liked it, anyway. It was a fantasy."

She laughed suddenly, then pushed her face against his

shoulder, wiping away tears. "I want to find Justin," she said tightly. "At least, I want to know what happened to him. We're not safe here; they could come searching among us at any moment, with their torches and swords. We might as well make use of the dark. If he's alive, it's what he'll be doing."

He took her potato, put it in one pocket, slipped the onion into another. "At least we're armed," he said dourly, and followed her slow, cautious path along the river into darkness.

Justin, Nicol, and a handful of the scattered remnant of the Griffin's Claw sat among rain-streaked slabs of marble, unfinished tombstones, and monuments in Evena's uncle's work yard. He and his family had fled, or been taken away; the house and the workshops below it were dark, silent. Justin, who had run into an inexpertly wielded sword, nursed a slash across his forearm, bound in the frayed, stained sleeve of a magister's robe. Nicol, holding a piece of the same robe to his cheekbone, was talking about messages, gathering places, as if, Justin thought grumpily, he were not sitting behind a tombstone in the mud, with his army in hiding and, in truth, more dangerous to itself than to the Basilisk.

"Music," Nicol said. "A ballad. You could hide a message in a ballad, recognizable only to us, sing it in the streets—"

"Nicol, if I so much as whistled in this city, I'd get my lips cut off. The guard is not in the mood for music."

"We must pull ourselves back together, fight for the House, now that we have the Griffin to fight with us." He seized Justin's arm in his fervor. "Think of it! Griffin Tormalyne returned, with all that power. He'll need us—" His grip loosened as Justin hissed. "Sorry. But think—"

"I am thinking. What I'm thinking is that for thirty-seven years arms have been forbidden in Berylon except to Pellior House and there was no one around to tell us that there is more to fighting with a sword than waving it around in the air. We should forget about fighting, and find him. Let him tell us what he needs us to do."

Gaudi, in the shadows behind Nicol, said uncomfortably, "I did that to you, Justin. I'm sorry. I wasn't looking."

"My point." Justin sighed. "If we're this dangerous to ourselves, we will be just as dangerous to Griffin Tormalyne. The House is dying all around us. He won't have a House to rule by dawn unless we help ourselves."

There was a short silence. Then Nicol asked calmly, "What do you suggest?"

Justin, rendered momentarily speechless by the question, answered haltingly, "We must gather ourselves together. You're right. All of us. We must find our families, help those still alive, find some safe place for them."

"The music school," someone suggested.

"It's still guarded. I went there earlier to see if I could find Giulia."

"Did you?" Nicol's voice sounded oddly harsh.

"No."

"What about Tormalyne Palace?" Gaudi asked. "They've already searched it."

"It's too dangerous. They'll be watching for us there."

"Iridia House," Nicol said. "They fought for Tormalyne House. We could ask them for help."

"Do we know anyone to ask?"

"Some of the magisters, if we can find them. If they're still alive. Hexel Barr has some family connection. I don't imagine they like Arioso Pellior any better now than they did thirty-seven years ago."

"What about here?" Evena asked, startling them as she moved silently among the stones. She had been rummaging in the house for food; she unfolded a cloth on the mud. "I found bread, some cheese, turnips, what smells like boiled mutton. They won't be watching this place. My uncle has rooms below the workrooms where he keeps flawed headstones, broken statues, marble coffins he's carving for people who want something elaborate waiting for them when they die."

"That might be useful," Justin murmured.

"Let's look," Nicol said promptly. "It's safer than sitting here in the rain."

They ate among yawning coffins out of which stone flowers had begun to emerge, among statues with cracked arms, unfinished smiles. A single lamp, left burning from the afternoon, showed them one another's weary, muddy faces. Nicol made his way rapidly through bread and a slab of tasteless mutton. He said, chewing, "We have to search at night. Tonight. Go to the houses of people we know, look for anyone hurt or in hiding. Take what food you can find, bring it back here. Justin, you search for Griffin Tormalyne. You know what he looks like. And the bard Hollis." He paused. "I had no idea they taught such things on that rock."

Justin nodded absently, wondering where in the dark, fuming city he was most likely to find Giulia. The school was guarded, the Griffin's Egg too close to the Tormalyne Bridge, and dangerously named, besides. . . . His own small, untidy rooms? He had found her there more than once, unexpectedly, waiting for him. Fear seized him suddenly, that she would go there and the guards, searching for those of Tormalyne House, would find her. . . . Where he might likely find Griffin Tormalyne, who spoke to ravens and charmed basilisks out of a pipe, he had no idea.

"I'll find him," he said, thinking: Giulia.

They finished eating and went out again into the night, leaving the lamp burning like a talisman among the coffins.

Four

Luna Pellior stood in the dark at Tormalyne Palace, listening.

She had walked alone through the streets of her father's city, smelling the bitter air from the smoldering fires, hearing in the tense stillness around her the occasional, descending scale of secret footsteps, a brief staccato scream. Those she passed saw her as a stir of dark, a ripple of shadow against the night. In the tangled, dying gardens of Tormalyne Palace, she did not need light; she saw as the moon sees, in a glancing reflection of light. She shaped the heavy, rusted chains across the massive doors with her hands, unbound them like ribbon. Carved griffins on the doors stared past her; they did not see her enter.

She walked curiously through the vast, empty rooms, their walls charred black like chimney stones. Cries followed her, seeped out of the past around her. She listened to them, but did not answer, left no more of herself among the ghosts than a movement of air, a rustle of dead leaves that had blown through the shattered windows. She had come to find past more tangible than memory to work with. In an upper room, with an immense hearth, she found a circle of ash. She bent, studied the fragments of bone in it. She reached for one, a fingerbone, and caught the ring that slid from it.

Air dragged at her, like the sudden rise of immense wings. In the garden, ravens stirred and muttered. She wiped ash off the ring and found the griffin stamped in gold. She put the ring on her thumb and the bone in her pocket, and rose.

She heard music then, distant and very strange, as if ancient voices stirred beneath the moon, spoke in forgotten ways. She stood motionlessly, hearing bone speak, stone, skin, a singing reed, a heartbeat, slow and steady, soft yet and undefined: the drum of mourning, or war, or the beginning of the dance.

She looked at the griffin, pale gold in her moonlight gaze, and smiled.

In Pellior Palace, she vanished into the hidden chamber. Her father slept uneasily behind one of its walls, as if he, too, heard the ancient songs. The imagery of his dreams, rich and terrifying, weltered through her thoughts, like things rising, half-glimpsed, out of deep, starlit water. She let them surface and slip down again, intent on her work. She laid the griffin ring on its broken finger in the center of a round mirror. Then she poured a circle of oil around the rim of the mirror and lit it.

A man's face appeared within the flame, worn and bloody, one eye closed, the other torn and empty, seeing death. He cried at her, a soundless word that splintered the mirror. Minute ravens flew out of the cracks, turned to ash in the air. She said the word on the ring: the Griffin's face appeared, broken in a dozen places. His eyes were closed; he held a clay flute to his mouth. Candle fire illumined half his face, and the white bird painted on the flute. She watched him for a long time. His music trembled in the air around her; she felt it, but she did not hear.

She reached into the dying flames, drew the ring off the bone and held it to her eye. Through the griffin eye, she saw the room around him: the marble walls, the long tables, the dark-haired man sleeping on the floor behind him. The Griffin lowered the flute abruptly then and turned, seeing what she saw. She put the ring down quickly and extinguished the fire, leaving only a smear of oil, a cracked mirror, a fingerbone to tell where she had been.

She heard the palace stirring around her as she stepped into it again. The windows in her father's council chamber showed her a smoky dawn. She went through the private door into his room; he shifted, aware of her in his dreams, and woke to see her.

He sensed the night still clinging to her, the spells. He said harshly, "Did you find him?"

"In a room," she said, "somewhere in the city. That's all I saw." She touched his hand, quieting his restless tossing, then went to the door. "Be patient," she said lightly. "I won't fail."

"You failed me once," he complained.

"Do you think I would dare twice?" She opened the door, spoke to the chamberlain and attendants waiting, red-eyed and sleepless, in the hall. She sent them for the physician, for breakfast. Taur, up early for once, hovering, looked at her hopefully. She turned her head.

"Father, Taur is—"

"No."

She left him with the physician and found Taur again, pacing, disheveled, a glass of wine in his hand. He seemed more relieved than discomposed by his father's refusal; he said only, "I suppose he is too furious to die."

She heard the regret in his voice. "I think he is," she agreed.

"The captain of the city guard came to me, wanting to open the bridges. I asked if they had cleaned out the rat's nest of Tormalyne House. He said some were still in hiding. So I said no."

"So our father would have said."

"Tell him I did that. Maybe he'll see me, then. It looks bad that he won't."

"He's ill," she said temperately. "He is not thinking clearly."

"He's thinking the way he always thinks about me. Maybe if I—"

"Maybe if you see him yourself and explain to him what you've done . . ."

"He won't let me in."

"He will," she said, her bright smile only slightly wan from sleeplessness, "when I explain why you want to see him."

Her father turned the color of the basilisk above his head when she gave him Taur's message. She watched him, impressed, half expecting flames to come out of his mouth, his eyes to change color and glow. He flung his breakfast to the floor and bellowed for his heir. Taur, calm as he came through the door, was met with a firestorm that turned him the shade and fragility of old paper.

"You spoke for me?" his father raged. "You gave orders? Must I kill you before you get it into your head that I am still alive?"

"No," said Taur, and "yes," and "but," the only words not burned to a crisp before they came out of him. Luna, listening gravely over a piece of needlework, flung him a sympathetic smile. Taur stared at her a moment, before his father's fury seized him by the hair again and shook him.

"Leave me! Send the captain of the guard to me. The bridges will be opened."

"But—"

"Get out!"

"Will you really open them?" she asked her father wonderingly, when Taur had crept back out.

"Yes," he said brusquely. "When there is one life left of Tormalyne House and his name is Griffin Tormalyne." He fell back then, exhausted, coughing. She rose to call the physician again; he caught her hand. "You will not leave this city in Taur's hands," he commanded painfully.

"No."

"There are things—I will show you before—if I die. When. Power that will pass to you from me. So that you will know my thoughts and wishes even after death." She was silent, gazing at him, her eyes opaque, for once not smiling.

"Power beyond death?"

"So that you will see out of the Basilisk's eyes . . . my

eyes." His hand loosened, freed her slowly. "Later. When I regain strength. Then I will give you your heritage."

She sat with him until he slept, the needlework idle in her hands, her eyes searching the familiar lines of his face as if she could find, beneath them, the shape that he would take past death. She touched her own face, wondering if that, too, would change in her eyes, if she would recognize herself, or even remember what she had once been.

He reached for her once, his own eyes closed, and murmured, "Your hand is cold. And your thoughts."

"I am a little tired."

"Find me Griffin Tormalyne."

"I will."

She called for Damiet after he fell asleep, left her sister sitting sullenly, contemplating their father. She rested for a while, then went back into the hidden room. There she shook the pieces of the broken mirror into a bowl and filled it with water. She passed the ring through flame and dropped it onto the shards of mirror. The piece of bone she floated on the surface of the water. She blew it gently, whispering a name with each breath, until the bone, turning and turning under the name, found the ring beneath it and refused to move.

"What shall I call you?" she asked. The water gathered colors, shapes from the splinters of the mirror: a raven-dark eye, a painted white bird, a drum, an eye socket black with blood, a hand, the corner of a blanket. "Speak to me," she urged. Bending, she took a sip of water and gave it back. "Speak. . . ." She heard music rising from the water, faint and sweet, then a voice, fragments of words. She saw an angle of an unfamiliar face: a dark brow, an eye the darkest shade of blue, opening senselessly as at a dream or a premonition. "What shall I call you?"

She heard Caladrius's voice: *Hollis*.

She broke the image immediately with water poured from a silver pitcher. The bone weltered out of its frozen position; she picked it up, and then the ring beneath it. She laid them on black silk. She poured the shards and water out of the bowl, all the scattered images, into a jar of blackened glass, and sealed it with wax. She knotted the bone and the ring in the silk, and tied the silk around her wrist, pushing the secrets up her sleeve.

Hollis, the Griffin said again in her mind. She inhaled deeply, as at some wild, sweet scent, and wiped the bowl clean of images.

Returning to her father's chamber, she found it filled with flowers, fruit, messages from Iridia House, Marcasia House. In an antechamber, she met with officials of the city pleading with anyone who passed for an audience with the prince. They clustered around her like birds discovering a crumb of hope.

The streets along the bridges were impassible, they explained. Full of carts, animals. No one could move and the stench was terrible. Fights broke out constantly over the rotting food in the carts. Fires were started anywhere, in the middle of streets, in doorways, on the riverbank; carts caught fire, threatened houses. Moored boats had been set adrift by the city guard so that no one could escape. The city was beginning to fester from its wounds.

"I will ask my father," she told them.

"Tell them to find me Griffin Tormalyne" he told her. "And then I will open the gates."

The moon saw her on the streets again, in the early hours

before dawn. The dead that the guard had left lying on their thresholds the night before had been spirited away, she noticed. The doors had been closed. Lights flicked here and there in darkened houses, brief and elusive as fireflies. This time she went where music was played, to the chained and guarded Tormalyne School.

She let the guards see her face.

"My father has sent me here," she said as they stared, stupefied, at her. "To find something belonging to Tormalyne House that he can use in his secret ways." She smiled her charming, golden smile that unlocked chains and opened doors. She spread her cloak to the noise they made, drew it into soft velvet folds. Her steps as light as leaves, she walked down the empty halls, hearing, all around her, phrases and echoes of the strange music that had welled up out of the broken mirror.

She heard human breath at last, deep and even, from the rooms where magisters slept. There was a spell over the door; it gave voice at her touch. She recognized its short, vigorous thrum: the picochet.

She stopped, hearing a sudden shift, an intake of breath. She was silent, a stroke of dark beneath a moonlit window. A candle flared. She felt the darkness searched. Someone grunted, "A mouse. Go back to sleep." She waited; the moon inched down into the window to watch with her. Finally the breathing was even again, thoughts quiet.

She stepped to the door, opened her cloak around the warning wails of the picochet, and muffled them, let them fade.

Hollis, she said in Caladrius's voice. *Get up. Come with me. Don't wake up, there is no time. Don't speak. Be still. As still as nightfall, as starlight. Put on a robe. Come with me. Come.*

He drifted out of the dark room like a ghost, stood waiting, his eyes closed, while she touched the magister's robe, turned its fabric as dense and heavy as sleep. She bound him in it, and then hid him behind his formless, flickering dreams, a patchwork of shadow and moonlight.

She left him there, while she went into the room to lay a gift for the Griffin on Hollis's empty bed: a ring and a bone wrapped in black silk.

Come, she said to Hollis. The guards, half dreaming beside the open doors, remembered only that she bade them good night as she left.

She was waiting for Caladrius when he came out.

Five

Dawn opened a red, swollen eye above the river, glanced across the water in splinters of light at the crowd massed and stirring beside the Pellior Bridge. Children wailed fretfully; dogs snarled and barked; birds like shreds of night swirled up from the waking and scattered over the city. Giulia, stretched next to Hexel, dreaming of bread, winced as a finger of light jabbed her eye. She had wrapped herself in a purple-and-white-striped awning that had come adrift from a stall. Hexel, already awake, stared morosely back at dawn. He wore a piece of tapestry that had flung itself at him out of a window during the night. The violence that had precipitated the tapestry from within the high room had been hidden behind sharply closed shutters. They had found the city by night even more perilous than by daylight. Footsteps were anonymous; sound distorted itself along the streets; screams and shouts echoed relentlessly against the stones. Even silence seemed dangerous; it was the language of the hunter, the language of the dead.

They had returned to the Pellior Bridge exhausted and hungry. Hexel did not dare seek shelter in his own house; Giulia was locked out of hers. She had gone to Justin's room, found it disheveled, empty. Hexel, with good sense, had persuaded her that she could not stay. He had found the houses of his closest kin unnervingly empty; whether they had died or taken shelter elsewhere, he could not guess. On the riverbank again, in the dark, they had shared bread and apples snatched from overturned stalls. Now the sun began to bake smells that the night had cooled; sweat, dung, rotting fish mingled with smoke, onions, roasted vegetables over the cooking fires of those who had scavenged during the night. Not all the scavengers had returned: some ate only bitterness that morning.

They had seen few other magisters or students at the Pellior Bridge. The name itself terrorized. Those they found extended relief and sympathy but few words; it was best, they felt, not to know, not to be known, in that mass of strangers. As the sun climbed out of the clouds into unremitting blue, the crowd grew still again, beaten under the threat of heat. They watched the motionless guard at the gate and hoped for hope.

Giulia, discarding her awning as the sun climbed, dreamed of green northern provinces, her grandfather's farm. There was music hidden everywhere around her, she thought: the country folk had carried songs into the city with them, a favorite pipe, small harps, dances. But under that burning eye no one sang, no one whistled; not even mothers dared a lullaby to a miserable child, lest the Basilisk hear. Giulia played the picochet in her head for comfort, and watched the water out of gritty eyes, thinking and trying not to think of Justin.

Hexel, unusually silent, seemed to find his own consolation in some enchanted place. He did not notice the crying children, the animals bawling for hay. His eyes, charred with weariness, were abstract, distant. Giulia touched him finally, wondering where he had gone, why he did not take her with him.

"Hexel. What are you thinking?"

He looked at her from that distant place and murmured incoherently. She watched him a little, wondering. The guards had doubled force at the bridge, fiercely determined to let no one cross. They still searched then, she guessed, for the vanished Griffin, who would not have come all that way, after so many years, to flee the city twice. He would die first, she thought, seeing his face again: a strong, unsmiling marble ghost in a music room. Justin would be looking for him, too, if he were still alive. And the fastidious Nicol, and pretty Gaudi, who had been taking voice lessons from Hexel. And half her opera chorus, the students and the strangers among them. If they were still alive . . .

But where? she demanded in sudden frustration. "Hexel." He did not answer. She continued anyway, thinking of them all. "Maybe the Griffin's Egg, the Tormalyne Bridge . . ." Those places, named aloud, seemed wildly improbable. No one of that House would survive in the northern part of the city. Of the four bridges, that one was easiest to close, and the most dangerous to risk.

Hexel spoke finally, startling her. "They have gone underground."

"Yes," she said a trifle testily. "But did they go alive? Hexel, where are you?"

"Listening," he said obscurely. He added, enlightening her, "And without that moonstruck girl and her demented voice."

Giulia considered Damiet, not without a grain of sympathy. "She did her best."

"Pish."

"What is opera without passion?"

"Art."

"Hexel—"

He ran a hand through his hair, dislodging debris. What he listened to evidently spoke beneath the surface of the water, sang within the needles of light, for his eyes did not move from it. "But without her, what do I have? It is not a love story, now. . . ."

She sighed. Light bore down at her, drying the streak of mud on her face; she felt sweat trickle through her hair. Hexel was growing light-headed with hunger, she decided. He did not babble in exasperation, or smolder with impatience; he remained composed, as calm as if he did not truly recognize the heat, the flies, the swamp of smells they sat in. His eyes were red, his chin stubbled, his clothes stained with dirt and sweat. If his despair had turned to music, to fantasy, then he was fortunate; her hunger had not.

She rose stiffly; he paid attention to that. "Where are you going?"

"Maybe someone will want my awning. In trade for food."

He reached absently into his pocket, produced a coin.

"Try that instead. Leave me the awning." As she stared at him in annoyance he put it over his head, shading his eyes, and disappeared again into his musings.

She searched the crowd, moving slowly, her head bent, trying to look as if she spent her life growing corn and shearing sheep. She traded his silver for a couple of roast potatoes, a half loaf of drying bread, some malodorous cheese, and a third of a skin of wine. She searched faces as she returned to Hexel, but found no one she knew.

Hexel had not moved since she left him, though the awning had slid over one eye. She straightened it and pushed the skin into his hand. "Drink," she said, settling wearily down, and showed him what she carried in her skirt. He drank and then his eyes went back to the river; watching it, he chewed a potato thoughtfully. She lay back, watched the changing of the guard along the bridge. The new rank looked as tired as the old, grim and unshaven, their uniforms rumpled, stiff with sweat and blood.

"That is," she heard Hexel say sometime later, "the only solution."

She closed her eyes against the fury of the dying autumn sun.

Hours later Justin woke, stared groggily at a marble face with one eye and half a mouth. In the perpetual dark of the workshop, stubby candles illumined coffins where, for lack of better accommodations, a few of the wounded of Berylon lay. They had been found in piecemeal fashion, the night before: stumbled over, or heard moaning on a doorstep. Those who could talk revealed a connection, however ancient or tenuous, to Tormalyne House.

Justin, lying under a workbench, wiped marble dust off his face and rolled upright. He found bread almost as hard as marble and a cup of sour wine, into which he dipped the bread. He tried not to taste what he chewed. Nicol, who never seemed to sleep, left the side of an old man calling fitfully for his wife, and came to speak to Justin. His lean face had gotten leaner, Justin noticed; the skin pulled so tautly across it that he seemed more hawklike than ever. His eyes glittered, bright and fierce with weariness.

"You have got to find him," he said to Justin.

Justin nodded, his mouth full. He had spent most of the previous night searching for both Griffin Tormalyne and Giulia, who were not in his rooms, or at the Griffin's Egg, or at the Iridia Bridge, or the Tormalyne Bridge. No one was at the Tormalyne Bridge, he had discovered; no one alive, anyway. The gates were shut; guards watched from doorways and windows along both sides of the street. He had nearly walked into their sight; they were that eerily quiet, looking for tremors in the shadows, listening for steps. Near dawn, slipping home, he had been able to pick up gossip. The prince was ill; Marcasia House and Iridia House were watching like cats to see if he would live or die; Griffin Tormalyne had not been found. The warehouses around the Iridia Bridge had been permitted to burn to the ground so that guards could more easily watch the crowds massed there. The city gates would remain closed until the Griffin was given to the Basilisk.

He would search at the Pellior Bridge for Giulia, Justin decided. He would walk in the dark among the sleeping, whisper her name, see what he could find besides a curse. He still had no idea where to look for the missing Griffin.

"Unless he's locked himself in the music school," he suggested.

Nicol read his mind. "They searched it before they locked it," he said tersely. "As we saw. What about his lodgings?"

"I looked."

"What about the bard Hollis?"

"Nowhere."

"I suppose Griffin would not still be in Pellior Palace."

Justin shrugged. Anything seemed possible. "They didn't notice him before. Maybe Tormalyne Palace."

"They searched it."

"Then it's searched. They'll guard it, but they may not go back into it."

Nicol thumbed a brow, looking, for once, uncertain. "Would he have escaped across the Iridia Bridge during the confusion of the fires? Or taken refuge in one of the other Houses? It seems strange that he has made no attempt to find us."

"Maybe he's safer without us," Justin said dryly.

"We're all he has left of a House," Nicol argued.

"Maybe he didn't come back to rebuild the House. Maybe he just came back to kill the Basilisk."

Nicol fixed him with a bird's unwinking stare. "Find him," he said, "and ask him."

It was one thing, Justin thought moodily, easing his way toward the Pellior Bridge, to acquiesce to the relentless urgency of Nicol's gaze. It was entirely another to be alone in the dark streets doing what was promised. He idled in the shadows of an alley across from Tormalyne Palace, studying it for a long time until he could make out slight movement near the main doors. He watched half a dozen guards pass through the gates, another half dozen come out, walk toward Pellior Palace. He could not tell where those inside had gone; earlier, at dawn, he had seen no one guarding the loose bar in the fence.

Griffin Tormalyne had hidden himself in plain sight for weeks. He survived in places no one expected him to be because they were so obvious. A handful of guards would not be likely to notice him in Tormalyne Palace, which was a huge, cold mausoleum, empty of everything but ghosts. It seemed at once obvious, and unlikely. So, Justin decided, he might well be there.

He continued his erratic, covert path to the Pellior Bridge, to search for Giulia first. She could not talk to birds, or summon monsters; she had no defenses against history. That she might be dead inside the music school, Justin refused to consider. That she might be languishing in Arioso Pellior's dungeons for the crime of inciting her opera chorus to rebellion, he could concede possible. But he did not want to dwell on it. As he neared the river the restless, desperate noises of hungry animals, the smells, the numb silence of waiting, rolled over him like smoke from the fires. He stopped, sensing the density of humans packed around this bridge, the enormity of his search. Fires burned here and there, drawing him on: he could at least look where he could see.

He lost track of time along the river. He walked beyond night, it seemed, in mud and stagnant smoke, whispering a name while he tried not to wake sleeping children, or step on burly farmers lying prone in the mud. The night was made of strangers' faces, hands, arms, partially lit by fire, feet he stumbled over. Eyes came clear sometimes, dark, expressionless, watching him, Once or twice, someone spoke at the name, seizing his heart. But it would be some other Giulia, who answered cautiously, listlessly, not expecting to be looked for. The moon watched him as well, a narrowed eye above the river, shedding little light upon the matter.

He tripped over someone's leg, received a weary curse. "Giulia?" he said mechanically; his mouth was dry, his voice hoarse with her name.

"Under the awning," the voice muttered.

"What?"

"Giulia."

"Giulia?"

"Yes," she said out of sleep, hearing her name spoken from behind doors opening abruptly down a long marble corridor. Justin fell to his knees in the mud as she rose up out of it.

"Giulia?"

He felt her arms, and then her mouth, whispering his name, over and over. "Yes," he said, his face wet, not knowing which of them wept. "You're alive."

"So are you. Justin, Justin—"

"I'm sorry about your opera."

She pulled back from him a little, trying to see him in the dark. He heard a sniff turn into a laugh of mingled amusement, astonishment, and despair.

"My opera . . . Justin, we've been here for days. I think. What should we do? Where can we go?"

"We?"

"You stepped on me," the voice breathed. "I wrote that misbegotten opera."

"You did," Justin whispered, trying to see the magister who had produced Griffin Tormalyne out of his music. He eased down, drawing Giulia with him, and said, more softly still, "Wait. Until it's quiet around us. And then I'll take you out of here."

An hour later he worked their way slowly, silently along the bank to the street, under the moon's slitted, midnight gaze. Past the carts and animals, the streets were dangerously quiet; he set a painstaking pace through alleys, gardens, over fences. The moon watched as they crept, shadow by shadow, toward Tormalyne Palace. Or he thought it was the moon, which had been at his back before, and not nearly so full.

He stopped so suddenly that they all collided. The moon, it seemed, had taken residence in Tormalyne Palace.

He swallowed dryly, finally recognizing light in a place unlit for thirty-seven years. "Griffin Tormalyne," he breathed. He heard Giulia start to protest, stop. They stared at the upper windows, that loosed a silvery glow like a reflection of the moon. Hexel spoke first, his voice thin as a cat hair in the silence.

"Can we get in?"

"But," Giulia whispered.

"There is no safe place anywhere in Berylon," he reminded her. "If he is signaling—"

"Or the guards. A trap, maybe."

"Who would be stupid enough to walk into it?"

No one answered. They began to move again, toward the beckoning light.

Six

Caladrius stood in the dark beneath Tormalyne Palace, trying to see. His wrists were bound by chains and cuffs of metal: gold, memory kept trying to persuade him, though in that place metal would be rusted iron by now. He recognized the air dense with horror and pain; he had no idea how he had gotten there. He had wakened abruptly out of some dream of terrible loss to find Hollis gone. A ring and a charred bone lay on his empty bed. Caladrius had recognized the ring. He had stumbled then into another dream. Someone had stolen his heart; he had to find it quickly, quickly. . . . Searching had led him to Tormalyne Palace, into that deadly room where, as far as he knew, Brio Hood still lay moldering on the stones at his feet. Why he had not been seized by the Basilisk's guards, and who had chained him to the wall, he could not remember. But he guessed.

He gripped the chains that held him, seeing her eyes in his mind: the Basilisk's eyes. He remembered the flick of magic in her fingers that had brought the stone basilisks alive to save her father. An agony of impatience and dread burned through him. He wiped sweat out of his eyes on one arm and tried to think. He could not believe that Arioso Pellior would be content to let him starve to death in the silence of Tormalyne Palace: He would want to watch Caladrius die. Perhaps Luna wanted something from her father, for which she would trade Griffin Tormalyne. But why she had taken Hollis, and left Raven Tormalyne's ring and his fingerbone like a message, Caladrius could not imagine. What was the message? he wondered starkly. The message was fire. The message was death, to the Raven and the Griffin. But what did she want with Hollis, if she had Caladrius himself? To present Griffin Tormalyne's heir as a gift to her father? The thought left Caladrius breathless, weak with fury and terror. His heart had been stolen, he would give anything. . . .

As if she heard his incoherent, piecemeal thoughts, she stood before him in the blackness. He did not see her; he only sensed her: someone else alive in that death-ridden place.

Her voice came out of the dark, cool, composed, as if she strolled through a garden. "I have taken your son."

"I know," he said numbly, feeling the blood beat painfully behind his eyes.

"What will you give me for him?"

"Anything. Everything."

"Tell me."

"I will give you my name. I will give you my life. If you will let him leave Berylon."

"I have your life," she reminded him.

He closed his eyes, gripping the chains. "Then what can I give you?" he pleaded. "You must want something. Or you would have given me to your father. You would not have brought me here."

"Oh, yes," she agreed softly. "I want something." She let him see her face then, luminous and beautiful, smiling and not smiling. He sensed her power, something vast and elusive, unpredictable, like the power in the hinterlands.

"Take it," he begged her. "You have my heart. I will do anything, give anything, if you set him free."

She was silent, studying him; he could not guess her thoughts. She turned away from him finally. "Follow me," she said, and he felt the weight at his wrists melt away, as if he had only imagined it there. She moved ahead of him through the dark; he saw her easily, moving surely, gracefully across damp, sagging flagstones, through the maze of rooms. He felt the blood pound again behind his eyes. She knew the place where he had been born as if she had claimed it for her own.

She spoke as they finally reached the marble stairs beyond the wine cellar and began to climb. "You saw your father die."

"Yes."

"You recognized his ring."

"Yes."

"Where were you?"

He swallowed, his mouth as dry as ash. "In the hearth."

"Why did you wait so long to return to Berylon?"

"I thought I was dead." She turned to look back at him.

He added tautly, "Another child burned and was mistaken for me. So I found it easier to make the same mistake than to remember what I had seen."

"And what made you remember?"

He shook his head, finding it difficult to answer. You are mine, her gaze reminded him. You have given everything to me.

"I began to dream of fire. I made a journey into the hinterlands. Unknown places. I remembered, there."

"And there you found that pipe."

"I dreamed of it there. I recognized it here in Berylon and took it."

"From the music school."

"Yes."

She was silent a moment, as if hearing the overtones of the lie in his voice. But she did not challenge him. "And what else did you play in the hinterlands?"

"Many things. Odd instruments."

"Do they all have such strange powers?"

"Some more than others. All respond, like the fire-bone pipe, to the workings of the heart."

They had reached the top of the stairs. She wound a path through some clutter of debris. He closed his eyes, feeling wood, ash, bone under every step.

"And so you left the hinterlands and came to Berylon. To kill my father."

"Yes."

"And to reclaim Tormalyne House?"

"I did not expect to live beyond your father's death."

He felt her glance again. "But you brought your son with you. To claim his heritage."

"I would never have asked him to inherit such bitterness. He made his own way here without my knowledge. He refused to leave me."

"It was he who played the first pipe, that summoned the power in it."

He had to swallow again before he could speak. "He didn't know—"

"But you knew."

"That it was deadly? Yes. I killed Brio Hood with it."

She led him across a broad room to another set of stairs; they began to climb again. It seemed to him that she walked up night itself, step after step carved out of darkness, so that the stone beneath his steps was always unexpected. She said, "Tell me why you killed my cousin Brio."

He told her as they reached the crest of night and turned to cross another plane. She said, "And then you returned to Pellior Palace, Master Caladrius, to give my sister Damiet a picochet lesson. And to listen to her proclaim her love for you."

"Yes."

"My father killed your father's children."

There was a question in the words, he realized; he tried to answer it, but found only confusion. She turned again to look at him, the faint smile in her eyes, as always, concealing what she saw.

"We three are our father's children," she said lightly, like a riddle. "We are what he has made of us."

She opened a door; they began to climb again. He could see, in the room at the top of the stairs, a faint, silvery glow.

He stared down, remembering the griffins carved into the marble on every step he climbed. He smelled the bitterness that still hung in the air after so many years. A question formed by fire and memory wrenched itself out of him.

"What will you do with Hollis?"

She did not answer.

He recognized the room they entered. Light revealed the massive hearth, the charred ring on the floor, the ash and bone within it. He felt himself grow invisible again, a ghost of his own past, a nameless child made of ash.

"What are you doing?" he whispered. She did not answer. The light came out of a crystal on one of the scorched, empty window ledges. Round and milky as the moon, it illumined the room and spilled silver into the night. He heard shouting from the gardens below, a muffled, repetitive thudding.

"They can't get in," she explained. "I have locked the doors until my father comes."

He felt the hollow where his heart had been, the dry, papery taste of ash. "Where is Hollis?" His voice refused to come; he spoke only the shape of words, but she heard him. She looked at him, her eyes flashing white, reflecting light, and did not answer, even when he screamed the question at her.

She was marking a circle with her footprints into the wind-strewn ash on the floor, when she stopped, mid-pace. She listened to some sound beneath the tumult at the door.

"Who is coming up from the dark to join us?" she wondered, and finished her circle. He watched her steps link themselves through the ashes of his dead, enclose the fragments of their bones. He closed his eyes and heard the song they played, fire-bone pipes, wailing sorrow and fury. Steps, slow and tentative on the stairs, caught his attention. He drew breath to shout a warning; her voice stopped him.

"Let them come. I want them."

He opened his eyes, stared helplessly at the open door, listening, with heart and bone, for Hollis. Hollis did not appear. Three faces came clear in the wash of pale light: all haggard, uneasy, oddly transfixed, as if they dreamed awake. He knew them. They saw him and their faces came alive, no longer spell-bound but struggling with wonder now, saying his name without words, until Justin spoke.

"Griffin Tormalyne," he whispered. "We've been looking for you." His head turned suddenly, as if Luna had just formed herself out of light. His voice came more clearly then, trembling. "You. What are you doing here?"

"Waking the dead," she said, and tossed a fingerbone and a gold ring into her circle.

Ash and bone and gold ignited; a figure formed within the flames. Caladrius took a step toward it, loosing the cry that the child in the hearth, being dead, could never make. But it was not the raven in the fire, he realized even as he took another step. It was the Basilisk.

He saw a coil of night, with a flaming crest and mad, restless eyes of lizard green and gold that seemed to draw life from everything they touched, and leave a shadowy husk behind. Its crest stiffened, flared with fire as it saw Caladrius. It hissed a warning mist of black, and rolled toward him out of the circle, stunning him with its gaze: Arioso Pellior's eyes, seeing at last the child hidden in the hearth.

He could not move. The world vanished around him, turned to memory. He tasted ash again, smelled the charred bones of the dead. He saw nothing but the Basilisk's mad, glittering eyes. *You are nothing,* they said. *You are mine now. You are dead.* He breathed ash, felt it whisper into his heart, drift into him, enclose his bones. I am nothing, the child made of ash thought, transfixed in the Basilisk's stare. I am dead. There was only this left to do: wait for the last ember that was his heart to flare and die, and then there would be only ash. He waited, within the silence of the marble hearth, while the terrible eyes drained memory out of him, his life, his name. Finally, he felt the spark within the ember flame, and he opened his mouth in pain to give his last breath to the Basilisk.

The raven flew out of the fire.

Caladrius felt it strike his heart. The clawed, rustling darkness burrowed into him, looked out of his eyes. It spread its wings, reached down with its beak to break a bone from one of them, out of which song poured like blood. He stared back at the Basilisk out of ravens' eyes, his father's eyes, and saw the death within the looming gaze. He heard his own voice in some fierce, harsh word of recognition. And then he felt the music of the fire-bone pipe playing through his bones, reshaping him with its song until he was the pipe, and the music, and the magic that had made both. He opened wings then, flew out of the flaming ember in the ash. He swooped and seized the deadly eyes in his claws, wrenched them out of the Basilisk, and dropped them into the fire.

The fires were gone; they had never been; there was only the charred circle on the floor enclosing ash and bone, the cold ash in the hearth. The raven flew out of him into the shadows, where Caladrius felt its black, secret gaze. He was trembling. Notes from the raven-bone pipe seemed to flow out of him still, as he moved, searching the room for the vanished basilisk. His fingers loosened from some stiff, unfamiliar position. In the silvery light, a few drops of blood on the marble gleamed black.

He looked at Luna. "What did I do?"

She did not answer, except with her smile, brilliant and weary, the mask she held to the world. He saw three faces beyond her, familiar and unfamiliar, as if they belonged in another tale and had gotten lost in this one. They did not answer him, either. They had been turned to stone, it seemed; they stared at him and could not speak.

He saw Hollis. The raven's song faded, stopped within him, then; he felt his own heart return. Hollis, standing near Luna, did not seem hurt, only stunned by what he had seen. Caladrius went to him, said his name; he touched his father, but could not speak.

The guards came then, furious and sweating, spilling into the room. They recognized Luna and hesitated. She said briefly, "Take them to Pellior Palace."

"Even the librarian, my lady?" one asked.

"He is Griffin Tormalyne."

She walked with them through the streets of Berylon, as though, Caladrius thought, she could not move past music, or fade into night. His mind still grappled with a confusion of images. The Basilisk had come out of the circle; the Basilisk had never been there; Caladrius had become a raven-bone pipe and outstared a basilisk; there had been no raven, no basilisk. Something had happened; someone had left blood on the marble floor. A raven had stolen something—a heart?—and dropped it into a fire which was only a memory of fire.

As if she heard his confusion, Luna turned her hooded head to look at him. He could understand nothing in her eyes; he could see neither death nor mercy. She was not finished, he guessed; she wanted something, but did not have it yet, and what she wanted was not him, not Hollis, not anything he could see.

She spoke softly, beyond the circle of the guards, her voice pitched for him to hear. "My father taught me many things when I was a child, Master Caladrius. I learned best how to see."

"I don't know," he breathed, "what I am looking at."

A guard, rough and edgy, ordered him silent. He walked quietly, watching the lights of Pellior Palace grow near, aware of little now but his steps, and Hollis walking with him. Then they crossed the threshold into light, and time stopped. He could hear Hollis breathing shallowly beside him.

"My lady?" a guard said.

"Send the captain of the guard to my father's chamber."

"Yes, my lady."

It was late, but the door to the prince's chamber was open wide, and candles burned along the walls, beside the bed. Damiet, looking cross, sat at one side of the sleeping prince; Taur yawned at the other. The physician, alarmed at the onslaught against peace, met Luna at the door.

"The prince has been taken with nightmares, restlessness," he said softly to her. "He complains of the basilisk in the canopy, but will not let us take it down. He must rest."

She smiled. "He will rest now. I have brought him Griffin Tormalyne."

The prince stirred at the name. The book closed abruptly

in Damiet's hands. She blinked at Caladrius, then her lips thinned and her head turned sharply toward her father. Taur rose quickly, leaned over the prince.

"Father? They have captured Griffin Tormalyne. Wake—"

The Basilisk opened his eyes.

It seemed to Caladrius that their eyes met for a long time before the prince turned his head away irritably and spoke. "Who is there? Taur? Why are you sitting in the dark? Did you say—or did I dream—bring me light!"

"There are candles everywhere," Taur said obtusely. "Look. Here is Griffin Tormalyne. Your librarian."

"Let me examine him," the physician said quickly, returning to the bedside as the prince called, with increasing frustration, for light. Caladrius, suddenly unable to find breath, saw the shadow of a raven spilling down from a candle sconce. He remembered the odd stiffness in his hands, the raven's sudden swoop and wrench, the death that it dropped into the fire. It, he thought, wide-eyed, motionless. I.

"I can't see!" the Basilisk cried. The physician, suddenly pale, looked across the bed at Luna.

"There is no reason—" he said incoherently. "I cannot explain it—"

Taur, his brows raised, passed a hand in front of his father's eyes. "A blind old basilisk," he grunted, surprised, and drew the Basilisk's venomous gaze.

"You think I cannot still rule?"

"I didn't—"

"This will pass, Taur. I will live to see again, and what I do not see is Berylon passing into your hands."

Taur's voice rose. "You have no choice! I am your heir! And you are no longer fit to rule. I declare myself—"

"I declare you nothing. You will inherit only the life you have led, and your sister's permission to continue it. Luna sees for me. Luna will rule, now, while I live, and after I die. You are all my witnesses. This is my will."

"You can't!" Taur protested. "Father, you are ill, get some sleep. You'll change your mind when you can see again."

"Luna!"

She came to his side, took his hand. "Yes, Father."

He turned his head restlessly back and forth, searching for light. "You found Griffin Tormalyne?"

"Yes."

"He is here in this room?"

"He is here."

"And I cannot see. . . . But I can hear. You know my wishes. Question him and then have him killed. I want it done here, now; I want to listen to him—"

"No!" Rising, Damiet threw her book across the room, knocking candles into the hangings. Servants batted hastily at flames. She stood over her father, stamped her foot. "Not Master Caladrius! He was kind to me. You killed his family—all this is your fault!"

"Then leave the room," her father said impatiently, "if you don't want to watch. Luna, you are my eyes, you are my mouth, your will is my will. Speak."

She looked at the guards. Silver flashed as one drew his sword before she spoke. Her eyes, reflecting firelight, suddenly transfixed them.

"I have not given you orders," she said. "You heard my

father. I rule." She gave them her charming smile, and then, lifting one hand lightly, she extinguished the unruly random fires in the hangings with a gesture. "You will obey me." She looked at Taur; he sat down slowly under her bone-white gaze. "You may speak. Speak."

"You can't—" he began furiously.

"Be silent."

He was, abruptly, swallowing words, trying to push them out; a jewel dropped out of his mouth; a moth, with death's-heads on its wings, flew out. Nobody spoke. A guard swallowed, touching his throat. Damiet watched in fascination, smiling faintly.

"At least," Luna finished, "until dawn." She turned her baleful eyes back at the guards. "I can do many things," she said softly. "My father taught me all he knew. I learned more than he taught me. I learned from him many, many faces of death. I can kill with a rose. With a written word. With the tip of the hand of a clock. You taught me these things, Father. Did you not?"

"I did," he said, still searching restlessly for light. "Remember that, if you are tempted to the least betrayal of her rule. She will be my eyes past death."

"I will help you see now," she told him, and smiled again, her eyes turning their lucent green in the candlelight. She moved among the guards; they watched her, uneasy yet entranced. "Go now," she told them. "Open the bridges. Unlock the music school. Let the dead of Tormalyne House be buried, and leave the living to me."

"Yes, my lady."

"And Griffin Tormalyne?" the captain of the guard asked.

She looked at Caladrius. He saw, like one last glimpse of life, the garden in her eyes, the fragrant light, the cool shadows and resting places. "I think," she said softly, "that Pellior House has tormented Tormalyne House enough." She turned back to the captain of the guard. "Let Lord Tormalyne and his son go free."

Taur, coughing, his hands at his throat, loosed a line of dragonflies. Stranger noises came from the Basilisk, who, struggling to rise, stared blindly at his daughter, his face purple, a vein throbbing furiously above his brow. He tried to speak, produced only a long, inarticulate word that ended in a moan. He stiffened in amazement, one hand groping at his heart. The blood receded in his face; it grew paler and paler as he struggled for one last word until, falling back, he met the gaze of the basilisk above his head. He said nothing more. Only his eyes, growing fixed and lightless, told them what he saw.

The physician, with a sudden exclamation, felt for his heartbeat. Damiet, her hands at her mouth, looked down at him in horror and curiosity; she shivered suddenly and moved closer to her sister.

"He's dead, my lady," the physician said incredulously.

"What killed him?" Damiet whispered. Luna lifted a finger, touched her father's motionless hand; she could not seem to speak.

"Kindness," the physician guessed blankly.

Luna looked silently at Caladrius, the mask of her smile fraying at last to reveal the strength behind it, the bitter love and weariness.

He bowed his head, blind himself now with unshed tears. "Thank you," he said. "My lady."

Seven

The Basilisk was buried without fanfare. Luna, considering the dead of the Tormalyne School, was crowned with a single flourish from the trumpets of Pellior House. Both ceremonies, Caladrius thought, were remarkable for their silence. He attended them at Luna's request, as Duke of Tormalyne House, though he still had to remind himself of his own name. The House, free at last to bury its dead, revealed itself to Caladrius little by little at various funerals. Students and magisters at the school were remembered with music from their cherished instruments. Standing under a cloudy autumn sky, with Hollis at his side, he listened to Nicol harp for one of the magisters and remembered the dead harper at Luly, who had called himself Griffin Tormalyne.

A sudden chill in the wind stung his eyes. He looked north across the burial field, as if he could see the vast, white, unfurling wing from which the wind had sprung. Ravens in the trees lining the field called to the dead in their raucous, ungainly voices. Caladrius, listening to the mingling of harp and raven, felt again the strange shift of his body into wings, claws, singing bones.

You turned into a raven, Hollis had said. *You tore the Basilisk's eyes out. Don't ask me to explain. That's all I know.*

What was left of Tormalyne House after it ventured out of hiding into Luna's city was an assortment of distant relatives, whose wealth lay in the vigor and determination of their children. They gave Caladrius what they could, in gratitude; he could see in their eyes that Justin's tale of the Basilisk's blindness and death had lost nothing in the telling. They saw the raven in him and told him so: he was, they said, very like his father. With unexpected grace, Luna sent him a small casket of ebony and gold in which to lay his own dead to rest. He waited until the final trumpet had sounded over the last of the dead. And then, with Hollis, he returned to Tormalyne Palace.

They filled the casket with ash and bone in silence, and then they argued.

"No more funerals," Caladrius said tersely.

"There are people still living who knew them," Hollis protested. "They've been lying up here unburied for nearly forty years. You've brought back honor to the House, and that's the way they should be remembered, with proper dignity and ceremony. You can't bury them in the garden."

"Why not? They died decades ago. The House did its grieving then." He gazed into the open casket, saw the child in the hearth buried in ash, watching the Basilisk kill. He closed the lid gently.

"Because," Hollis said behind him, "you are not just burying your memories."

Caladrius turned. He smiled suddenly, put his hand on Hollis's shoulder. "Then you bury them. You may be better at this than I am."

"Better at what?"

"Ruling Tormalyne House."

Hollis slid out of his hold. "No," he said, with something of Caladrius's own unflinching gaze. "You are the heir of Tormalyne House; you can't go back to living on that rock. If you want the House to survive, you must stay. You fought for this."

"An empty palace and a casket of ash."

"Freedom."

Caladrius was silent. Rain blew on a gust of wind across the window ledge; in the gardens trees soughed like tide. Ash brushed across the floor where the nameless child had lain. He could still see a curve of Luna's footsteps in the ash.

He said slowly, meeting Hollis's eyes again, "Then I will need all your help. You saw what I have become."

Hollis said it after a moment, reluctantly. "Bard."

"I thought I knew once what the word meant."

"So did I."

"All I know is where to go to understand it."

Hollis closed his eyes, struggled with words. "Now?" he demanded incredulously.

"Soon. I'll see you settled first. I won't be gone long."

"How do you know? You know what they say about the hinterlands."

"I'll come back," Caladrius insisted. "But I need you here, in my place, for a while. The Griffin's son, to handle matters of the House. What House we have, and what little we have to handle it with." He picked up the ebony casket, gave it to Hollis. "This first. I saw them die. I'll never bury what I saw, but I would try. You do what's best for the House."

"This first," Hollis said, and handed him his father's ring.

Nine magisters in black, with black ribbons trailing from their horns, lifted them in a fanfare for the dead that Veris Legere found among the manuscripts Caladrius had been sorting. What seemed to be the entire House attended the ceremony to place the bones and ashes of Raven Tormalyne, his wife, an unnamed child, and a dog into the vault that held the rulers of Tormalyne House. Luna sent Veris Legere to attend also. Caladrius spoke to him afterward.

"I never thanked you," he said. "You let me leave the Hall of Mirrors, that day."

"What I saw," Veris said slowly, "was between you and Arioso Pellior."

"You took a risk."

Expression, brief and intense, touched the dispassionate face. "So did you. Master Caladrius."

A few days later he was summoned to Pellior Palace.

He waited for Luna in a quiet council chamber, in which he noticed hanging on a wall a tapestry with a hole in it where an animal's eye should have been. While he was investigating it the block of marble behind it began to turn silently. He moved away, startled. Luna came out from behind it, carrying a rose.

"It's a secret chamber," she explained, sealing it again. "Where my father taught me things."

"To kill with a rose," he said, his eyes on it. She smiled.

"This one heals," she said enigmatically, and went to give it to an old woman he had seen waiting outside the door.

He drew breath, remembering the terror of that night she had found him, the mystery of it. She returned to him, her eyes cool, smiling faintly, though her voice was grave. She wore black, for her own dead. She seemed composed as ever; but he glimpsed the constant watchfulness that she had kept hidden behind her wayward smile.

"Master Cal—" She stopped.

"I hardly recognize my own name," he commented.

"Who named you Caladrius?"

"My great-uncle did, when he found me alive. He had some desperate hope that the child he gave it to might learn what to do with it."

"Indeed, he was right," she murmured. "I sent for you for three reasons. The first is to tell you that I have asked Veris Legere to return the music taken from Tormalyne Palace to the palace or the music school, according to your wishes."

"Thank you," he said, touched. "I am grateful. The school could give it better shelter than Tormalyne Palace. As you know, it may be some time—perhaps even a generation or two—before the palace will be a suitable place for much of anything."

"That is the second reason I sent for you. To discuss reparations for the damages done to Tormalyne House by my father." She held up her hand as he began to answer. "I know," she said gently, "you will tell me that no price can be put on such suffering. But I hope you will at least accept a few chairs to sit on in Tormalyne Palace. Windows to keep out the rain. Someone to clean the soot off the walls."

He felt the raven in his bones again, his hands turning into something other. "And the third reason?" he asked steadily.

"The third reason," she said, and stopped again. She linked her fingers. He saw an unfamiliar expression in her eyes, the first hint of uncertainty. "My lord Tormalyne, you and I have some very unusual powers. I hope that we will be able to live peacefully in Berylon. The third reason I sent for you is to assure you of my good intentions. And to ask you how far your unusual powers extend. My father could not have turned into a raven."

He answered her unspoken question first. He went to her, drew one hand free from the other, and raised it to his lips. "I owe you my life," he said simply. "And my son's life. I trust you. But I can't answer you. Not yet. I must leave Berylon first. And I leave Hollis under your eyes."

Her brows rose. "Where are you going?"

"North."

"For how long?"

"I don't know. No one ever knows."

She was silent, studying him, not smiling now, letting him glimpse again some sweet, green shade in her eyes, where leaves trembled with light but did not let it fall. "I hope, my lord Tormalyne, that you will let me know when you are leaving."

"I will." It seemed to him that his name had come to him at last, from some untroubled place, perhaps from within the leaves. "My lady."

• • •

In the Tormalyne School, Giulia was collecting manuscript sheets that had been scattered through halls and chambers during the invasion of the Basilisk's guard. Around her, students and magisters picked up books, mopped mud and spilled water off the floors, repaired battered doors, patched and restrung instruments. She put a pile of music, in hopeless disarray, with other piles of music in front of students who were trying to sort it; they glanced up and groaned. Justin, trailing a broom, appeared behind her as she turned. He snatched a kiss. The students groaned again.

"Magister Dulcet, I can't find the viol part to this piece anywhere."

"Magister Dulcet, the bust of Auber Tormalyne fell over and broke its nose off."

"Magister Dulcet . . ."

"Giulia," Justin said. "Come to the Griffin's Egg tonight. Play with us."

She thought about it, exchanging one chaos for another, and smiled suddenly. "Yes." Her smile faded. "But where," she wondered, "has my picochet gone?"

She searched, hoping that it had not met its fate in the streets. She gathered music as she looked in practice rooms, under tables. She found it finally in Hexel's study, where it had slid beneath his harpsichord. He had not seen it, she guessed; he had not tossed it out the door.

She found Hexel there also, unexpectedly sitting at his desk with a pen in his hand, another woven through his hair. He barely noticed her until she spoke.

"Hexel," she said, amazed. "How can you be inspired in all this confusion? What are you doing?"

He looked up at her and smiled. "Changing the ending," he said, and went back to work.